ECHOES OF MAYA

KELLY VINCENT

*For everyone who needs to find the strength to face down evil
and win*

PROLOGUE

The girl thought about the strawberry fruit snacks that awaited her in the cabinet at home as she turned the corner to cut through the creepy alley behind the Chinese restaurant. She came this way every day after summer school, even though she almost always ended up running at the end to get out faster. If she didn't take the shortcut, it was a really long walk around the block.

She passed the dumpster and then the large black grease bin that you couldn't get too close to because they always missed the opening, making the whole area slick. It grossed her out as always. Halfway down the alley, the hair on the back of her neck rose and her stomach twisted. She stopped, pulling on her backpack straps.

This was worse than normal. Should she go back the way she came?

This was dumb. Everything was fine. She stepped forward again.

But the feeling worsened with each step. Soon she would have to pass another dark alley that branched off this one. The one she always rushed past.

She broke into a run toward the other end, wincing at the slapping sound of her shoes on the ground. She wished she could teleport to the street.

1

———

Lauren

I plopped two tomato slices on top of the lettuce on my burger, then added a third tomato for good measure, trying to ignore the Fourth of July sun beating down on the back of my neck. Well, everywhere.

"Are you sure you don't want two more, Lauren?" Gabriel teased.

"Yeah, you always eat so many tomatoes!" Maya echoed.

"Shush, both of you." I squirted some ketchup on top and dropped the bun in place, then moved along to the chip bowl. I hadn't really wanted to come out of the nice, air-conditioned house to hang out with a slew of neighbors, but at least Gabriel and Maya were here to make it tolerable. My other best friend, Tenny, said she'd try to drop by later, but she had her own family thing. I scooped some of the dill cucumber salad I'd made onto my plate and dropped a handful of chips beside it, covering the rest of the American flag, and glanced at Gabriel, who had his ever-present grin on his face. We'd grown up next door to each other and I was still a little heartbroken over learning he was gay. It was some consolation that I was one of the few people in the world who knew.

Maya was my eight-year-old stepsister, who had the energy of a jet engine.

"Here you go!" she said, dropping two more slices of tomato on top of my bun. Gabriel cracked up as he piled his own burger with pickles.

"Gross, now my bun is wet, Maya." I slid them off the bun. We were technically stepsisters but I'd known her her whole life and practically raised her. I'd always thought of her sort of as mine, in some abstract way.

"What kind of chips are they, Lauren?" Maya asked, standing on her tiptoes to see.

"Just regular, unfortunately."

"No barbecue?" Gabriel asked.

"Nope." I backed up from the table and ate a chip. "I got us a blanket."

I looked toward our house. It was small and tan, and the siding and white trim looked worn, but not too trashy. My parents were talking to Gabriel's mom—they'd been best friends forever—and there were some other neighbors around. As soon as it was dark, we'd break out the sparklers and do some fireworks in the street.

Maya ran past me toward the blanket, a ratty old Barney thing I'd put in the corner of the yard in front of the boxwood shrubs. Maya plopped down, half her chips sliding off her plate. "Oops!"

I grinned. So much energy. I loved it.

Gabriel and I sat down on opposite corners. He pulled three cans of Coke out of various pockets and tossed them to us.

"Can you open it for me, Gabriel?" Maya said, fluttering her eyelashes, which made us all laugh.

"You don't have to flirt with me to ask a favor, niña." He opened it and handed it back.

I opened mine and took a swig. I wished I didn't like sugar so much, but there was no denying it. My thighs would give my secret away, if I bothered to try to keep it a secret. I took another swig and crossed my legs and scootched around to get more comfortable.

"Did I tell you I registered for all my classes, Gabriel?" I asked.

"No. What are you taking?"

"The obvious—English, pre-calc, Western Civ, and of course I'm taking Spanish." Gabriel had been on my case forever to learn it. He always said I was lucky to have a close friend who was fluent, but I hadn't been interested earlier. Now I saw the practical value.

Maya took a bite of her burger and a big blob of mustard dropped out of the sandwich onto her belly. She looked down. "Oh, man."

Gabriel handed her a few of the many napkins he'd brought and she tried to wipe it off but ended up just spreading it around.

Gabriel and I laughed. "Dana's going to be so happy," I said.

Maya kept wiping and Gabriel turned back to me. "I know you're not just taking four classes at OAMS."

"No." The Oklahoma Academy of Mathematics and Sciences was a final-two-year high-school run by the state. You had to apply to get into it, but tuition and room and board were fully covered for all students. Gabriel had graduated from there last month, so he did know what he was talking about. "I'm also taking inorganic chemistry, botany, and art."

"You'll like the art teacher," Gabriel said. "She's super nice. Do you remember who any of the other teachers are?" He crunched down on a chip.

"No idea."

"Let me know when you find out, and I can give you tips. Most of them are actually not bad. A lot of them have PhDs. It's kind of like being in college." He stretched his legs out in front of him.

"You've told me all this already, Mr. Broken Record." I squeezed my burger to squash it down and my finger split the soggy top bun, sending the halves onto the plate. "Shit!"

"You're not supposed to cuss," Maya said, pretending to be serious.

"I know, sorry, but it's your fault. The tomato juice soaked all the way through. Stupid cheap buns."

"You're supposed to be setting a good example for me." Maya smirked at me.

"I think, overall, she does, niña," Gabriel said, tapping her toes with one of his black Pumas.

It was sweet of him to say that. He knew how much I'd watched her growing up. Our parents worked a lot. Plus he was there for a lot of it, giving me breaks by playing *Mario Kart* with her. I pulled my t-shirt out from my waist. "Look, I'm setting an example of not pouring mustard on my shirt."

Maya cracked up while I tried to piece my burger together.

Gabriel laughed. "You know she has to make her own mistakes to learn."

"Exactly!" Maya said.

"Then you're taking a step in the right direction," I said,

picking up the barely-together burger and successfully taking a bite.

Maya was still giggling, but we dug in and ate for a bit. Maya told us about the goings on at the two-week summer camp she'd just finished and Gabriel went over his own course list for his first semester at college. We were lucky because we already lived in Burnside, a suburb of Oklahoma City, and that's where Gabriel's college, the Oklahoma Institute of Technology, was—which also happened to be the campus that housed OAMS. OAMS required students to live in the dorms, but we could go home on weekends. Gabriel was going to be living at home while at OIT to save money. He'd wanted to live in the dorms, but his mom thought they should save some of his scholarship money for other living expenses. Things were tight for them because the money he'd been getting from the government because of his dad dying had stopped when he turned eighteen earlier this year.

I lay back, head in the grass. Gabriel and Maya were talking some more about the camp and swimming in the lake and how cool that was. As hot as it was outside, I felt peaceful. Everything was good. I was excited about OAMS, Gabriel was starting college, and Maya was going into the gifted and talented program at school.

"Look, it's the Three Musketeers!" I sat up to see one of our neighbors. "Hi, Mrs. Jansen." I gave a little wave.

"What grade are you going into, Maya?" she asked.

"Third!"

"You'll be graduating elementary school in no time, sweetie. Gabriel and Lauren, you're both starting on your own big adventures, aren't you?"

"Yep. In four years, I'll be some kind of engineer." He laughed. "The hard part is figuring out which type."

"You'll figure it out. You're a sharp one." She turned to me. "And that fancy school will be lucky to have you, sweetie."

"Thanks. What's Morgan up to?"

"Still auditioning all the time and waiting tables." Mrs. Jansen laughed. "It's the old cliché for actors, but she seems to be having a good time."

"That's fun," Gabriel said. "I think she's doing everything she's supposed to."

Mrs. Jansen nodded. "Okay, I'll let you get back to your conversation. I need to get a recipe from your mom." She tottered off toward the patio.

"Is Morgan going to be famous?" Maya asked.

"Maybe," I said. "She's pretty, and she's really effusive."

"What does that mean?" Maya asked.

"She expresses herself a lot," I explained.

"Sort of like you, kiddo," Gabriel said.

"I'm effusive?" Maya asked, grinning.

"You definitely are," I said. I picked up one of Maya's flip-flops and threw it at her.

Maya caught it and threw it back, and soon we were tossing both flip-flops at each other and laughing.

"How are you all doing?" Dana, my stepmom, appeared. "Oh, Maya, you've made a mess of your shirt. Let's go inside and change it. Give me all your plates."

We handed them over while Dana rolled her eyes at Maya's mess and smiled at us. "Charles will be here a bit later." Maya clapped happily and took Dana's hand, and they went into the house.

Uncle Charles was Maya's biological father's brother, and he was around, but he worked in the oil fields so we didn't see him all that often. He was a nice guy and always gave Maya candy. And me, also, if I was there.

"Guess who we ran into at the DQ yesterday," I said. "And who is coming over tomorrow to hang out."

Gabriel rolled his eyes. "You texted me right afterward. I don't know what you see in that guy. He's a douche. Even his name is douchey. *J. T.* "

"But I haven't told you *in person*." I laughed. "You're just jealous because he's straight."

"Okay, I will acknowledge that he's an attractive ... young man. But. Douche."

"Have you ever seen eyes in that particular blue?" I mused. They really were pretty. "Usually blue eyes are normal blue, but his are more like teal."

"I have not, and I don't care." He stretched his legs out and leaned back on his hands. "Eyes do not make someone interesting."

"Oh, I beg to differ."

"I'm beginning to question my assessment of you as not shallow."

I splayed my fingers on my chest and feigned offense. "How sayest thou?"

"Oh, God." He put his fingers to his forehead. "Not Shakespeare again. I thought you got over that last year."

I laughed. "It's kind of how they talk in the Bible, too, you know."

"I've only read the Bible in Spanish."

"Well, you're missing out on archaic English."

"I think I'm okay with that." He nodded thoughtfully. "So ... are you going to try to impress JT with your cooking?"

I laughed again. "I probably will. I'll bring you something of whatever I make." Cooking was kind of my thing. I'd probably make cookies in the morning and something for lunch.

He grinned at me and rubbed his stomach. "Yay."

Out of nowhere, Maya threw herself across the blanket, making both of us jump.

"You're back, kiddo," Gabriel said.

"I'm going to get us some pie," I announced.

"Great, Maya can get sugary cherry goo on her new, clean shirt."

"Perfect." I got up, wiggled my half-asleep foot and limped over to the table. I shooed some flies and cut three pieces. When I looked back, Gabriel was tickling Maya's feet, an old pastime of theirs.

With Maya getting older, I was kind of glad he was gay. There were some creepy guys out there. I was so glad I'd never have to worry about Gabriel. I walked back.

"Pie!" I handed them out and we all dug in.

2

———

Gabriel

Thursday morning, the sociology professor wrapped up what she was saying about the complexities of race in America—she wasn't wrong, but it would take more than a single unit in a semester class to do it justice—and I loaded my spiral notebook into my backpack, which had seen better days. It was a faded black, and near the top, there was this random tear whose origin was a total mystery.

"Hey. Gabriel, right?"

I looked up to see—OMG, it was Will, the guy I'd been obsessing over from afar since the first day of class. His dark, curly hair was even hotter up close and his eyes were definitely green, something I'd been trying to confirm for weeks. I mentally gulped and somehow produced a confident smile. "Hi. How are you?"

"Good, good." He spread his palm across his chest, which looked pretty solid under his white t-shirt. "I'm Will."

"I ... knew that." I laughed awkwardly. "Nice to meet you."

He was smiling at me, those green eyes shining. "Do you have another class right now? I thought we could get a coffee, maybe talk about class."

"Oh, you want to get a perspective on race from the person of color, huh?" I teased.

He laughed, his grin absolutely infectious. "Come on, let's go. But actually, I do have a clue. My dad's Black. I just take after my mom and pass on my own. My brother doesn't."

"Oh, wow." I felt like an idiot. I zipped my backpack and jumped up, and we headed toward the door. "Sorry, I was trying to be funny."

He laughed again and looked at me as we walked. "No offense taken. You probably wouldn't be surprised at some of the other stuff I've heard."

I nodded ruefully. "Probably not."

Now that I was looking again, I could kind of see it in his face. But I was not saying that shit out loud.

Besides, as it happened, I liked his face. He had a strong jawline and looked kind of rugged.

"Where do you want to go?" I asked.

"Student union?" he suggested.

"Sure."

We headed toward the building exit, neither of us talking. I wanted to say something, but everything I was coming up with was either stupid or way bolder than I could really be out loud. I was not going to tell him I'd been wanting to hang out since the start of the semester.

"What's your brew of choice?" he asked.

"I'm more of a smoothie guy."

He pushed open the building's front doors and the brisk

fall air hit us. "Smoothie? Really? What's wrong with a thick black brew?"

"It doesn't sit well with me." We trotted down the steps to the sidewalk. The real reason I couldn't drink coffee was because of Papá. He taught me to like it, and we'd drink it together despite Mamá being annoyed because I was so young. After he died, I couldn't go near it because it reminded me too much of him. But this isn't something you tell someone you're supposed to be flirting with.

"Your loss."

The sidewalk was busy with people going both directions, with lots of dodging involved to make progress. I glanced over to where the Happy Hollow was in the lawn across the street. It was a small dug-out pit lined with stones, a perfect den of privacy for horny couples. Maybe Will and I would end up there sometime. I wondered if there would be a line, given how popular it was supposed to be.

Will's eyebrows were raised as he looked at me. He must have spotted the daydreamy look on my face.

"What are you thinking about?" Will asked.

I regained control of my smile and toned it down. "Uh." I reset my brain and looked at him. "Maybe I'll tell you some day."

"I'm going to hold you to that."

Did he just *wink* at me? Lauren would be so impressed with me for flirting with a hot guy. I was always such a chicken.

My stomach was doing flips, but we just turned right toward the union like everything was normal.

"So, what do you think of the class?" I asked. "Dr. Wetherspoon?"

He nodded thoughtfully. "It's actually kind of cool, way

more interesting than I expected. Like, learning that all these things I've seen in the world are recognized concepts that have names."

"Same. It's also kind of jarring to see a white person acknowledging the ones about race."

"Yeah, I know." He laughed "But that idiot who insisted race was always biologically detectable from a person's features ..."

"She was all, 'Those are all socially constructed meanings that you're assigning to people's features.'" I said in a haughty way, and sort of imitating the professor's voice, which made us both laugh.

We had to dodge a group of frat guys hogging the sidewalk.

Once we were past them, Will said, "I know. He's not going to do well on the test. What's your major?"

"Mechanical engineering. But I'm not sure if I'll stick with it." We turned left and headed toward the union's back-door entrance.

"Oh, nice. I'm undeclared at the moment." He shrugged, seemingly unconcerned.

"If I do want to change, I have to keep that major as long as possible because I have a scholarship through the department." There was so much at stake with college that I couldn't make a bad step. I had to get it right or I could end up wasting so much money.

"Oh, so you're a smart guy." Will opened the door and held it for me. It led right into Booth Forest, a large area filled with these tall wood and green booths

"Mostly just organized." I went in, and it was loud from all the conversations echoing throughout the room. Some people turned to look at us, but nobody seemed alarmed by the sudden presence of a couple gay guys. If they knew. Did people know? I'd never really officially come out, but people often guessed. Still, it hadn't ever really been a problem for me. What about Will?

I glanced over at him. He caught me looking and gave me a sideways smile. We'd just passed through Booth Forest and into the food court area.

He touched my shoulder. "Do you want to split up so you can get your smoothie and I'll get my coffee, and we can meet back here?"

"Sure."

We went our different ways, but once I was in line and had ordered my smoothie, I looked over at him in line. He totally caught me looking and winked at me again, which about made my heart nearly stop. I turned quickly back around, face heating. He was obviously way more used to being identifiably gay. If we got together, I'd have to get used to that.

I could get used to that. I totally could.

We met up at the entrance to Booth Forest and smiled at each other again, making me feel giddy.

He looked into the room. "Let's find a spot."

I followed and we had to walk down a couple aisles before finding an empty booth, but we snagged it. When I sat down, I tossed my backpack into the corner, where it landed with a heavy thud.

"What do you have in there?" Will asked.

I adjusted the backpack against the wall. "I have to drop some books off at the library, plus I always feel like I should bring every relevant book for my classes."

"Okay, let's see them," Will said.

I unzipped the bag and looked at him. "Are you a reader?"

"Sometimes. I like fantasy, like, the newer stuff that isn't always about only white people."

I laughed and pulled out three books and set them on the table. Two Batman graphic novels and an old sci-fi in Spanish.

"Batman, huh?" He gave me the side-eye. "I'm more of a Marvel guy."

My eyebrows shot up in excited surprise. "Do you read comic books?"

He shook his head. "I never have. Is that a problem?"

I laughed. He was obviously teasing from the glint in his eye. "Well, if you're interested in trying them, I have the perfect starting point for you. Have you heard of *Watchmen*?"

"The movie?"

"Oh, my God, no." I splayed my hand across my chest. "The graphic novel. It's way better. Dark, but good."

"I usually like stuff that's a bit dark," he said.

This was awesome. Maybe I could get him into comics and I'd have someone to talk about them with. Lauren had never liked them. "I'll bring it on Tuesday," I said. I raised a finger and cocked my head to the side. "But be aware, there are rules about how to read it."

He laughed. "I'm not a rule-follower, Gabriel."

"Well, you have to, or I won't let you borrow the book." I tried to look very serious and utterly failed because of how happy I felt.

He made me pull out the other books in the bag and teased me relentlessly about my mom's Spanish romance novels, but I hadn't felt this good in a while.

～

Lauren

My botany lecture ended and I headed to the front desk, where I was scheduled to meet a prospective student and her mom for a tour. I volunteered for this the first week of class after I found out you could get out of P.E. to do it. They liked how easy it was for me to talk to people, a skill not everyone here had. You know, with all the nerds.

Before turning the corner toward the front of the classroom building, I spotted JT coming out of a classroom. His blond head towered over everyone, sort of the same way he dominated any room he was in. I adjusted my shirt and cursed myself for not stopping at the bathroom to put more lip gloss on.

But I shouldn't have worried. We'd been together for months.

A smile stretched his face when he saw me. I went up to him and kissed him on the mouth, his light day-old stubble brushing my chin.

He put his arms around me for a second, but then pulled back and took my hand. "What are you doing out of class?"

I explained about the tour.

"See you at seven thirty, then?" he asked.

"Yep," I said, despite the twinge in my heart. Why couldn't he ever meet after school like everyone else? Where did he go every day? Was he sneaking around with someone?

He squeezed my hand and headed off to his last class.

I shouldn't complain, even in my head. He was perfect, and I was lucky he was into me. I'd been admiring him since I first saw him freshman year at Burnside High, and running into him in July was just great luck. We'd been officially together since mid-July. He'd become a bit of a fixture at my house over the summer, even helping out by staying with Maya when Gabriel and I had to do something. He usually came over on Saturdays when I had to watch Maya, which was most of them, including this coming weekend. I was planning to make my onion pizza, which was JT's favorite.

The prospective student and her mom were waiting by the front desk when I got there. The girl had on jeans, a yellow cardigan, and some brandless shoes. Her straight brown hair was unsettled and clearly not designed to impress. No makeup. Obviously awkward—like half the kids here. She'd fit right in with them. Her mom was wearing nice slacks and a pink blouse and had on normal makeup. I always wondered what moms like that thought of their unkempt daughters.

"Maddy?" I asked.

Maddy turned and looked at me before looking at the ground again. But her mom smiled.

"Welcome. I'm Lauren Baxter. I'm a junior here, and I'll be giving you the tour and telling you about the school."

The mom said hi and Maddy smiled shyly and gave a little wave.

"Nice to meet you both." I walked closer to the windows to get out of the way and they followed me. "First I'll give you an overview and you can ask questions, then I'll show you around the classroom building and the dorm."

We started down the hall.

"I'm sure you already know a lot of this, but one of the rules is that we aren't supposed to leave the college campus without permission."

The mom nodded. "And by college, you mean OIT, right?"

"Yeah. OAMS doesn't really have a 'campus.' We just have this building and the dorm you passed on the way here from the parking lot. But the Oklahoma Institute of Technology does have a whole large campus, and it's sort of our adopted one."

"Great. Thanks for clarifying."

I continued as we walked. "OAMS students have to live here during the week. Friday after classes they can go home, but they have to be back by Sunday night at eight thirty. Most students stay here most weekends."

"And there's no fee, even for room and board, right?" the mom asked.

"Correct. The state covers everything."

After that, I showed them around the front, where all the administrators' offices were. We turned the corner and I took them to the large lunch room. "They bring us lunch here during the week, mostly sandwiches, but Tuesdays and Fridays we get hot food. The shepherd's pie is the best. Breakfast and dinner we get at the college cafeteria. And on weekends, lunch too."

"Maddy has a gluten sensitivity," her mom said. "Will they be able to accommodate that?"

"Definitely. The cafeteria, too." This just made me think of JT again, because he was a picky eater and always asking for little things from the staff. I'd see him next at the cafeteria. My stomach flipped at the thought of kissing him again.

"Great," the mom said.

We moved on down the hall and looked into a couple of empty classrooms. We went into the second one and I showed them the various tech we had: computers, specialized tablets that could project, several AV tools.

"This is impressive," the mom said.

I glanced at Maddy, who looked a little bored. I gave her a smile and she returned it, albeit shyly.

We walked to the art studio at the end of the hall, but there was a class in session so we didn't go in.

We headed back toward the front of the building and down the opposite hall. "The music room and auditorium are down this way." The music room wasn't in use, so we went in. The teacher was there, and Maddy chatted with her because she was an oboe player.

After they were done, I said, "Let me show you the dorm." Our two white brick buildings shared a lawn, making an L shape with each other.

As we crossed the grass, the mom asked, "Can you talk a little about safety? We're worried about the missing girls."

There had been several girls who'd gone missing in the area recently. It had become big news when a sixth grader disappeared on her way home from school a couple weeks earlier.

"Well, we have the run of the campus, but it's pretty safe. There are blue lights all over the place where you can run to and call for help if you need it. They have a microphone and speaker connected to the campus police. But those missing girls are all younger, too."

"That's true," the mom said. She still looked worried.

I worried about Maya, but we never let her out alone, and that seemed to be what happened with all the missing girls. Somehow, they'd end up on their own, walking home from school or something like that. Maya would never do that. And right now, I had other things to keep my mind occupied—primarily JT, but also the insane amount of homework that was always waiting for me.

3

Gabriel

I was at home Saturday evening, texting Will and working on calculus homework. I was lucky Mamá didn't want me to get a part-time job, since I got the scholarship. She was always stressed about money, but she wanted me to be able to focus on school. I sometimes thought her life would be easier if she would just find a guy to marry, but she never got over Papá being killed any better than I had. We sometimes still talked about him like he was coming home from Afghanistan soon.

My phone dinged on the couch next to me, but I forced myself to finish the calculus problem I was working on before I could touch the phone.

It was excruciating. The phone dinged again. But finally I finished and picked it up.

—*I've gotta go to work*—

Well, that was a buzzkill. Not what I wanted to see. I picked up one of Lauren's snickerdoodle cookies she'd brought over earlier. JT was over, so of course she wanted to impress him with her cooking. It was embarrassing how much he would gush over the things she made. She was good, but still.

—I'll talk to you after I get home— Will added.

He worked in the college's library and apparently his boss wouldn't let him use his phone during work hours, which was ruining my life even though this was only the second time I'd had to deal with it. He'd worked Thursday, too. That was actually why our coffee/smoothie date—was it a date?—ended. He'd had to go to work.

Will was really cool and had seemed to enjoy hanging out with yours truly. He was definitely a potential boyfriend in my mind, even though we hadn't seen each other since Thursday. We'd texted all day yesterday. I knew I needed to chill out, but that's where it seemed to be heading. I scrolled back to our first texts.

—I'm almost to the library and will have to go dark— he'd texted after leaving the student union.

—It will be good for me to have a chance to do some homework— I said.

There were some laughing emojis, and then a message saying he was turning his phone off. Eventually, several hours later, *—Okay, I like books, but I don't like student athletes coming in, handing me a list of books, and asking me to get them for them. I mean, no—*

—Do they do that?—

—You'd be surprised at how entitled they are— he answered. *—My brother definitely is—*

His brother was a walk-on for the basketball team.

—You're pretty entitled— I texted.

—In what way?—

—You think you're entitled to my texts— I added some laughing emojis.

—*I think this is more of an equal partnership thing*— he said, which made me laugh.

I responded with more laughing emojis, feeling like I was being ridiculous.

He texted —*You do owe me though*—

—*What?*—

—*You have to guess*— He included a winking emoji. He had stepped up the flirting a bit, and I was both nervous and excited.

I also had no real idea how to respond properly. —*I couldn't possibly guess. I'm a very innocent boy*— That sounded very flirty, even though it was also literally accurate.

—*That doesn't have to always be true. We'll talk about it sometime*—

Being so inexperienced was really annoying, but it wasn't like I could fix it on my own. I couldn't have an actual relationship with myself. I set the phone down. I needed a break from all the hoping-it-worked-out, and from my calculus. I headed into the kitchen to heat up some leftover enchiladas Mamá made for dinner last night. She almost never made them with salsa verde, even though she knew it was my favorite, so I was really looking forward to these leftovers.

Once it was in the microwave, I went to get the mail, still smiling.

The arrival of the electric bill was an immediate stressor, even though this month would be lower than September because AC season was fading and it hadn't gotten cold yet. But then, as I was coming back in, I saw JT leaving Lauren's house. He looked smug and I hated him. Something was seriously off with that guy. He looked up and smiled at me, managing to look even more smug.

What was up with Lauren? What did she see in that guy?

I ignored him and decided to see if Lauren and Maya wanted any of the enchiladas. There were more left in the pan. I walked over and rang the doorbell. The front room lights were off and nobody answered the door. Maya wasn't supposed to answer the door on her own, but what was Lauren doing? I rang the doorbell again, but nothing.

Was she already in bed at this hour? So weird.

Feeling a bit lonely, I went back home, dropped the mail on the kitchen counter, and grabbed my enchiladas out of the microwave. I sat down on the couch, put my feet on the coffee table and turned the TV on. It was on a local channel and by chance they were talking about OIT. Something about sports.

I took a bite of enchilada—yum—and watched as they switched to a hospital scene with some of the big basketball players there, talking to cancer kids. I wasn't into sports, but some of these guys were ... very nice to look at. They were wearing shirts that covered their biceps, which was unfortunate, but it was still obvious how fit they were. All these giant guys were sitting in this big room with a bunch of kids clustered around them. They looked hilarious in those kid-sized chairs. Honestly, I was probably closer in size to the oldest kids than to these guys. Being short was really annoying.

After a bit, they interviewed this blond guy named John Johnson. Apparently he was a big guy on the team, nick-named Hoppin' John. I didn't like the look of him and he reminded me of JT. Guys like that were so arrogant, and he was obviously full of himself.

"I'm just happy I can change a kid's life. These little guys go through so much, and they need a break from everything."

Blah blah. I had achieved a few things in life, too, and

you didn't see me going around like I was God's gift to humankind. All he was doing was visiting them. The kid he was talking to was in bed and had a tube running up his nose, although, admittedly, he did look excited to meet John.

I hated performative philanthropy. Famous people were always doing that stuff. Walking around like their mere presence was life-changing. I mean, college athletes weren't usually wealthy yet, so maybe I was being harsh. But seriously, just because he's a good athlete, we're supposed to believe he's this great person? I didn't buy it.

Lauren

Halloween night, I made a quick dinner of chicken noodle soup for Maya and me. I'd been roped into taking her trick-or-treating because both my parents had ended up having to work. I was a tad annoyed at having to come home on a school night, which wasn't the norm.

After we ate, I helped Maya get into her pirate costume. It was pretty cute, actually—black boots, red and black striped leggings, and a flowy white shirt. The best part was the upright plush parrot that was stitched to her left shoulder. We put on a flashing ankle light for safety.

"Hold up your sword," I told her before stretching my jaw in a giant yawn. Another week with not enough sleep. OAMS' homework load really was no joke.

Maya lifted the cheesy plastic cutlass. "Arr!"

I snapped a photo, Maya's red bandanna bright against her dark hair. She was so excited that it was infectious, and I was no longer annoyed at having to take her. She was too cute.

The truth was, I'd been kind of frustrated with her because every time I babysat on Saturdays, I'd have JT over, but Maya would always be in our space.

Tonight was like the old days. As an eight-year-old, I'd loved getting a new baby sister more than anything. From her first steps, she'd always followed me around as if I were the sun.

Looking at her now, growing up so fast, I shook my head and texted the pic to Dana like she'd told me to. She'd been really disappointed she had to work and couldn't take Maya out.

The sun was starting to fade by the time we left the house. We stopped by to show Maya's costume to Gabriel and his mom, Adelita, and they said appropriately admiring things and took their own photos.

"You look positively dangerous," Gabriel said.

"I do?" Maya said, stricken.

"It's good, Maya," I explained. "Pirates are supposed to be dangerous."

"Oh yeah," she said.

"Have fun tonight, *mi peligrosita!*" Adelita said, making Maya smile.

Then we headed out—but not before Maya grabbed a banana Laffy Taffy from their bowl. Plenty of other kids were trick-or-treating, parents in tow. Maya went up to each house on her own and came back to show me her spoils. She had the same old purple plastic pumpkin I'd used when I was little.

After the first few houses, I got my phone out and played my puzzle game. I stuck one of Maya's pieces of red licorice in my mouth and sucked on it for a while. This stuff was so good, I didn't know how Maya could hate it so much. But she did, so I got all of it. Which was great, but I'd really rather be celebrating Halloween differently, like going to a party with a boyfriend.

After several houses, we caught up to a group of other third and fourth graders. One of them called her name, and after they all excitedly showed each other their candy hauls, she stayed with the pack.

I sent JT a text. —*What are you doing?*—

I followed the gaggle of kids to several more houses, avoiding the parents, because who wanted to talk about school and where I was going to college with a bunch of adults? I glanced at my phone. Why hadn't JT texted me back? I started another game.

I'd seen him at school today and everything seemed back to normal, but Saturday was weird. He'd come over with some beer, and we'd been drinking stealthily, and somehow I'd fallen asleep on him. I woke up and he was gone and it was late.

Maya ran over with more licorice and I stuffed a piece in my mouth.

"It's so gross, Lauren," she said.

"Nope, it's awesome."

She went back to the group and we went to the next house.

"Lauren," said someone behind me.

I spun around and saw JT.

"What are you doing here?" I was so surprised I forgot to smile. And then I panicked a bit because I hadn't touched up my makeup before coming out.

"I was just out for a run."

I clocked what he was wearing. "Only you would run in jean cutoffs," I said, laughing. He also had a brown t-shirt with the chemical formula for caffeine on the front, which was more normal.

"It was all I had. Tomorrow's laundry day. Anyway, I came this direction because I thought I might catch you and get to see you again." He grinned, which made his eyes crinkle.

That made my night. I kissed him. I slid my hand across the back of his neck, breathing in his familiar guy smell. He wrapped his arms around me and pulled me in close—so close that I felt a hardness in the front of his shorts, which shocked me. Was that because of me? That idea was both terrifying and intoxicating.

He disentangled his tongue and leaned back. "You taste like candy."

I laughed. "It's the red licorice Maya's been giving me all night. She doesn't even want it in her bucket, so I get every bit of it."

"I like it." He let go of me and backed away and I was instantly two degrees colder.

"I texted you," I said.

"Oh, it must still be muted." He pulled his phone out to glance at it. "I didn't notice."

"That's okay." I stepped forward and took his hand. "I was just wondering what you were up to. Now I know." Not with some girl.

He smiled and squeezed my hand before dropping it. "Listen, I'd better get going. I want to finish my run so I can get back. Don't want to get caught off campus. But I'm glad I got to see you again."

"Yeah, me too." I loved that he sought me out. Not a lot of people prioritized me.

He gave a little wave and took off running. I didn't know why he couldn't stick around. Getting caught off campus wasn't really that big a deal. At least from what I'd heard.

I turned back around and watched the kids ring the next

doorbell. The pirate dropped a handful of candy into her bucket and the group headed across the yard to the next house.

I covered my mouth in another yawn and followed along the sidewalk before pulling out my phone to text JT again.

—Miss you already—

I stared at the phone, waiting for a response that didn't come right away like I'd hoped.

Maya got so excited on the way to the next house that she jumped up and down. It made me smile. She was so cute.

Even after four more houses, JT hadn't replied. Of course, if he was running, he wouldn't feel it. Or hear it.

After the next house, the pirate ran over to the group of parents and held up a Butterfinger to a woman in a witch costume who leaned down and smiled. "Look what I got, Mommy—my favorite!"

It was a little boy, not my sister.

Oh, my God—where was Maya?

4

Lauren

Instant panic burned my throat as a sudden breeze sent leaves swirling through the air.

Now that I really looked, it was obvious the pirate wasn't Maya. There was no parrot. The pants were black and loose. The head scarf covered the boy's whole head. And he was carrying a canvas tote rather than a pumpkin.

Where had she gone? She wouldn't have just wandered off on Halloween night.

Or maybe she had—maybe she'd gotten ahead of the group and was just at the next house.

I looked at the kids again and she definitely wasn't with them. There were princesses and zombies on the street, but no Maya. My heart started racing and I rubbed the back of my neck and continued scanning the area. But Maya was nowhere.

Could she be hiding? It wasn't like her, but she'd been a little different lately.

I looked around. "Maya?" I called.

Those missing girls on TV flashed into my mind. What if somebody had taken her? My heart sped up even more.

"Maya!" I called again, looking around more frantically now. The two moms I'd been shadowing looked over at me.

"Have you seen my sister?" I barked out while running toward them. "She's the one wearing the other pirate costume. She was just here, but I can't find her anywhere."

Witch Mom said, "Where did you see her last?"

"It was a few houses back. I'd thought she was this pirate." I motioned to the one who'd held up the Butterfinger, then added, "I thought she was still with the group."

Maya must have just run ahead. Jesus, this was so dumb. What was she thinking? I'd wring her neck once I found her.

"I'm sure she's around. Let's go ask the kids," said the other mom, who was in jeans and a tucked-in green tee. The moms followed me to the group of kids who were making their way to the next house. On the way, the woman asked, "What's your sister's name?"

"Maya."

"Oh, you're Maya's sister," Witch Mom said. "She's a sweet girl."

Jeans Mom put her hand on a ballerina's shoulder. "Have any of you seen Maya?"

The ballerina said, "She showed us her candy."

"She is a pirate, too!" the pirate said, holding up his plastic sword.

Witch Mom crouched down and said, "Yeah, she is. Did any of you see where she went? She's not with you anymore."

They were quiet, and several shook their heads until Captain America finally spoke up. "I saw her running away."

My racing heart nearly stopped. "Running?" But then I calmed again—she had just run ahead.

The boy nodded, looking down.

Jeans Mom gasped. "Elliot, why was she running? What was she running from?"

"I don't know. She just ran really fast."

"Where did she go?" Jeans Mom said, her voice very tense.

"Past that house." He pointed down the street—the same direction JT had gone.

Past the house? Not to it? Jesus.

Maybe JT had seen her! Maybe Maya had even followed him since she was so interested in him. I was frozen in place, completely uncertain what to do next. I didn't even know if I should be annoyed or panicking.

Witch Mom stood back up and rested her hand on the other woman's arm and looked at me. "Honey, she probably just went ahead. What's your name?"

"Lauren," I answered.

Jeans Mom's eyed the hand on her wrist and didn't say anything.

"Okay, we need to figure out where she went," Witch Mom said, letting go of the other woman's arm. "We should call the police." She was all business now.

Jeans Mom quietly said, "The missing girls."

Somehow, involving the police was terrifying. She wasn't *really* missing, was she? I turned in the direction Maya had gone.

My heart fell into my stomach like a heavy stone and panic won the contest, making my stomach cramp. It couldn't be. Really, it couldn't—Maya had just been there. I sped off, scanning the street and calling Maya's name.

"Lauren!" one of the women called.

I ignored her. When I reached the end of the street and didn't know which way to turn, I pulled out my phone and called JT.

Thank God he answered this time. "Have you seen my sister?!"

"Just with you," he said, breathing fast. "I thought you were watching her."

"I am! She ran off after you left. Or maybe before. I don't know!" Suddenly I was annoyed again. "My parents are going to kill me for losing her!" I folded over, palms on my knees, totally out of breath now. Where would Maya go? Why would she run?

"Try to calm down a little, Lauren. I'm sure she's around. You'll find her." It sounded like he was still running.

I glanced at the phone feeling a little betrayed. He wasn't being helpful. "Would you come help me find her?"

"Lauren, you know I can't." His words came out between heavy breaths. "I've already been pushing it to go out to see you. I have to get back to the dorm, or at least on campus, soon. But don't worry, I'm sure she'll turn up. Why don't you go check at home?"

"Okay, fine. Thanks for being such a great boyfriend." I almost tossed the phone away.

I took a right onto another of the neighborhood streets and started running again, calling, "Maya! Maya!" There were still kids everywhere, but no Maya. And it was already so dark.

People were staring. "Have you seen a girl in a pirate costume?" I called to the general crowd of people, but no one answered. I kept running.

A pirate! I skidded to a stop. It had to be her.

Thank God. Relief flooded me so fast that I doubled over from queasiness.

I looked back up. White shirt. Black bandanna. All-black pants.

Not Maya. My stomach roiled again.

Where could she have gone? My heart was flying, and not just from the running, and my mouth was dry. I headed back, turning back onto the street I'd come from, when I saw Witch Mom running toward me, phone in hand.

"Lauren!" she called. "Have you called your parents? The police are on their way, but someone needs to go to your house."

Oh, God. Dana. This woman was right—I needed to call Dana. I dialed her at work.

"Dana, I can't find Maya!" I blurted.

Dana gasped. "What do you mean?"

"I mean, she disappeared when we were trick-or-treating." I was still breathing fast, and I was terrified about what Dana was going to say.

"How could you lose her?"

"I don't know! There was another pirate and I confused them. One of the kids said she ran off. I don't know why!"

"Where did this happen?" Her voice was high and fast.

"I don't know the name of the street—we're not that far from home."

Witch Mom interjected, "This is the 1500 block of Crest Road."

I repeated it for Dana. "The police are coming but they said you need to go home so someone's there."

Dana called to someone in the background and had a short conversation. Then she came back on. "I'm on my way." The call clicked off.

I bent over, resting my hands on my thighs, head spinning.

A cop car pulled up and stopped across the street. A

Black cop with a shaved head came over. Jeans Mom said, "This is Lauren. It's her sister who's missing."

"Can you tell me what happened?" he asked.

I explained as quickly as I could, anxious to keep looking. The cop nodded and asked for a photo of Maya, so I sent it to the number he gave me, and then more cops showed up. I was ready to get going, but then another cop started talking to me, wanting me to give the full story, and any information I could about where she might have gone.

"I've already told this several times. Can't we just start looking for her again?" I rubbed the back of my neck, my whole body charged with tension. "Is someone looking for her?"

He barely glanced at me. "We need all the information. We're currently arranging a search."

I looked around. Other cops were talking to the moms. There were some men milling about, some neighbors, talking to other cops. Nothing looked organized. What were they doing?

Right then, Dad showed up. "What's going on?" he asked, his voice high.

I relaxed a tiny bit because I knew something would start happening now. But he was going to be so mad at me. "Maya ran off and we can't find her."

He started talking to the cop, who asked him a bunch of stuff, but then they started talking about the search.

"Lauren, I want you to go home," Dad said. "Wait there. Nathan and Charles are on their way to the house. We'll find her."

"Dad, I want to help look!" Why was he keeping me out of it?

"No," he said, his voice cracking. "I don't want something to happen to you."

That stopped me. He was really scared. This couldn't be this bad. We would find her, wouldn't we?

One of the other officers gave me a ride. I stared out the window while she asked me questions about Maya.

As soon as we pulled up by the curb, I jumped out and ran up the cracked sidewalk and onto the brick path that led up to the house. My foot caught on a loose brick and I threw my hands out but still ended up sprawled out, face smashed painfully on the grass.

I pushed myself onto my knees and looked up at the porch. Maya wasn't there. Oh—what if someone *had* taken her? I stood and rubbed my sore cheek and nose. Dana ran out. "Did you find her?" Our uncles, Nathan and Charles, stood behind her.

I shook my head. She went back inside, looking panicked and angry. I was going to be in so much trouble. Maya would feel really bad about it. Why had she run off? What in the world was she thinking? How could she do this to me? They'd probably ground me for months—and make me come home every weekend, and I'd never get to see JT except during the week.

But how could I be thinking about that? Maya was *missing*. Oh, my God.

The uncles stepped out and started talking to a cop behind me. Right then Gabriel came out of his house and hurried over, phone in his hand. It dinged but he didn't look. "What's going on?"

"Maya's missing!" My voice broke. "She got away from me when she was trick-or-treating. She ran off for some reason and I don't know why!"

"What happened?" His voice was sharp with concern.

"I don't know! It's so weird—she was happy, and then one of the other kids said she literally started running away!

I didn't notice at first because her pirate costume was like one of the other kids' she was with, and I thought he was her." I put my hand on my stomach, feeling completely sick.

Gabriel's phone dinged and he typed a quick text and put his phone in his pocket.

"Gabriel, come on, we're going to search." Nathan stood next to us, still in his work shirt from Don Pablos.

Gabriel grabbed my arm. "Come on."

Nathan held out his hand. "Your dad said you stay here."

"I want to go!" What was with all these people telling me what to do?

He shook his head. "No. We don't know who's out there."

"This is so stupid! I can help!"

"Come on, Gabriel," Nathan said.

Gabriel looked at me, desperate, but he followed Nathan over to where some men were gathering. Of course it was all men, like the rest of us don't have working feet and eyes.

How could I lose her? God, this was the worst night of my life. Where was she?

I watched them leave and went into the house, still feeling like I could throw up at any second.

There were already other cops in the house talking to Dana. I stood in the kitchen, watching everything. I was really starting to panic. She'd been gone too long. Where in the world was she? All these people were coming and going in the house—cops, neighbors, other people. Dana was crying and a neighbor whose name I didn't even know was consoling her.

And then I was crying. I went back to my bedroom to get away from all the people and sat on the bed. No texts or messages from JT.

I texted Tenny, my other best friend since kindergarten and also my roommate at OAMS.

—OMG, Lauren! Where is she?— she answered.

—I don't know but I'm so scared right now— The crying got worse. How could I let this happen? If only I hadn't been so focused on JT. God, how could I?

—Should I come over?— Tenny asked.

—You probably shouldn't— I put the phone down and lay back on the bed, still crying. It dinged a couple more times. I picked it up. Just more sympathy from Tenny. She wanted me to tell her as soon as they found her so she could relax.

I texted JT. *—Call me?—*

After several minutes, he actually replied. *—Can't right now. U find your sister?—*

—No!! They are still looking—

—Oh no. Good luck. I'm sure it will be fine—

"Good luck"? That's all he could come up with?

But then again, he probably didn't know what to say. Did he feel bad for being with me when Maya disappeared? I tossed the phone aside.

There was only one thought in my head right now— Maya, where are you?

Gabriel

My heart was pounding a mile a minute as I headed off with the other man I'd been sent to search with. Nasim. The man's name was Nasim.

"Maya!" I called, looking around, my entire head laced with cold, sharp tension.

We were heading into downtown. I'd been this way a bunch of times because I used to walk to the 7-Eleven for candy all the time, and I couldn't tell you how many times

Lauren and Maya had made the trek with me. They had good choices of Laffy Taffy. Maya's favorite was the banana ones.

But nothing looked normal tonight. The whole world had a wavy sheen to it through my panic. There were trick-or-treaters everywhere, confusing things and stressing me out so much. I kept looking for Maya to be hiding in plain sight, but none of the pirates were her. The car in the driveway of the first house on the right looked foreboding, a big dent in the back passenger side marring the already dull silver. I headed toward it anyway and Nasim followed. He was walking a little slower—the man didn't know Maya, so obviously he didn't have the same sense of urgency I had.

At the first house, I ran up to the fence and peered over it, calling Maya's name again. Nasim was looking over the fence of the house across the street, also calling her name.

He had to be in his thirties, but I didn't know much about him, except that he was a professor at OIT and lived in the neighborhood. He had on jeans and a brown polo shirt, and I wondered if he was a creeper. Could he have had something to do with this? Where had he come from, to be out helping with the search?

I ran to the next yard while Nasim trotted to the next one on his side of the road. He was obviously a decent person, out to help. Or maybe he was covering his tracks. No. God, I was so terrified it was making me paranoid. We kept going, checking one house at a time, calling maya's name, dodging kids and parents just out having fun.

Surely Maya was just hiding. She must have gotten spooked by something. But it wasn't like her at all. She wasn't normally a scared kid. I could not get rid of the burning terror coursing through my veins.

A couple people came out of their houses, and Nasim

explained what was going on while I kept checking the backyards on my side of the street, scrambling from house to house, feet numb in my stupid Crocs. I couldn't stop my mind from spinning up horror stories, and I was sweating through the fear.

A second man had joined Nasim, and they kept going down the street. By the time we got to the end of the road, I realized I was crying.

I wiped my eyes, grinding my teeth in frustration and stress. How could this be happening? Where was she?

"Gabriel, let's turn left," Nasim called from across the road. He narrowed his eyes. "Are you okay?"

I realized I'd just been standing there, wiping the tears off my face. I nodded and scrambled to follow the guys. This was the last street before a commercial one, and we made it down the entire row of houses with nothing to show for it but sore throats. Grungy cars, run-down houses, a couple of hastily tossed-aside bikes, and too many places for a little kid to hide.

Or be hidden.

Where *was* Maya?

We turned onto the commercial street, starting with the 7-Eleven on the corner.

I went inside, the string of bells hanging on the door handle clanking sharply in my ears. A young woman with black braids stood behind the cash register.

"Have you seen a little girl in a pirate costume?" I asked, more panic in my voice than I'd meant.

The woman shook her head. "Nope, just people buying gas, cigarettes, and lottery tickets tonight. You know Power-ball's up now."

"Oh." How could the lottery still be happening? "We're

looking for an eight-year-old named Maya. If you see her, please keep her here and call the police."

"Oh no, she's missing?" She sounded genuinely concerned and glanced at something on the glass near the door.

I nodded and followed her line of sight, turning toward the door. It was a flyer with a picture of the last girl who'd gone missing. My heart dropped again. We had to find Maya.

I went back outside and found Nasim and the other man spread out, looking into the other businesses on the road, but they were all closed. We just checked the doors and peeked inside. A watch repair shop, a pawn shop, a nail salon, and a deli, all with locked doors and nothing visible from the windows.

Where *was* she? Had one of the other searchers found her? I realized I was gritting my teeth and tried to relax, but my jaw was locked in tension. We crossed the street and checked a couple of other businesses before getting to an alley.

I turned down the alley. There were a couple of cars parked behind the nearest business, with a junky gate leading up to some stairs and an obvious upstairs apartment. I checked under and inside the cars, but there was nothing. It was dark, with only the light from the main street and one dull light over the apartment's front door.

There were a couple cars parked next to the stairs—a beat-up blue sedan with orange bungee cords dangling from the back and an old silver BMW. I went to look behind them when something caught my eye. Something was flashing. The blue car's trunk was slightly ajar and a light was flashing inside it. I lifted the trunk.

Maya.

"No!" I jerked back and tripped on my feet, crashing backwards onto my ass and elbows, and then my head hit the ground with a crack.

The other men came running around the corner. "What happened?" Nasim asked. "Are you okay?"

The image was burned into my head. Maya, eyes frozen open, a line of blood trailing down out of her mouth, a cut on her forehead, her arm thrown back unnaturally, knees bent, the striped leggings torn, blood streaks on the oversized white shirt.

I couldn't breathe.

"*Ya Rabb!*" Nasim said when he saw her. "No!"

"Oh my God, is this her?" the other man asked.

"Yes," Nasim said while I nodded, still on the ground.

My stomach lurched and I rolled to the side and threw up the horrible SpaghettiO's I'd had for dinner.

"Here, get up," the other man said. He reached out a hand for me, but I didn't take it, instead pushing myself up off the ground. There was something sticky on my hands and I wiped them on my jeans.

I couldn't even face the trunk, but Nasim was on the phone with the cops. Any second now, they'd be here and this would be real. Maya would really be dead.

I cried, face in my hands, head pulsing with pain.

Then the cops were there, coming around the corner after the sounds of running boots on the ground.

They ignored me and raced up to the trunk.

But then everything slowed down. Because Maya was gone. Nothing seemed so urgent anymore.

"Is that from her?" someone asked.

I felt a jerk on my shoulder and turned to see a white cop with a buzzcut, looking at me and pointing down. I blinked, not understanding.

"The puke," the cop said. "Is it hers?"

"No," I said, my voice thick. "It's mine."

I vaguely heard one of the other men say I'd found her, and then two cops were talking to me. My head throbbed and my vision was blurry even though I'd wiped the tears away.

"How did you know she was there?" the buzzcut cop asked.

"What?" I didn't understand the question.

"Why'd you know to look there?" the second cop asked.

"I ... didn't. I just saw the trunk ajar and I opened it. There was a flashing light. From the light on her ankle." I glanced back at the car, Maya's black boots just visible out of the corner of my eye. Fresh tears formed.

"You're going to have to come talk to us." The second cop had black hair and looked a little Asian, something I knew was weird to notice.

My head continued to throb and I needed to get home. I couldn't be here. I started walking toward the entrance of the alley.

"Where are you going?" the first cop asked.

I held my head in my right hand. "I ... need to be at home." My voice was almost unrecognizable. Thick and deep and laced with shock. But I didn't stop or turn.

"You're the neighbor, aren't you?" the cop asked.

I nodded and turned back onto the street.

"Don't go back to Mexico."

Mexico? We were Guatemalan, not Mexican. And I was born here, and so were my parents. My feet were numb and damp from sweat, squeaking in the Crocs. I headed toward home.

Who was going to tell Lauren and her parents? I couldn't imagine.

Lauren

I was so on edge waiting to hear any news about Maya. Dana made me wait in my bedroom because she was so pissed at me, completely blaming me. Not that she was wrong. Dad seemed more worried and wasn't paying any attention to me. I didn't care, I just wanted Maya back. My head throbbed from the tension and crying because it was horrible to just sit here and do nothing. I'd texted Gabriel a couple times but he hadn't responded. JT didn't respond to my texts either, so I was just sitting at my desk, staring at the wall.

I was staring at the photos that lined the bulletin board on the wall, with shots of me with Maya, Gabriel, Tenny and now JT.

I heard a tapping on the window and jerked my around —Maya!

But no, it was Tenny. My heart sank, but I opened the window.

"I'm sorry, I didn't know if you needed me," Tenny said. She'd obviously been crying. "I'm so worried! What's happening?"

That's when I heard Dana scream. It made me jump out of my skin, and I was terrified. Tenny's eyes widened. I ran into the hall.

"Nick, how?" Dana shrieked and then just wailed. I'd never heard her like this.

What did it mean? Had they found Maya? Was she hurt?

I peeked around the corner.

Dana was crumpled on the floor next to the couch with Dad crouched down consoling her. A couple of neighbors were standing close, like they'd been talking, but they were all just standing behind the couch with their heads down. The two women were crying. The man looked lost. A cop was talking into a radio near the front door, but I was in a fog and couldn't hear anything.

Why wasn't anyone doing anything?

It finally hit me—they had *found her*. And she wasn't okay. They weren't doing anything because there was nothing that could be done.

I was frozen in horror.

Dana and Dad saw me then, and Dana said, "Get out of my sight! I don't ever want to see you again! She's gone and it's your fault!"

I took a step back and stumbled, my stomach in turmoil. I barely made it to the toilet, where I threw up all the red licorice candy Maya had ben giving me all night.

Dana was still yelling. I knew I'd better leave. I scrambled across the hall to my room. At first I didn't know where to go, but then I realized I'd just go to the dorm.

I threw my shoes on and looked at Tenny, still standing in the window, wide-eyed. I immediately burst into tears.

"She's dead," I said to Tenny, the words almost impossible to say.

Her eyes were still huge and her mouth was hanging open.

I started climbing out the window because I obviously couldn't go through the front room again.

Tenny grabbed me by the shoulders, and we burst into tears in an awkward hug. A couple of cops had watched me climb out the window but said nothing as Tenny took my hand and we took off toward the dorm.

The tears were coming nonstop. Maya was dead and it was my fault. They were all right. I could barely hear anything and almost walked in front of a car when I started to cross a street, but they honked and Tenny pulled me back. It was four blocks to the OIT campus, but then we had to cross it to the southeast corner where the OAMS buildings were.

Tenny and I didn't utter a word the whole way. When we got there, the dorm was locked up because study time had started, but one of the staff downstairs saw us and let us in. They looked concerned, but neither of us could say what had happened out loud. We knew we were in trouble. They let us go upstairs, but warned us that the dorm mom was going to come up.

I opened our room door slowly, still in a daze, and we both went to our desks and sat. I slumped, head in my hands.

"What ... happened?" Tenny asked.

I shook my head and tried to form words. "I don't know. Nobody told me anything." I started sobbing. "It's all my fault."

Tenny obviously had no idea what to do or say, which I understood , because that was exactly how I felt too.

"Was that Dana that yelled at you?" she asked.

"Yeah. She said she never wants to see me again." Tears dropped onto my jeans. "And I don't even blame her."

"Lauren, you didn't do anything wrong. Kids get away from their families all the time. You know I lose Samuel about five times every summer."

Like me, Tenny grew up watching her siblings. But she was wrong. I didn't notice for *so long*.

Tenny came over and hugged me from behind, and we bawled.

5

———

Lauren

The car is blue and the trunk is open, like a dark and gaping wound. There is something inside it, and orange bungee cords dangle from it like they'd had a purpose before.

∿

Lauren

I woke with a start to an alarm. I fumbled in the dark to get my phone turned off because that's where it was coming from. It was 5:00 a.m.—why was it going off?

"What's going on, Lauren?" Tenny asked groggily.

"I don't know. My alarm just went off."

"Okay."

We lay there quietly, both knowing the situation of the world we had just awoken into. But then I remembered I'd been having a dream. There was a blue car with something in it. But I couldn't tell what it was.

"Are you okay?" Tenny asked.

I immediately started crying. "No." I was not okay and I never would be again. I had let Maya get killed. But I still didn't know what had actually happened. Was she taken by the same people who'd taken the other missing girls? If so, why had she been found and the others hadn't? And what was done to her? It was making me sick, imagining all the worst things.

Tenny didn't say anything, and I knew she was crying, too.

We stayed quiet. I think she slept, but I just lay there, tears rolling down my cheeks for the next hour and a half.

Gabriel

Tuesday morning I could not get myself out of the house. Mamá went to work in the morning, but I just sat on the couch trying to figure out what had happened to Maya. Why had she run off? How had she ended up in that trunk? She was obviously hurt before she was put in there—was she hit by a car? Did she crawl into the trunk? Nothing made sense. But I could not get the image of her out of my head.

Had she suffered? She must have. She was so beat up.

I wrote down all the questions on individual pieces of paper I tore out of my spiral notebook. But as much as I stared at them and moved them around on the coffee table, nothing made sense.

Lauren had texted me last night and I hadn't responded. I was so mad at her. I still didn't understand how she could have let this happen. I was convinced that it was her obsession with JT that was responsible, somehow.

A knock sounded from the front door. I got up and looked out the glass.

Two men. Who would be here?

I opened the door.

It was two bald white men I hadn't seen before.

"Gabriel Canul?" the older one said. He had a clean-cut, peppery beard.

"Yes, that's me." My entire body vibrated with nerves.

The younger guy held up a badge and said, "We're investigating the death of Maya Roberts-Baxter."

Hearing it out loud made me sob. But then my heart started beating like crazy. Did they think I was guilty of something? I hadn't thought about it, but that's what that guy was implying last night, wasn't it?

Both of them looked at me, apparently alarmed.

"Sorry," I said, wiping a couple of tears away. "I just can't believe it. I'm completely destroyed. I love Maya." Should I have said "loved," instead? I felt like everything I said would be held under suspicion.

"Do you mind if we come in and talk to you?" the older one asked. "I'm Detective Hansen and this is Detective Tolui. We understand you were the one who found Maya."

That felt like a punch to the gut. "Uh, sure." I looked back at the room and suddenly felt self-conscious. The old, decrepit flower-print couch and two wingback chairs that had seen better days formed the sides of a rectangle around the coffee table.

I turned back to the door and stood to the side to let them in, then they took the chairs and I sat on the couch, painfully bumping the table leg with my toes first.

I immediately felt cornered, with one of them on either

side of me. But I needed to hold it together. I hadn't done anything wrong, and I needed to give them any information I had, even if I didn't think it was important, so they could investigate and find the real killer.

"Gabriel, walk us through your night," Detective Hansen said.

I nodded. "Okay. My mom and I took shifts managing the candy bowl and I worked on homework on the couch in between. Lauren and Maya came by to show off her costume, and I got my annual picture."

"Oh, can we see?" Detective Tolui asked.

I felt self-conscious again. Why did they want to see it? I didn't want to show them, but I figured I'd better. I picked my phone up off the table and realized all my notes on Maya were just sitting there, along with the spiral notebook. I pulled up the picture of Maya, smiling happily, and it made my heart stop and brought tears to my eyes. I showed it to both of them.

"Lauren's sure cute," Tolui said.

That made me stop. "What?"

"She's in that picture, too. Was that an accident?"

"We're all friends. She was just ... in it." This was just making me more and more nervous. Also, that rage I felt at Lauren flared again. How could she lose Maya?

"So Maya wasn't getting in the way?" Hansen asked.

"Getting in the way of what?" I was so confused.

They both just looked at me.

Oh. *Oh.* God, this stupid shit again. "Lauren's not my type."

"What, not young enough?" Tolui asked.

"What—oh, my God! No! She's a girl. Jesus." What is wrong with people?

"You're gay?" Hansen asked.

I stared at the table. Too many people in Oklahoma thought being gay made you a pervert. "Yes."

They both nodded, like they understood something important.

This was idiotic. I needed to get them back on track. But the relationship idea stirred something in the back of my mind, and I remembered seeing JT leaving Lauren's on Saturday. And that smug look. That was one guy who'd have a reason to want Maya out of the way. It's not like the two of them could get up to anything with Maya around.

God, what if it was him?

Both of the officers were looking at me. "Have you talked to JT? Lauren's boyfriend?"

"Joseph Comstock?" Hansen asked.

"Yes."

"We talked to him, yes," Tolui said.

They weren't going to give me anything.

"Why don't you finish telling us about your night," Hansen said.

"Okay." I ran my hand through my hair and pulled my feet up on the couch, under me. They were cold.

"You were doing homework after Lauren and Maya left," Tolui prompted.

I nodded and talked through how I saw all the activity outside and I'd gone out to find out what was going on, and that's when I'd found out Maya was missing, and joined the search effort. I'd felt like I had whiplash, because I'd been in such a good mood, texting Will while working on homework, and then everything happened. As I was talking to the cops, I was feeling panicky as I walked them through the searching, and I cried again when I talked about finding her.

"It was the worst moment of my life," I said flatly. "Even worse than when I found out my dad had been killed." But then both horrors came rushing in and I had to wipe more tears away. Why was there so much death in my life? What had I ever done to deserve it? Two wonderful people, gone for no reason, while there were so many horrible people still here. Including the one who'd killed Maya.

JT's name floated across my mind again. But he would have been back at the dorm, wouldn't he? This all happened well before curfew, though, so he could have been out and about.

Tolui was saying something.

"Sorry?" I ran my hand through my hair again, an old nervous habit that was coming back with a vengeance.

"Do you have any ideas about what might have happened?" he asked.

I shook my head. "She looked so beat up. It was obvious that she was put in that car after ... whatever happened. Did she get hit by a car? She had that cut, and the blood from her mouth, and her arm looked horrible, all unnatural." I had to close my eyes and catch my spinning emotions. How bad was this? Could it be even worse? "Did they ... mess with her?" God, please no.

"You know we can't divulge information from the investigation," Hansen said. "But we do believe she was hit by a car."

"It must have happened close by, right? There are all those businesses around there. There must be security cameras."

Tolui nodded. "We're looking into that. We're just wondering if you saw anything in that area that gave you pause."

I shook my head. "I was so focused on finding her."

"Okay. Let us know if you think of anything else."

Hansen reached into a pocket and handed me a business card. "And don't leave town."

"I'm not going anywhere. This is where I live, and it's the middle of the semester." Now I was stressing again. They still thought I was involved somehow.

They stood up, somehow in unison, and I followed them to the door, happy to shut it on them. In the most polite way.

I had a really bad feeling about this, on top of being destroyed and having all my classes and everything else to worry about.

I remembered what I went through when Papá died. I was a wreck and started struggling in school. I had one teacher who really helped me, but it was a very hard time. I couldn't sink into that again this time. I couldn't afford to let my grades slip, as shitty as I felt.

Somehow I had to keep it together and keep my scholarships.

Lauren

I woke to someone knocking on our door. I felt immediately alert.

"Lauren?" It sounded like the dorm mother.

"Yeah?" I said.

"Your dad's here, sweetie. Go ahead and get your stuff, as you'll need to leave with him. I'm really sorry about what has happened."

"Okay," I called. I didn't get up right away and instead remembered the dream I'd been having when the alarm had gone off earlier.

"I can't believe Dana made you leave," Tenny said, her voice thick.

"I know." Then I did get out of bed, got dressed, and packed a bag. I went to the bathroom to brush my teeth and headed downstairs.

"We didn't know where you'd gone," Dad said when I got to the front desk. He looked rough.

The RA on duty waved at me to let me know I was checked out, and we left.

"Dana told me to leave."

"She didn't mean it." He pushed open the front door and we went through the foyer and onto the pavement. "She was just upset."

I didn't point out that they didn't seem to care that I was upset too. I knew she blamed me, and I doubted that had changed. But she wasn't wrong, so it's not like I could complain. We walked down the path toward the car.

I blamed myself, too. But also, why did that boy have to be dressed like a pirate, too? Fuck.

"Why are you here?" I finally asked.

"You need to be at home right now." He opened his door and I followed suit.

"Nobody told me what happened, Dad. I still don't know."

He turned the key to start the car and it sputtered. This was a works-on-the-second-turn kind of car.

It caught on the second turn. He leaned against the steering wheel. "We don't really know. It looks like she was hit by a car and put in the trunk of another car. She might have been strangled, too. It doesn't make sense."

"Strangled? What? Why?"

He shook his head. "We don't know, Lauren."

At least he didn't say, Thanks to you.

We drove home in silence. When we got there, Dana was in bed and she stayed there. Dad said the police were coming by at twelve. I ate some cereal, staring at the kitchen wall while I ate.

We ended up sitting on the couch, waiting for twelve o'clock, saying nothing. At one point, he took my hand and held it, which didn't seem weird, even though it totally was. We sat that way for a while and it made me feel a little better. Like I wasn't so alone.

He squeezed my hand and said, "Lauren, somebody strangled my little girl. Why?"

"I don't know, Dad." I put my head on his shoulder. He was shaking a little, probably from crying.

A knock sounded, as if in the distance. Dad raised his head but didn't move or let go of my hand. Another knock. He rose and slowly made his way across the room, opening the door to reveal two men.

They introduced themselves as Detectives Hansen and Tolui. Hansen wore a blue blazer and was shorter than Dad while Tolui towered over them both, with eyes heavy and dark. Dad didn't move from the door while the two men stood just inside it, glancing around.

Hansen motioned at the kitchen table and said, "I'm going to just grab a chair from in here." They both moved into the room, and Tolui sank into the recliner that suddenly looked a lot more tattered than I remembered. He was mostly bald, with a few blondish hairs hanging on for dear life. Dad finally shut the door and made his way back to the couch.

Tolui said, "Thank you both for being willing to talk to us. I am very sorry for your loss." He looked at each of us in turn when he said this, and it seemed like he meant it.

"What we really need from you today, Lauren, is a clear picture of the events leading up to Maya's disappearance."

"But I already told the cop last night," I said in a thick voice. Dad patted my arm and left his hand there, making me a little calmer.

"We just need to go over it one more time. To see if you can remember anything you couldn't last night." Tolui pulled out a small notebook and pen. Hansen followed suit.

The notebook was disconcerting. It made it all the more real. And terrifying. "Okay." I nodded and closed my eyes for a moment, waiting for the wave of nausea to pass. Over the next few minutes I went through every detail I could remember, explaining how I thought I was watching Maya but it turned out to be a different kid. I had to close my eyes again at that point, but tears slipped out anyway. Dad squeezed my arm.

Tolui nodded. "Could you talk a little more about what happened when your boyfriend got there—this is Joseph Comstock, right?"

"He hates that name. He goes by JT."

"JT, okay. Good. What happened when he got there and when he left?"

"So. I guess I was looking at Maya when I heard someone say my name. I turned around and saw him." Drainage had collected in my throat and I swallowed. "I was really surprised. I didn't know why he would be there, but I was glad because I was pretty bored and whatnot." I was a horrible person. I started crying again and looked over. "I'm sorry, Dad."

He just patted my arm and his eyes focused on a point beyond Detective Hansen. It was still really weird that he had his hand on my arm. Maybe this meant he didn't blame me. I couldn't remember the last time he'd touched me, even for a hug. He just wasn't a touchy-feely kind of guy.

God, I missed JT. He would comfort me. It was just last night that he'd had his arms wrapped around my waist, but it was a lifetime ago.

"So what happened while he was there?" Tolui asked.

"We talked for a bit."

"Anything else?"

"We kissed." I blushed and felt like a child for doing so.

"So you were probably a little distracted?"

I nodded, closing my eyes and wishing I hadn't been. Jesus, it really was all my fault.

Tolui was quiet for a moment while he wrote on his notepad. Hansen looked up from what he was writing and said, "How did you feel about having to watch your sister?"

"What? Oh. It was okay. I have to watch her a lot when our parents are working. Not as much now as I used to because I'm away at school during the week and sometimes weekends. Now Uncle Charles does it more."

"Charles?" Tolui asked.

"Charles Roberts," Dad said. "Maya's biological uncle."

Tolui cleared his throat. "Can you clarify that?"

"Charles is Maya's uncle through her biological father. James Roberts. His brother."

"Where is her father now?"

"He died before she was born," Dad said.

Tolui scribbled another note down. He glanced at Hansen, who nodded and said, "Lauren, it can't be fun getting stuck babysitting all the time when you want to have a life."

I gaped at him. My stomach roiled again.

Dad looked up. "Hey, she's a good kid. She loves her sister."

"I would *never* do anything to Maya." My voice cracked.

Hansen nodded, writing.

After glancing over at Hansen, Tolui pulled a sheet of paper out of his pocket and stood to hand it to me. "Have you ever seen this car?"

It showed two different shots of a grungy old blue Geo Prizm parked next to a silver car. I knew the model of the car immediately. The one picture I had of my bio-mom showed her standing in front of her own ancient Prizm—a red one. In the photo, she was holding baby me and smiling. This was not long before she took off. A familiar ache in my chest started up, like it sometimes did when I thought about my mother. Why had she really left me?

I blinked. The second photo showed the back of the car. I could see the dark gap between the bumper and the trunk lid that meant that it was slightly ajar.

All the blood drained out of my face. The dream. "Were there orange bungee cords on this car?"

Dad jerked a little and looked at me.

Tolui frowned slightly and narrowed his eyes. "What makes you ask that? Did you see the car?"

"No." Why had I blurted it out? Now I'd have to explain everything.

"What then? Because you're right, there were bungee cords that previously held the trunk closed. But they were removed at some point last night before this picture was taken."

I opened my mouth to start talking but realized I had no idea what to say. I couldn't believe in a dream. I was a rational person.

"Lauren?" Tolui prompted.

"It will sound insane." I looked anywhere but at either detective's face. The tattered recliner, the TV sitting in front of the fireplace we never used, the wobbly black coffee table we'd recently brought home from a garage sale.

I was quiet for another moment. Tolui said, "Go ahead."

I glanced at Dad, who was looking back intently. "I had a dream last night with this car in it. The bungee cords were dangling."

"A dream?" Tolui asked.

I nodded. "But it doesn't make sense. I must have seen it some other time. Maybe at a store or something? Burnside's not that big. Where was this?"

"Yes, that's certainly possible. It was by the 7-Eleven a couple blocks from here. But you don't remember where you might have seen it, or know anything else about the car?"

I shook my head.

"Please try to think of any other connection to this car either of you might have had," Tolui said.

"Is this the car you found her in?" I asked, needing to know for sure.

Tolui nodded. "It is a vehicle of interest."

Dad looked down and made a little noise like a small groan.

Oh, God.

Dad's hand was heavy on my arm, a dead weight. I'd let everyone down.

6

———

Gabriel

I walked into my sociology class Thursday feeling sick to my stomach because I kept thinking how great it would be to see Will, and that felt so wrong right now.

Will waved at me and smiled, but it was not a flirty smile. He knew what had gone down. I didn't text him at all after I'd told him Maya was missing Monday night, and he'd kept texting occasionally. Tuesday he tried again, and I finally responded after the cops left. He'd already found out from the news, but he told me he was sorry I'd been the one to find her. I walked across the room and he pulled his bag off the chair he'd been saving for me.

"Hey," he said. "How are you?"

The question called up a surge of emotion and I had to take a deep breath. I sat down and said, "Not good."

He nodded. The room was relatively quiet while people were filing in. I felt like all eyes were on me, which was ridiculous. Even though I'm sure a lot of people had heard about Maya, nobody knew it had anything to do with me. Or did they? Did people here even know about it at all?

Will patted me on the back, awkwardly but kindly.

"It's so hard to focus on things. I'm so behind on the readings for my classes. I just want to know what happened." I pulled my notebook and pen out, opening it to the next blank page.

Will nodded. "I know. It's just such a weird thing, the way everything happened."

I'd filled him in on everything, and honestly, I was kind of surprised he wasn't pulling away the way guys usually do when there's a chance of emotion. He knew how upset I was, but he'd still been brave enough to ask how I was doing. Maybe he was the right guy for me. I wondered if we'd really get together. I hated myself for being a little excited about that idea.

He smiled at me again, supportively, just as Dr. Wetherspoon greeted the class.

I'd just been staring at him, having all those thoughts, so I blushed and stared down at my notebook.

The next thing I knew, Dr. Wetherspoon was talking about prisons.

How long would the man who killed Maya—it was almost always a man—spend in prison? It better be his whole life. Or maybe he'd be executed. Oklahoma still did that. But didn't they usually have to be serial killers or something? Or just not white. Could I end up on death row? A rush of panic went through me and I forced myself to get back to the present.

Dr. Wetherspoon was actually talking about capital punishment now. Apparently it wasn't really a deterrent. And sometimes it cost more for someone to be on death row than to spend life in prison because they got so many appeals.

I tried to write this down, but my hand was shaking and I just wanted to cry. I pulled my phone out and pulled up the picture of Maya in her costume. It was the last picture on my roll because I hadn't taken a single one since then.

When would they find him and put him away?

I couldn't get myself to focus. I must have looked out of it because Will gave me encouraging smiles on three separate occasions. Then he wrote something in the top corner of his notebook and pointed at it.

I can send you my notes, it said.

I mouthed "thank you," and looked at Maya's picture again. How could somebody do that to her?

Will tapped my arm and I looked at him, but then I heard, "Mr. Canul, care to share with us what has you so enthralled?"

Dr. Wetherspoon was glaring at me, and everyone but Will was staring.

"Um." I was blushing again. I didn't want anyone else seeing that picture. It was mine and I was still mad about what the detectives had said about it. The photos that were in the news were the one Lauren took of Maya in her costume, and her school picture from last year. I held the phone against my stomach.

She walked over and held her hand out. I just sat there, withering away while my heart tried to beat its way out of my chest.

"Come on. If it's porn, it's nothing we haven't all seen before."

Oh, my God, was she going to show it to everyone? Not Maya. Nobody else should get to see this picture of her. It was my last moment with her.

"Mr. Canul."

God. I handed her the phone but stared down at my desk.

She was silent for a beat, then asked, "Why do you have a picture of the girl who was just murdered?" She sounded alarmed and suspicious, and you could feel a wave of disgust go around the classroom, but I was frozen silent.

"He knew her. They were neighbors," Will said after a pause.

Dr. Wetherspoon set the phone on my desk and said, "Start paying attention in my class."

I nodded miserably and locked the phone, then crammed it into my pocket, safe from prying eyes. She was as judgmental as the cops. Why did people think I was doing something wrong? I felt queasy.

There were only five minutes of torture left, and Will and I walked out in silence, all eyes on us.

Once we were out of the building, Will said, "I'm going to talk to her. She has office hours tomorrow."

Students were walking all around us, going on about their business like everything was normal.

"Don't," I finally said. "It doesn't matter."

But his jaw set. I knew he disagreed with me.

"Do you want to go get a coffee?" he asked. "Don't you have a class later today?"

"I do. But I forgot my wallet." Just then a sharp, cold wind rushed across us. Winter was coming. Things were about to get even worse.

He shivered. "Come on, I'm buying. But I won't buy you a smoothie. Have you tried matcha?"

I shook my head and he took my upper arm and pulled to get me walking.

I guessed I was going to try matcha. Will being so insistent on being there for me was making me feel better. I didn't know what he saw in me, though. I didn't feel like anybody who mattered.

~

Lauren

I'm standing next to the passenger side of an old, junky truck. The window is down and a man wearing a mask that looks like a normal face frozen in a wide smile but with silver eyes turns toward me from the driver's seat. He says, "Come sit next to me." He pats the seat and I see that he has strong hands.

I'm glad he wants to spend time with me because he seems happy. I open the door and crawl in. It seems to take forever to make it all the way to the seat. His hand is still resting there, right next to my hip.

"Do you like to be tickled?" he asks.

"Yes!" I say, because it's always fun.

He starts tickling my side and it makes me laugh and I try to get away. I move so far that I fall off the seat and out of the truck because there is no longer a door. I look down and can't see the ground. I jerk to a stop, my feet dangling in midair, and he drags me back into the truck slowly by my hair. It doesn't hurt, but it feels weird.

Once I am nearly back in the seat, he grabs me around the waist and places me back where I was before. When he moves me, I look in the back seat and see there are black and white kittens crawling all over the place. A little girl in a pale pink dress sits there, petting one of the kittens in her lap.

"Kittens!" I call out. I'm not interested in the girl.

"They'll be there. Now where were we?" He is still turned

toward me and puts his left hand around my waist and starts tickling me again with the other. I laugh and squirm again, but I can't get away because he's holding on tight.

Lauren

I woke with a start, my phone alarm going off. I was so confused because I hadn't set it. It was still light out. I'd been sleeping again.

That dream. What was that? Why was it so vivid? It felt like I was still in the car with the kittens. And that creepy girl in the back. And the guy. He gave off a bad vibe.

I sat up, groggy from so much sleep. It was Thursday afternoon, and every day of the week was worse than the last. Dana wasn't leaving the bed, and Dad and I hadn't spoken in more than a day. He was gone all day and even some of the nights, probably working extra shifts for Uber and Lyft. That's what he did when his mom died a couple of years ago. When Gabriel's dad died—they were best friends—he'd actually taken off for a week. Dana and I still had no idea where he went. He'd just shut down emotionally. I was dealing with it by sleeping. Normally I handled stress by cooking, because it always made people happy, which made me feel better. But I couldn't bear to cook now, because who would eat it? I'd tried to read a novel, but I couldn't follow the story. I'd also tried to read for school, but had the same problem.

In desperation, I'd finally gotten my pre-calc textbook out and started working on the homework problems Tenny had sent me, instead of eating breakfast this morning. I'd been at it for three hours, and I'd finished all the homework and the unassigned problems in the section we were in, then I went back and started problems in the sections we'd previously studied. It was weirdly therapeutic. There was a clear right and wrong, and a clear way—or ways—to get from A to B. Everything made sense, even if it was hard.

I'd been at it all day. I'd worked all the way back to the front of the book. I was actually in the slow-kid pre-calc—the year-long version, where most of the kids at OAMS took the single-semester versions because they could then take three semesters of calculus and test out of two years of college calculus at Oklahoma colleges. I wasn't going to look at math again after high school.

But for today, it had kept my mind off Maya. And the fact that Gabriel hadn't responded to any of my texts. And that all JT was giving me was well-wishing sentence fragments.

But I needed to move. I slid my chair back from my desk and stood up, nearly leveled by a sudden cramp in my lower back. I fell back into my chair.

And burst into tears. Tenny had offered to come over every afternoon this week, but I kept saying no, because what would we talk about? But at least she cared about me enough to offer. Everyone else hated me, except maybe JT, who didn't care at all.

They all blamed me for Maya. And they were right. Would they ever forgive me?

I couldn't see how. Maya would never come back. I could never do a better job of watching her. I shouldn't even be here. If I'd never been born, this never would have happened, and Maya would still be here. Or if my mom hadn't left. Or if Maya's dad had never died. My dad would never have gotten together with Dana, and I wouldn't have gotten to be Maya's big sister.

Something I was completely unworthy of.

Light was filtering in through the blinds, hurting my eyes, so I closed them. I rested my face in my hands, tears slipping through my fingers. I didn't know how to have these feelings. What was I supposed to do?

The bottom drawer of my dresser had all my journals in it. My current one was at school, but all the others were in there. All my thoughts about Maya. All the cute things she'd done and said over the years, because I obsessively recorded everything in my life that I enjoyed.

I pushed on the spot on my back, which was tender to the touch. But I stood up again and it seemed okay, so I went over to the dresser and pulled open the drawer. I'd gotten hooked on Moleskine notebooks a couple of years ago. I picked up the red one and checked the date. February 22 to August 12 last year. I opened it at random and landed on an entry from June 13. Summer was just getting started and Maya was still only seven, but she was obsessed with jigsaw puzzles, and that's what we were spending our days doing. Plus she was learning to read chapter books on her own because she wanted to be like me. That day, we'd built a puzzle of a basket of kittens. She'd knocked the lid with a bunch of pieces in it off the table and tripped and landed knee first on several pieces, so they ended up bent. When I ran my hand over the finished puzzle, some of these pieces popped out because they stuck up and had caught on my hand. Maya found this hysterical for some reason. She often laughed way more than any funny thing warranted.

Oh, my God, I missed her. How could she be gone?

I fell onto the bed and I looked back at the day's entry. She'd read three of those Magic Tree House books that day. She loved them, and she loved to go back through the special journal I had to record the books we read, because I made a big deal of listing hers and decorating them with markers so it looked like they were in a fancy frame. I had a full summer's worth of those.

I dug out another journal, from this year. Flipping through, I stopped at the July 4 entry where I'd drawn a picture of the shirt Maya had gotten the mustard on. Dana managed to get the stain out, of course, but it would forever be in my journal.

I skimmed a few more pages, stopping when I got to the one with a drawing of an upside-down DQ Blizzard, red spoon sticking out. That was the day we ran into JT at DQ. Maya and I had been sitting on a bench outside, talking about something boring that she found interesting—why couldn't I remember what it was? How could I already be forgetting everything? I scanned the page and read what I'd written.

She was blathering about the OKC Thunder—Dad had promised her we'd go sometime, and she was currently fixated on basketball even though no one else in her life cared about it—when I heard, "Hey, don't I know you from Burnside High?"

I looked up and about had a heart attack.

It was JT. We'd chatted and I'd told him I was also going to OAMS. I was ridiculously excited but trying to play it cool.

He grinned at me before looking at Maya and crouching down. "And what's your name?"

"Maya," she said through a mouthful of vanilla ice cream, because DQ didn't have her favorite, strawberry. There was a ring of brown around her mouth from the chocolate coating. She was swinging her legs off the blue bench.

He stood back up to look at me and asked. "Are you babysitting?"

"Yeah, but she's my sister."

"Huh, you two don't look anything alike."

"Technically, she's my stepsister." I liked that he was thinking about how I looked.

He reached down and patted Maya on the head. "That's a pretty name. Maya. I like it."

She grinned and continued working on her ice cream cone.

We chatted more about OAMS and exchanged phone numbers. Two weeks later we were hanging out—I'd made a carrot cake for us and that seemed to seal the deal. Before school started, we were officially together. Everybody liked him.

I shut the journal and closed my eyes. Besides me, he was one of the last people to see her alive. At least among people who knew her.

Or had he seen her. Was she already gone by that time? No, because she had just brought me more candy and I'd watched her go to the next house, so she was still there when he showed up. I was surprised she didn't come and say hi—she loved him. Or she had. She'd been a little less interested in him the last few weeks. It had been nice because it gave us more semi-alone-time.

Oh, God, I was horrible. How could I have lost track of her like that? All I'd had to do was watch her and keep her from running away.

I opened up the texts in my phone and looked at Gabriel's. Or my many texts to him, unanswered. Would he ever forgive me? I didn't know how to function with none of my people talking to me. Except I had Tenny, and she was the best friend someone could have. I texted her to see if she could come over after all. I didn't know what we'd talk about, but maybe it would just be good to get a hug. I hadn't had one since Tenny hugged me Monday night. Maya always made it a point to give me a hug goodnight, even if she was mad at me. I would never again see my favorite person in the world. I had no idea how to live like this.

7

Gabriel

"**I**'m gonna beat you, Gabriel!" *Maya says as both of our cars round a corner in* Mario Kart, *bouncing on the road.*

"No way, niña!"

The road looks familiar. It looks like it's part of the game, cartoon style, but I realize it is Crest Ave., two streets over, where Maya went missing.

Wait, where is she? She left me in the dust. I speed up. Suddenly trick-or-treaters line the road, going from house to house.

I try so hard, but can't catch up with Maya.

~

Gabriel

Mamá and I came out of the house Friday morning and I stepped off the porch as she locked the door. I looked over at

Lauren's house and saw Nick and Lauren trying to help Dana to the car. She seemed to be struggling to walk and was audibly sobbing. Lauren couldn't hold her up, and Dana fell to her knees in the grass.

I ran over and helped Nick get Dana to her feet. She was falling apart, crying so hard she was groaning.

"Sweetheart, you have to do this," Nick said to her, sounding dead. He looked at me and nodded, and we literally carried her to the car while Lauren raced ahead and opened the door. We got her into the front passenger seat and belted in while she just cried and cried.

Her obvious pain had me tearing up, and I hazarded a glance at Lauren. She also looked teary. I couldn't believe we were going to the funeral of the most vibrant eight-year-old who ever lived. I remembered the weird dream that had woken me up this morning, playing *Mario Kart* in our own neighborhood. It was probably telling me I would never get over this.

Mamá was behind us and leaned in to hug Dana and whisper something I couldn't hear. She always knew the exact right thing to say to make someone feel better, even when there shouldn't be any possible way. Dana nodded slightly and Mamá said something else, then stepped back and gently shut the door. She put her hand on my shoulder and said, "You ride with them. She absolutely has to go inside."

I got in the back seat behind Dana. Lauren walked around and got in on the other side and shut the door. She was wearing a black dress that looked a little small, and I guessed it was from the last funeral she went to, her grandma's, a couple years ago. She looked at me but I looked away. I just could not talk to her right now. I had never been so angry at somebody I cared about before. When

Papá died, I was really angry with the world, but this was different. I didn't know who the Afghanis were who'd killed him, so there was no one specific to blame. It still surprised me that she did this, but Mamá had taken my burgeoning hatred of all Afghanis and Muslims that had formed, and told me not to hate entire groups of people, and that people in desperate situations do desperate things. The civil war in our own Guatemala had devastated the country, with hundreds of thousands dead. Some of our family had died, and some had been involved in awful things.

What Mamá said made sense, but this was different. Lauren was supposed to be watching Maya, and she hadn't. I wondered if she'd been on the phone, distracted by a gooey love conversation with JT.

The only sounds on the drive to the church were the tires on the road and Dana's crying, though she was relatively quiet now.

I snuck another look at Lauren and she was crying, and despite my anger, my heart broke a little for her. I knew she hadn't meant to lose Maya. As much as I loved Maya, Lauren was her sister and it had to be much worse for her. I reached over and squeezed her hand quickly, all without looking at her. I just couldn't.

When we got to the church, Nick idled in front of the building. "Lauren, can you park the car? We'll go in from here."

"Okay," she said in a strained voice.

Nick put the car in park and the two of them got out, so I did, too. Lauren stood outside the driver's seat while Nick and I helped Dana out of the car. She also had on a black dress, but it looked wrinkled, and her hair wasn't perfect like it usually was. She was like a zombie. We helped her get to the entrance. I glanced back and Lauren was driving off to park the car.

Should I have talked to her? I couldn't get past my anger. But I didn't hate her. I would probably forgive her one day.

Someone opened the door for us and we got Dana inside. She was shuffling, but moving. We got her down to the front left pew and the two of them sat down. I went to wait for Mamá near the back. I'd never been in a Presbyterian church before. It was so bland, nothing like the Catholic church I'd grown up in.

People were coming in—mostly neighbors, some parents with kids Maya's age, Lauren's friend Tenny and her mom. She waved at me but they kept going.

Mamá came in and we moved up and sat in a pew on the right side. She put her black purse next to her side.

I saw Lauren walk past so I started looking around. There was a metal urn on a table at the front. A large picture of Maya stood next to it. It captured her laughing about something, her open mouth revealing a missing front tooth. The photo must have been from the summer because her skin had that faint pink tone of too much sun. One of her ever-present black braids was off her shoulder like she'd just swung her head around. Behind her was a merry-go-round in the park that was just down the street from us. Where Lauren and I used to take her all the time. Jesus, I couldn't believe she was really gone. I clutched my stomach to contain the queasiness.

Mamá gripped my arm. She whispered, "Thank you for helping Dana, niño. How was she?"

Other people were talking, but it was very low, so I whispered, "She was doing a little better."

"She's really not handling this well. I don't think I've ever seen anybody so destroyed. I'm probably going to have to help her quite a bit. I might have to take some time off work."

"Yeah. I think she will need it." Mamá was a home health aide, so caring for people was who she was.

The pastor headed up to the pulpit and everyone quieted.

I couldn't really focus on what he was saying, other than how a light was put out long before it should have been, which was obviously true. I think he did know Maya, because Dana came here sometimes. Lauren used to go too, when she was younger.

Then it was Lauren's turn to speak, and she went up and stood behind the lectern, notecard in hand. Her hand was visibly shaking, which made me feel bad for her, but then mad again. But then I worried about her because she hadn't started yet. She looked at me and I gave her a nod of encouragement.

She blinked. "Maya was my little sister and there was no other girl like her." She stopped and her eyes looked watery. She wiped them with her free hand. "Anyone who knew her would know how much she loved books. I started reading to her before she was even a year old, and as soon as she was on my lap, she would stop squirming and stare at the book like there was nothing else in the world worth looking at."

She paused again and visibly took a breath. "She was reading on her own by kindergarten, but she still loved me to read to her. Honestly, if we were together, there was about a fifty percent chance we were reading. And we were together a lot."

She cleared her throat and her voice turned husky. "Just last week, I noticed that she had organized her entire bookshelf, color-coding books and separating fiction from nonfiction. She was our little librarian. I was always sure she'd grow up to be a writer. I loved her so much."

She looked up and out at the audience, looking unbalanced and lost. The pastor went back up there and patted her on the shoulder. She sat back down.

Poor Lauren.

Then Nick got up, leaving Dana's mom to hold her up. He went up to the podium to say something himself. He just ended up talking about how Maya was a sweet little girl who only ever had nice things to say about her friends, and how they were all going to miss her so much. He started crying about halfway through and didn't stop. His brother, Nathan, had to get up and help him back to the pew after he went the wrong way. Then a woman who must have been Maya's teacher got up and talked about how generous Maya was. When she was finished, the pastor started his sermon. And I just sat there, destroyed, crying like I'd never stop.

~

Lauren

The funeral eventually ended and we filed out. There was a woman standing near the back of the church looking at her phone, and I had no idea who she was. She watched us as we passed her. It was weird, but my brain said, *She's a journalist,* but I was a wreck and forgot about it by the time we were outside.

Tenny was suddenly by my side. Her brown eyes were slightly puffy and glistened with fresh tears. She hugged me, and it was good, but it didn't touch all the guilt I constantly felt. She took a few steps back to her own mother and waved, her face as sad as I'd ever seen it. I had to catch up to Dad.

Grandma Cooper, Dana's mother, gave me the nastiest look as I hurried to the car. She'd always hated me—I never knew why—but now it was worse.

But I didn't care about Grandma Cooper. What I did care about was Gabriel, who also hated me now. The only thing I could think about was that maybe it wouldn't be forever, based on him squeezing my hand in the car.

JT couldn't make it to the funeral. He couldn't miss class because he had to talk to the teacher about an upcoming paper. Like he couldn't figure out how to get the info another way. He was obviously not the good guy I'd thought he was.

We got home, and while Dad and Gabriel got Dana into bed, I went into the living room. There were people there to give their condolences, but they did when Dad came back in, and then left. Grandpa Baxter sat in the recliner, looking uncomfortable in his black suit. I sat on the couch. Neither of us said anything.

Soon afterward, Dana's parents came in with some of the flowers from the service, which they set down on the TV in front of the fireplace. I got up so they could take the couch. I went into the kitchen to get a couple of chairs, assuming Dad would be back. I stood there staring at the several casseroles that people had already brought. There was also a stack of cards on the counter. I definitely understood trying to make people feel better with food, but now it was just a horrible reminder. And once all the food was gone, there would be all these stupid food containers. Did you try to return them? Throw them out? Absorb them into your own kitchen and get reminded all the time?

I dragged two chairs into the living room and went back

to grab a couple more because Uncle Charles and Uncle Nathan were supposed to be there soon, too. Grandma Cooper was setting a large platter of sandwiches that someone must have just dropped off onto the coffee table, where everyone stared at it. The grandpas leaned forward to take sandwiches, and she sat down next to Grandpa Cooper on the couch. I sat in one of the chairs I'd brought out.

We all silently stared at our feet, the only noise the sound of chewing. I wished the sandwiches didn't have lettuce. I remembered Maya in her costume and had to close my eyes again while tears formed. It was just a few days ago that she was not just alive, but full of light and joy that only she possessed.

For some reason, I remembered the night of the fire, three years ago. We were on vacation, at a motel. The smoke alarm had woken me with its wailing, and at first I was really confused. But when I noticed a sharp, acrid smell, I knew what was going on. We'd done stop-drop-and-roll practice enough in school that I knew about fires. Maya and I were alone in the room because our parents were at the bar with friends and they'd left us reading. But it had gotten dark and we'd both fallen asleep. Suddenly Maya sat up, eyes wide with confusion and fear.

"Come on, Maya! We have to get out!" I ran to the door of the room and the smell was even worse. It made my eyes burn, and I coughed. My heart was beating like crazy and I held my breath and put my hand on the door. It wasn't hot, so I opened it, but smoke just poured in, so I slammed it shut again, my pulse off the charts. I wasn't sure what to do, but we couldn't go out that way.

Maya was now standing on the bed. Then she started coughing, which got me going again. My eyes were watering and my heart was racing. I ran over to the window. We hadn't shut the blinds and I remembered that we were on the ground floor. We were looking out onto a parking lot.

Maya was coughing, and then she started audibly crying.

I looked at the window and saw there was a sliding lock, so I tried to open it but it wouldn't budge. I wasn't strong enough. I scanned the room, coughing. I needed something with leverage. I grabbed the TV remote and kind of wedged it between the glass and the side of the lock. It actually kind of fit in there.

Maya's crying had intensified and the coughing was crazy. It felt like I was choking.

I spotted the little desk lamp, which had a heavy-looking base. I unplugged it and used it as a hammer on the remote, which was still jammed between the lock and window, and amazingly, there was a popping sound and the lock moved. The remote went flying in pieces, and I used the lamp base to push the lock all the way open and jerked the window to the side.

We were both coughing like crazy, and now I could actually see smoke flowing out the window. I ran to grab Maya and raced back to the window. There was shouting and suddenly Dad was on the other side of the window. He ripped the screen off and I handed Maya to him and he helped me clamber out, over the AC unit. Maya and I continued coughing. It was only after I was outside that I could see fire trucks and police cars and flashing blue and red lights bouncing off cars. I hadn't heard or noticed anything but Maya.

We both ended up at the ER, but we were fine. A hoverboard in the room across the hall had caught fire and no one was in there, which is why it was so bad in our room. Everybody acted like I was such a big hero.

And it had all been so pointless. I'd saved her just to be the one to lose her in the end.

I looked around the room at the grim faces.

The frown on my face sank all the way into my soul.

The pungent stink of lilies got to be too much and I felt like I had to do something. "Does anyone want coffee?" I asked, standing up.

Both grandpas shook their heads. "Grandma, do you?"

"Do not call me that," she snarled. "You know you are not my granddaughter." The tips of her ears glowed red.

She might as well have slapped me. "Oh." My face went cold as the blood drained out of it. How could she say that? Especially right now? I glanced up at Grandpa Baxter, who looked over at Grandma and rolled his eyes. His way of trying to be supportive.

Grandma's hands were on her knees and she took a deep breath. "A coffee."

I numbly walked to the kitchen and started up the coffee maker. Dad would want some, too. But Grandma couldn't seriously think I was going to make her a coffee.

It was obviously true that Grandma wasn't my biological grandmother. But I'd been calling her that ever since Dad had married Dana. She was never a particularly nice woman. When I was eight years old, I was playing on her walker when she was recovering from knee surgery. She'd said, "Stop that! You're so fat you'll break it!" As if a slightly pudgy little kid was somehow bigger than a full-grown woman whose weight did not break the walker.

I wiped my eyes. My tear ducts didn't rationalize away Grandma's meanness. I heard Dad going into the living room. I poured two mugs and added a healthy dose of milk to mine. When I got back into the room, I handed Dad the black coffee.

"Thanks, honey." He offered me a half-hearted smile.

I sat down and sipped from my mug.

Grandma glared at me. "You didn't bring mine."

I looked at her over the lip of the steaming mug as I took another sip and said nothing. I honestly didn't know what to say, so I settled on, "No."

"Child, you are a monster!" Grandma said, spittle flying. Grandpa Cooper put his hand on top of hers as if to calm her.

"Wait a minute, Delia," Dad said, right as Grandpa Baxter said, "Hey!" Dad continued, "What's going on? Don't talk to Lauren that way!"

"You know it's all her fault!" Grandma's ears were even redder.

Dad shook his head slowly. "No, it's not. Someone else did it."

I couldn't stand to look at her anymore and scanned the room. Grandpa Baxter was looking at the carpet and Grandpa Cooper's hand still rested on Grandma's, although he too was staring at his shoes.

"Maya's not—wasn't even your daughter!" Grandma's shrill voice sounded far away.

"Yes, she was! I raised her from birth!"

"Tell yourself that all you want. She wasn't your blood. Go ahead and tell yourself now that *your* daughter's not a murderer."

Dad launched out of his chair, spilling coffee down his leg. "You need to leave."

A knock sounded at the door and it slowly opened, revealing Uncle Charles sticking his head in, his long black hair hanging in front of him. Dad jerked his head at the sound and Charles narrowed his eyes and came in. But quietly. He had another vase with more flowers in the crook of his arm.

"Fine," Grandma said, lifting herself off the couch.

Grandpa Cooper stood with her, looking even paler than usual, and said, "We are going to say goodbye to our daughter first."

Dad and I watched them go back to the bedroom while Grandpa Baxter stared at the floor some more. Did he agree with her, or was he just avoiding emotion again? I started to cry. Charles was standing with his back to the wall behind the door, unmoving. He held the vase to his chest with one arm while the other hung by his side, fingers tapping his leg.

"Lauren, don't pay attention to her," Dad said. But it was too late—I was already a mess again, because it was sort of true. I hadn't murdered her, but it was my fault it happened. How had I missed Maya running off?

Charles slowly moved toward the fireplace and put the vase on the TV beside the other one. Then he took one of the empty chairs, looking at everyone but saying nothing.

The doorbell rang and Dad went to get it. It was yet another casserole and a "Sorry for your loss" exchange. He took the dish to the kitchen and came back quietly.

Grandma and Grandpa were out the door a few minutes later with not even a sideways glance toward me.

Grandpa Baxter said, "That woman." He shook his head.

"I know." Dad set his coffee down on the floor in front of the couch. "Come on, Lauren, come sit on the couch with me." He nodded at Maya's uncle and said, "Charles."

Uncle Charles nodded back.

I sank into the couch. When Dad sat back down, he said, "Seriously, honey, don't listen to her. Yes, you made a mistake, but every parent, sister, whoever out there has made mistakes when watching a child. Most of us are just lucky to get away with it."

It was nice of him to say, but I didn't really believe it. It didn't feel true.

The front door opened again and Uncle Nathan, came in bearing still more flowers. After looking around, he gave a general nod toward everyone, put the flowers next to the others, and sat in one of empty chairs. "It was a nice service, Nick."

"It was," Dad said.

Grandpa Baxter and Charles both nodded in agreement, though Grandpa was looking at the floor and Charles was looking out the window, his hands by his sides. I wondered what he was thinking. His parents were dead, and his only brother, and now Maya. He didn't have anyone left.

It was so horrible. And what about Uncle Nathan? Would it push him over the edge like Grandma Baxter's death had? That had been when he ended up in the mental ward before. And he was pretty close to "Maya Girl," as he called her. He and Charles both were both a big part of our lives.

We sat there for several more minutes, nobody talking. I was waiting for somebody to nod again. Then Grandpa Baxter said, "Well, I'd best be getting back." He walked over to me, where I was still slouched on the sofa, and patted me on the shoulder. "I don't think it's your fault, either. Everybody makes mistakes."

I nodded. But Dana surely did. And she was right, no matter what Dad and Grandpa said. More tears started forming.

Grandpa walked over to the door. "Bye."

"Bye, Dad," Dad said, barely above a whisper. "Thanks for coming."

Grandpa nodded and left.

Nathan glanced at me and stood up. "Yeah, Nick, I should probably get going, too. Lauren, don't worry about what that bitch thinks."

Charles stood to follow him out, but first walked over to me and patted me on the back. "It's not your fault, Lauren. Nobody who matters thinks that." He nodded at Dad one last time and was out the door.

I didn't believe any of them. And I didn't know how to deal with this.

8

Lauren

I'm petting a tiger. The bright sun reflects off his dusty orange and black stripes. He makes a funny noise, like he's clearing his throat. I know what he's doing—big cats don't purr. They make this weird sound instead. While I'm rubbing the tiger's head, he brings his head up fast and whacks me in the chin and I fall backward. I laugh because the look in his silver eyes says he's very sorry.

A little girl in a pink dress holds out her hand to help me get up. She has black hair and I don't recognize her, but she seems familiar. I go back to the tiger and pet him some more. This time he's more careful.

A hand touches my shoulder and I look back to see a tall man. He's wearing a mask that makes him look like an older teenager. He has on jeans and an old red-striped t-shirt. "It's time," he says.

He takes my hand and leads me away, but I don't know what it's time for.

We leave the tiger enclosure and find a park bench next to an ice cream cart. We are at the zoo. He tells me to sit down and buys me an ice cream cone. "Your favorite," he says, handing me a cone with a scoop of strawberry ice cream.

I start eating the ice cream and he sits next to me. He watches me. Then he reaches over and starts tickling my tummy. I laugh and squirm but hold on to the ice cream. He keeps tickling.

Then his hand moves lower on my tummy and then even lower, and he tickles me there. I freeze. The scoop of ice cream rolls off the cone and lands on his arm before sliding onto my knee and down my bare leg. I can't move but I'm holding onto the cone so tight it breaks. He pulls his hands back, licks the ice cream on his arm, and laughs.

~

Lauren

Monday, my phone alarm went off at 5:00 a.m., volume all the way up, waking Tenny and me.

"Lauren, what are you doing?" she asked in a tired, scratchy voice.

My heart was racing and I struggled to get it turned off, my hands like hams. "I don't know. I didn't set it."

"Ugh."

I doubted she believed me, but she wasn't going to be mean. "It's off. And the only alarm set is the right one."

"Okay. Goodnight again."

"Night."

While I was lying there waiting for my heart rate to slow down, I remembered the dream. The alarm was what woke me from it. What a gross dream. It started just a little weird, but then it went all the way to gross.

And why did it have to be strawberry ice cream? Maya's favorite. God, I missed her so much. I started crying again, the guilt so raw I felt cut open. How could I live with myself after what I did?

It seemed impossible.

My mind went back to that night, to JT and how his arrival was what distracted me. He'd completely abandoned me after it happened. I mean, who could blame him? He probably knew it was my fault. But I couldn't imagine having a boyfriend right now, anyway, especially one who knew how horrible I was. I would break up with him when I saw him next. It would be for the best.

I thought of how Gabriel would be glad JT was gone.

Which of course reminded me that Gabriel was obviously done with me. He knew it was my fault and couldn't forgive me.

He was so right. I wiped my eyes, although the tears were still flowing, and turned over on my side. I yawned, and somehow it didn't take too long to fall asleep again. Maybe I just couldn't tolerate being awake and aware of the new world I lived in. And the monster I was.

The next thing I knew it was six thirty, and the alarm was sounding, unwelcome again. Tenny and I got through the morning preparation without talking—even under normal circumstances, we weren't morning people and had an agreement to just not talk unless absolutely necessary.

I was working on my eyeliner in the mirror when Tenny got back from the shower, hair in a towel and dripping purple caddy in tow. She put it on her desk and actually spoke.

"Lauren, are you sure you want to go back to class? I know they will let you miss some more days."

"I can't go back home," I said.

"Because of Dana?"

"Dana, and everything. I can't imagine being there anymore." Tears welled in my eyes just thinking about how Maya would never be at the house again. At least my eyeliner was waterproof.

"What about just staying here? Do you want me to talk to Ms. Patton again?"

The dorm mom had come by the night we got back to the dorm after curfew. She looked as devastated as Tenny when I told her what happened and told me that I could take as much time off as I needed and that she would support me.

"I think I'm just going to be better off trying to stay busy. The last week has been horrible. And it's already going to be hard to catch up."

"Okay," Tenny said skeptically. "Let me know if you change your mind. But, um, it might be kind of weird today. People have been talking about it."

I stopped and turned to look at her. "About Maya?"

"Yeah." She sat in her chair and squeezed the towel some more to dry her long, black hair. "Everyone obviously feels bad for you, but you know how people are. Not particularly sensitive."

I nodded. I didn't know what to expect. So we were quiet again until I broke the rule myself. "I'm going to break up with JT today."

"That's good." She started brushing her hair. Even though it took a while, she always let it air dry.

She'd never liked him, either. He gave off a bad vibe, she'd said. I didn't say it, but he obviously wasn't trying to transcend stereotypes of teenage boys.

Thinking of him made me thinking of Halloween night again, and Maya in her costume. My eyes welled with tears as I remembered what Gabriel and Adelita had said when we stopped by. She probably hated me as much as he did.

I wiped the tears away. I needed to get it together. I didn't want to break down in class. I would just have to try my best to not think about her when I was around other people. That would have to be confined to my bed, with the lights off.

Eventually, I went down to the downstairs girls' lounge to check my mailbox, even though there was no reason for me to have any mail. There were some senior girls in there chatting. They stared at me but didn't say anything. I sat down at one of the tables to wait for Tenny so we could walk to class together. The girls had the TV on Good Morning America and were lounging on the ugly couch.

I stared at the show but didn't absorb any of it. I opened up my laptop and pulled up Google to search for news about Maya again. I skimmed a few articles, but there was nothing new. I suddenly remembered the strange woman at the funeral. Was she really a journalist? Why was she there? I checked each article to see if it included the writer's head-shot, trying to see if any of them looked like the woman from the funeral. But I couldn't tell.

The girls got up and left, and the next thing I knew, JT strolled in.

For some reason, the first thought I had was that boys weren't supposed to be in the girls' lounge. But then I also realized I felt absolutely nothing for him. It was like everything I ever felt had never happened.

"I wanted to see how you were doing," he said. "Someone told me you were in here."

"I am." It was so weird to look at someone I'd wanted for two years and finally got, and realize that was all gone. I remembered that I needed to break up with him.

"Listen." He wrung his hands and grimaced. "I know the timing is bad, but I don't think we should be together anymore."

"What?" What was happening. He was dumping me? What had I done wrong?

"It's just clear that we weren't good for each other." He still had this grimace on his face, but it was by far the fakest grimace I'd ever seen. "I think it's better to call it now rather than letting it drag on."

I stared at him, just dumbstruck. What kind of guy is that much of a douchebag?

"Okay," I said. The shock had faded and I was back to not caring about him.

His eyes flashed. "That's it?"

"Yup."

I could tell he was pissed. I guess he wanted me to beg or something. I looked back at my laptop screen and he turned to leave.

Tenny came racing in and stopped when she saw JT. "Oh, sorry."

"It's okay, Tenny," I said. "He's just leaving after breaking up with his girlfriend a week after her sister was murdered."

Her eyes were wide and JT slunk past her.

"Oh, my God, *he* broke up with *you*? What an asshole!"

"I know." I stuffed my laptop back into my bag and stood up. "It threw me, but I guess it saved me the effort of doing it myself."

We headed toward the side door out of the building.

Tenny pushed the door open. "I'm glad I got here before he left. He's such a horrible person! I knew I was right."

We crossed the lawn toward the classroom building, freezing in the morning cold. Now I'd have to face everyone else.

Gabriel

Will had somehow convinced me to go to an LGBTQ Student Alliance meeting Wednesday night, and I was meeting him outside, the promised graphic novel in hand since I'd forgotten it before class. As I approached the building, I saw him standing there in jeans and a white t-shirt, no jacket. He was actually kind of buff. I hadn't noticed before.

"Thanks for coming," he said as soon as he saw me, a smile on his face. He gave me a half hug, patting me on the back, and I belatedly reciprocated. "How are you?" he asked.

"Okay." I'd seen him in class the day before. I'd accidentally looked at the professor when I walked into the room and she smiled at me, which was confusing and made me feel a little panicky, reliving last week's phone incident.

I'd sat down next to Will, who'd seen the whole weird exchange, and he immediately said, "So, don't be mad ..."

At that, I wasn't mad, just scared. I must have looked it, too, because he said, "No, no, it's not bad. So, I went to her office Friday. And I kind of told her what was going on, and that you aren't some pervert."

I just stared at him, shocked. He hadn't mentioned this in any of the texts he'd sent me since Friday. "What did she say?"

"She said she was sorry for your loss but you shouldn't be looking at your phone in class."

That actually made me laugh a bit, which made me feel guilty. I shouldn't be enjoying myself right now. I was in mourning. I mentally regrouped. "Do you think she believed you?"

He nodded. "Yeah."

I figured that was a good thing, and soon class got started. I took some notes, better than last week, but I was still distracted. And in the back of my mind, I was still worrying about the police, too.

After class, Will had talked me into trying this meeting. And here we were. It was his first one, too.

"Did you bring me a book?" he asked, glancing at it in my hand.

"Oh!" I'd totally forgotten, I was so distracted by him. "Yes." I held it up and he took it but I didn't let go. "I have to give you the rules first. You have to read exactly one chapter every day, no more, no less, until you're done."

"That's it?" He took it when I let go and started flipping through it.

"Yep."

"What if I want to read more than one chapter?"

I shook my finger at him. "Nope."

He laughed. "Okay, I'll follow your rule. But just because it's you."

That warmed my heart, even though he was teasing. "I didn't make it up."

"Don't tell me that. Then I'm not as motivated to follow it."

"Oh, I totally made it up. Just last week."

"Okay, good." He hit the spine of the book with his other palm. "Ready?"

"I guess so." We headed in. There were about twenty people in there, milling around, some looking like average Joes or Janes off the street, but then there were plenty of people who wouldn't be welcome in a country bar.

We were standing in the door like a couple of noobs. My heart was beating a little fast. This was the most out I'd ever been. I really should come out. But it was just hard in the

Latino community. I wasn't super-involved, but Mamá was, and it would make it hard for her. She went to church every weekend.

"Excuse me," someone said, squeezing between the door frame and me.

"Oh, sorry," I turned toward her and we moved away from the door.

She smiled and her lip ring moved with it. "Hi. You're new. I'm Simone."

"Hi, I'm Will," he said, then added, "This is Gabriel. He's shy."

"I'm not really shy," I protested.

"No worries," Simone said and laughed. "Most of us are at least a little awkward."

Will and I laughed.

Simone had short spiky hair and a wallet chain hanging off the side of her jeans. And she didn't seem awkward at all. She turned toward the front of the room. "Orion!" she called.

A guy—no, a person—turned and waved. I couldn't tell. They were slim and wearing jeans and a hiking jacket.

Turning back to us, Simone said, "Orion's nice. They'll get you started. I'll see you around."

Orion started walking over, a big smile on their face.

"Welcome!" they said when they reached us. They shook hands with each of us and we went through introductions. Orion was a junior and was happy we'd found the group first year.

"Come sit in the front," they said.

We dutifully followed, and soon the meeting started. It turned out that Simone was the president and Orion was the VP membership. We had to introduce ourselves to the group,but everyone seemed friendly.

Simone talked about the activities that were planned for the next few months. They met every Wednesday night at the student union, just for fun, nothing organized. There was going to be a fundraiser in January and an outing to a museum and a queer-owned pizzeria around the 39th Street District in Oklahoma City in a couple weeks.

It suddenly hit me that Maya would never get a chance to go to either of those places. My heart sank. I'd been feeling good and had actually forgotten about her. How could I? We still didn't know what had happened to her. Or at least I didn't. Maybe they'd told her parents. Maybe Lauren knew, and if I talked to her she'd tell me.

But I couldn't. It wasn't really her fault. I mean, it obviously wasn't really her fault. I lost track of Maya one time when we went to the grocery store. I found her three aisles away, pissing off a woman by petting her service dog. I really needed to text Lauren again.

Will patted me on the leg. I glanced at him and he gave me a reassuring smile. He must have known I'd gone down a mental rabbit hole.

What did I ever do to deserve this guy? It was unreal. I smiled back and tuned back into the meeting. Simone was talking about the fundraiser, which would be at a grocery store somewhere. It was all very mundane. So different from living in my head, trying to figure out what happened to Maya.

To be fair, that's what I'd be working on when I got home. But I still didn't know how to get more information. I would look into what I could get from the police. There was that law that meant they had to give you certain information if you requested it. Maybe I could do that.

9

Lauren

I was walking back from dinner Thursday night with Tenny and her boyfriend, Brandon, crossing the parking lot from the cafeteria toward the dorm. Tenny and Brandon were chatting about something funny that had happened in a class today, but I wasn't really paying attention. It had been ten days since Maya. Gabriel had finally texted me last night, but I decided I couldn't talk to him. His message just asked how I was doing, and he started a long apology about not contacting me for so long. I didn't read it all. I was horrible, and I didn't deserve him if he was going to be nice to me.

We were almost at the dorm when I noticed a woman who seemed familiar standing at the corner of the building.

I realized with surprise that it was the woman from the funeral. That just made me flash back to standing on the stage, trying to talk about Maya, and my heart fell apart and I teared up. She was the possible journalist. She had on black pants and a dark green blazer. And dark Pumas, which seemed out of place. Why was she here?

I narrowed my eyes as we continued toward the end of the lot.

She spotted me and started heading to the point where we were going to step onto the curb.

"Who is that?" Tenny asked, cutting Brandon off.

We were all watching her as we approached.

"She was at the funeral. I don't know her."

Now we were ten feet apart and she was watching me. There was no doubt this wasn't just a coincidence.

"Lauren Baxter?" she called.

We stopped.

"Yes," I said cautiously. Who in the world was she?

"My name is Candace O'Brien. I'm an independent reporter investigating the missing girls in the area." She was playing with a pen in her hand.

This was even weirder. I could sense Tenny's concern.

"Okay, but what does that have to do with me?" I asked.

"I think your sister's case may be related." A small notebook peeked out of her blazer pocket.

I jerked back in surprise. "Why? The police never said anything."

But maybe it was possible?

"There's obviously more to it." Her gaze felt like it was boring into me.

"She is the right age," I said quietly, queasiness creeping in. "But why haven't the other girls been found?"

"I assume something didn't go as planned with Maya," Candace said.

Planned? Had somebody really planned to kill my little sister? My stomach was roiling.

"The reason I think it's related actually has to do with

something else. Did you know about ...." Candace paused, glancing to the side.

"What?" I said, heavy dread lining my stomach.

She turned back toward me and looked sad. "The assault."

"What?" What did she mean. When they killed her?

"They released the autopsy report today. She was sexually assaulted before that night."

"What?!" Tenny and I said at the same time. We gaped at each other in horror.

"Oh, my God!" Tears filled my eyes and Tenny was the same.

"How?" Tenny asked, looking between me and Candace.

"They are going to be investigating this to see if it's tied to the murder. They may want to talk to you again."

I couldn't speak. Tears were rolling off my face. I glanced at Brandon, who was grimacing and pale-faced.

Tenny hugged me, which helped ground me.

"When did it happen?" Tenny asked Candace.

"Within the previous week or so."

Tenny held tight on my arm and I tried to think who Maya had been around. Dad, people at school. I don't think either of the uncles came by that week.

"I don't know how it could have happened," I said. I was numb with horror.

But maybe one of the uncles did come by? Or even Dad. No, there was no way Dad would do that. Maybe I didn't know the uncles that well. Neither of them was touchy-feely, and wouldn't someone who assaulted kids be more like that?

Oh, my God. Maya.

"What is it you want?" Tenny asked Candace, sounding way more assertive than normal.

"I wanted to ask Lauren about the night Maya went missing and the prior week."

"I don't want to talk to you," I said. I just wanted to get to my room and lie on the bed and cry. Even though I couldn't do that. I had too much to do.

Candace nodded, smiled, and said, "In case you change your mind, let me give you my card." She reached into her pocket and handed me a green business card.

I took it and glanced at it, seeing her name in white text, along with a phone number and email. I'd toss it in the trash as soon as we got to our room.

"You may know more than you think," Candace said. "Often cases like these are solved based on a tiny bit of information that doesn't seem important."

Tenny pulled on my arm a little and we walked away.

"Contact me," Candace called.

"Oh, my God," Tenny said. "I can't believe ..."

I closed my eyes for a second, trying to regain a sense of being connected to reality. Obviously, Maya being murdered was the worst possible thing that could happen. I didn't know something else could make the whole thing so much worse.

"That was weird and horrible," Brandon said, taking Tenny's hand. "I'm really sorry, Lauren."

"I know. I can't believe it. Poor Maya." My voice cracked when I said her name. "I mean, how did it happen?"

I was in a daze all the way back to our room. I fell onto my bed and just lay there, thoughts of Maya's last week in my head, even though I wasn't there for most of it. If I'd still been living at home, would it have happened?

Tenny had stayed downstairs to talk to Brandon, but a couple of minutes later she came into the room. She sat on the edge of my bed—she had the top bunk so it wasn't very accessible—and I moved my feet up so she could curl up at the foot of the bed.

"Do you have any ideas?" she asked, pulling her knees into her chest. "Who has access to her? The uncles? Men at school? What about JT?"

"I can't imagine any of them doing anything to her." I pictured my sweet, hilarious little sister—how could anyone do something like that to a little girl? I wiped tears from my eyes. "None of them give off a bad vibe."

But Tenny knew more about this because of her own uncle.

"To you, maybe," she said. "But you know JT had a bad vibe to Gabriel and me. I think he's a sociopath."

Her statement made me queasy. Could it be him? It couldn't. I took a breath. "So, I don't know. It can't be. But I'm so confused. I can't think of anyone she was around that week. Except Saturday. When JT was over."

She didn't say anything, which I knew meant she was considering it.

But he couldn't. Even he wasn't that bad.

Or maybe he was. He did break up with me a week after she was murdered, which seemed like something a sociopath might do.

I felt like I didn't know anything.

Gabriel

"I'm gonna beat you, Gabriel!" Maya says as we round a corner in the Mario Kart version of our neighborhood.

"No way, niña!"

We're on Crest Ave. and the trick-or-treaters are out. Maya hits the gas and I trail after her, dodging all the superheroes and princesses.

She's getting ahead of me. I see her take a sharp turn onto another neighborhood street and try to follow, but I lose traction and my tires on the right side of the car lift, and I flip over and over.

She's gone.

~

Gabriel

I woke with a start. The game! Why couldn't I find her? I felt the loss again, such pain in my heart. Then I looked at my watch and saw it was November 11. Veteran's Day. Which was always hard because I still missed Papá so much.

I closed my eyes and lay there for a bit, focusing on my breathing to try to get past the pain. Eventually, I leveled out and got up. I showered and shaved, but I couldn't stop picturing racing through the *Mario Kart* game in my own neighborhood, chasing Maya. And why did I have almost the same dream twice?

I decided to wear a collared shirt as a nod to celebrating Papá's memory. He always liked to look presentable and didn't own a single t-shirt except a week's worth of under-shirts. Mamá had let me keep some of his shirts when he died, even though they hadn't fit back then. I'd grown into them. I slipped a blue striped one on.

I had chemistry at ten and it was already nine thirty, so I had to get going. I packed my backpack with my notebooks, the book I was reading for English, and my chemistry book. I was meeting Will in the afternoon, so I had some time to kill after my last class.

Phone in hand to text Lauren again since she still hadn't responded, I opened the front door. The first thing I saw was a car parked at the curb with the two detectives sitting in it. Looking at me.

I panicked for a second and almost went back inside.

But I hadn't done anything wrong. I had nothing to hide. I steeled myself and locked the door and walked down the path toward the sidewalk.

The younger one—Tolui, I was pretty sure—said out his open window, "Where are you going? You're looking snazzy today."

I stopped, right before the sidewalk. "Class." God, I was nervous. And why did he have to mock Papá's shirt?

"Why don't you come in and talk to us."

Why wouldn't they leave me alone and look for the killer?

I was shaking, but I knew my rights. "I don't have to talk to you. I didn't do anything wrong."

Tolui arched his eyebrows. "Did you know Maya was sexually assaulted sometime before Halloween?"

"What?" I jerked to face him as I was hit with a wave of nausea that nearly doubled me over.

"Do you know anything about that?" Tolui asked.

"Oh, my God. No! What happened?" I couldn't even think.

"We were hoping you would tell us."

"I would never hurt her!" But then things were crystal clear. "It was JT. I saw him leaving the house the Saturday before. The whole house was dark when he left, and he had that smug expression he wears around." My lip curled instinctively. I was still nauseous. I couldn't believe it. How could he hurt Maya?

From the other side of the car, Hansen said, "JT

Comstock has nothing to do with this, Gabriel. Stop bringing him up."

I closed my eyes in frustration. What was wrong with these guys? I straightened my shoulders and decided I was done. "I'm not talking to you anymore. I didn't do anything wrong and I don't know what happened to Maya, before or on Halloween night."

I started walking down the sidewalk and the car followed along for a bit while Tolui watched me. Finally, he said, "Don't go anywhere, Gabriel." Then they hit the gas and sprayed dust everywhere, like some stupid cop show cliché.

I hadn't answered and just kept walking. But my heart was going a million beats a minute, and I felt sick about Maya. It had to be JT.

I trudged my way to class, arriving eight minutes late so the professor looked at me for a long second, and I slunk to my seat.

10

———

Lauren

I'm walking down a long, dim hallway. It looks like I'm in a hotel, with wide green and maroon diagonal stripes stretching into the distance. There are doors, but I can't read the numbers. They're too high up. I see a tall, stocky figure walking toward me. I keep walking, hearing nothing but my feet on the carpet.

There's a light shining from behind him and I can't see what he looks like at first. But as he gets closer, I can tell he's wearing a smiling plastic mask, jeans, and a black t-shirt. He has blond hair and looks vaguely familiar but I can't place him.

He stops a few feet in front of me. I can see that his silver eyes are part of the mask, which surprises me, and he reaches out a large hand. I take it and he turns around to lead me back the way he'd come.

We walk for ages. Along the way, I look up and the mask is still smiling, but he doesn't turn toward me. As we move, his hand starts to get hotter and hotter and I think it will burn me, but he holds on too tight so I can't let go.

Finally, we get to the end of the hall. It's a large room with a giant TV and several couches positioned in front of it. A dark-haired little girl wearing a pink dress that covers her knees sits on one of the sofas, bouncing her legs against it. She looks odd—a little shimmery, almost like she isn't really there. The man leads me, hand still burning mine, to one of the other couches and sits down, dragging me with him. I fall onto his lap but scoot off and sit beside him. He's so big next to me. He lets go of my hand.

"Hi," he says, the mask smiling down at me. I look up at him, unsure of everything. I turn my head toward the TV, which is displaying flowing colors and shapes that don't look like anything.

"Look at me," he says. I do. He takes my hand and puts it on something, pressing down with his own hand to hold mine in place. I look down and see it's on the front of his jeans. Why does he have something hard in there?

"Do you like that?" he asks before moving my hand up and down.

~

Lauren

Saturday was family day, but obviously my family wasn't coming. But I was downstairs, anyway, as moral support for Tenny dealing with her family. We were standing at the fancy glass punch bowl Ms. Patton had put out, drinking cherry Kool-Aid from tiny paper cups.

We were quiet and somber even though there were other students and their families talking and laughing around us. I know we were both thinking about what should have happened—Maya should have burst through the door followed by my proud dad and Dana, who would both hug me and have me show them around.

"Hortencia!" we heard from the front door. Tenny's mom. Tenny hated her real name, but her family insisted on using it.

Tenny's little brothers came running over and hugged Tenny, who naturally hugged them back. I stared at them and realized I now had no siblings in the world. Tenny's oldest brother was Maya's age and looking at him was excruciating.

Then Mrs. Garcia hugged her, and her dad was right behind her. They greeted me and her mom asked how I was doing. I shrugged and she gave me a hug. "I know it must be hard. You are doing your best."

I nodded even though I could feel the tears welling.

Then Mrs. Garcia said, "Come here and let's have a picture. Would you take it, Lauren?"

I took the phone and waited for all of them to get into view. "Ready? On three. One-two-three." Before I could press my finger on the camera button, I flashed back to the last time Dana had taken a picture of Maya and me. It was on the Fourth of July, and once it was dark, Dana had taken a picture of Maya, Gabriel, and me holding our sparklers. I could still see it in my mind. My heart hurt so much it made me queasy.

Gabriel had texted me several more times, but I was going to spare him dealing with someone as horrible as me. I would hate it if he tried to make me feel better.

I tried to smile to will the pain away and snapped the photo of Tenny's family and handed the phone back, watching the boys slip out of their mother's grasp and head toward the TV. Everything felt fuzzy.

"Thank you, Lauren." She looked at the picture. "Wait,

boys, come back! Can you take another one? Armando's eyes are shut in this one." She handed the phone back.

It was horrible to hear her obsessing over minor imperfections when all I wanted was Maya to be here to be in photos at all. I was still queasy. I had to take another five shots before both boys looked okay. Actually, Armando still appeared a little manic because he was trying so hard to hold his eyes open after getting scolded four times. But that kid had more energy than Maya, so even image-conscious Mrs. Garcia had to give up.

Tenny showed her family around the dorm and the campus, and I decided not to trail around after them, so I got another cup of punch and watched the room. All the little kids were running around the common room sporting red Kool-Aid mustaches. But not Maya.

I leaned against the wall next to the punch bowl and thought about the newest dream again. I'd had it right before my phone's alarm went off at 5:00 a.m. again, shocking us awake. We decided I would just have to turn my phone off before going to bed. I hadn't told Tenny about the dream yet. It was as repulsive as the last one.

I shook my head and I looked around. There were so many people milling around and coming and going in all directions that it was a little crazy. And there was JT, across the room. I felt a little sick, hating him but also somehow missing him, which made me feel even worse. He was talking to a petite senior girl I didn't know and a little girl about Maya's age and seemed really into the conversation. A lump formed in my throat and I had to fight the urge to cry. Maya had been an innocent and it was so unfair that she was taken. And nobody had been punished for it. Maybe nobody ever would.

Now JT was standing next to the girl and chatting with

her whole family. They were all as short as she was, except the dad who was maybe five seven. The little girl looked up at JT and he patted her on the head. I couldn't hear what they were saying, but the mom laughed at something JT said and his contagious grin did its thing to the group.

I took a sip of my punch. It wasn't fair. It looked like those parents thought JT was as great as mine had. He was the master of charming adults. Even the dad was laughing at something he'd said. I really wanted to know what they were talking about. But there was no way to find out.

Then a chill went down my spine. Was he only talking to them because the girl had a little sister?

I couldn't watch this anymore. I took a final sip of my punch, tossed the cup in the large gray trash can, adjusted the trash bag that had fallen slightly inside, and went up to my room.

11

———

Gabriel

"I'm gonna beat you, Gabriel!" Maya says with a giggle.

"No way, niña!"

We're bouncing down Crest Ave. again and trying not to hit the trick-or-treaters.

She turns a corner and I chase her, slowing just enough to make the sharp turn onto the next street. By the time I make it around, she's out of sight on the short street. I race to the next intersection, but somehow she's disappeared.

∼

Gabriel

Sunday morning I woke from the dream with a start. I would never have thought that a recurring nightmare could be set in *Mario Kart*. I would never be able to play that again. Probably not even the Wii at all.

I got up and prepared a bowl of cereal for breakfast. I sat

on the couch, a couple of my textbooks stacked on the coffee table. I ate the cereal and thought about the dream. Was it telling me what happened, in a slightly contorted way to fit the game we played so much? But it didn't tell me anything. Was that because I didn't know?

I hated dreams. They were stupid.

I put the cereal bowl on the table and texted Lauren again, but she still wasn't responding. Maybe she was punishing me for ghosting her for so long. I picked up the chemistry book and tried to read.

It soon became clear that it was hopeless. I was going crazy trying to figure out what had happened. Maya was assaulted at some point, then got hit by a car, and then strangled and put in a different car. What had happened? And the police didn't seem to be doing anything to figure it out, except harassing me.

Which was terrifying.

I tossed my chemistry book to the other end of the couch, picked up my phone, and lay back. It was a bit early to be texting Will on a weekend morning, but I didn't care.

—*What's up?*— I texted.

It took a bit, but then those three dots appeared. Eventually, he replied —*I'm still asleep dude*—

—*But you're texting me*—

—*I'm very skilled, I can text and sleep at the same time*—

I laughed a little. Then I remembered Maya and the smile was gone.

—*Now you made me get up*— he texted. —*What are you up to?*—

—*Trying to study*— I didn't want to tell him I was obsessing over this dream and Maya in general. I didn't want to wear out his sympathy.

—*Boring. Let's meet for coffee at 1*—

That made me smile again. I didn't know why he liked me, but he obviously did. That sort of felt amazing, even if everything was dampened by Maya and the cops.

—*The union?*— I texted.

—*Yep*—

I sent the hundred-points emoji and decided to try reading for sociology. There was a test Tuesday, and although I'd already read most of the material, there were a couple of articles I needed to get through.

But between Maya and Will and all my emotions going all over the place, it wasn't happening. I put on jeans and a shirt and then grabbed my Nikes. I was going to try and retrace Maya's path and see if anything jumped out at me. Maybe I'd see something that would trigger a memory that would help me understand.

Without really thinking about it, I headed over to Crest Ave. I got to the spot where the dream always started, and stared at the street. It looked familiar now, even if it wasn't cartoon-style and there were no kids running around in costumes.

Sadness leveled me. I had to close my eyes to catch my balance. Reality slammed me when a car honked and I realized I was standing in the middle of the road. I moved to the side and the car passed me.

Then I started walking down the side of the street in the same direction we always went in the dream. This was an old neighborhood. Most of these houses were fairly small and many needed some upkeep. Our house had fallen into the same situation because Papá wasn't around to fix it up. I was going to have to step up and do it.

I was passing the houses so much slower than in the dream, and nothing was happening. I wasn't seeing or thinking anything useful. But I kept going, kicking some trash that lined the curb and scanning the houses, desperate for anything. An older woman came out of a house and picked up a newspaper from the driveway, giving me side-eye.

I got to the end of the street and stood there for a moment, looking around. It was just a neighborhood intersection, nothing special. I turned right, the way Maya turned in the dream. Just more old houses until I hit the intersection Maya turned at, where I'd flipped in the second dream. But walking, it wasn't a problem to make the sharp turn.

And that was it, all I had from the dreams. I kept going, walking the length of the street. Halfway down, I realized I was close to the 7-Eleven. My heart sped up and I got suddenly hot. When I got to the intersection, I could see it at the end of the street. I also saw the alley where I found her. We'd come at it from a different direction that night.

I turned and walked down the street, anxiety building, until I was across from the alley. The building jutted out enough that I couldn't see the cars. I crossed the street and walked into the alley.

There was the spot. The car wasn't there, but the image of it, the orange bungee cords, and the light flashing from inside the trunk landed hard in my mind. I felt sick.

A wave of desperation washed over me. I was instantly crying. Just standing there in an alley, crying for Maya, and the rest of us who missed her.

After a while, I left, glad nobody had come into the alley and seen me crying. It was already eleven thirty, so I figured I'd head over to the union and wait for Will there.

It was about a twenty minute walk, which gave me more time to think. The little gift shop was open so I went in and got an OIT branded notebook and a fancy pen, bought a smoothie, and headed into Booth Forest.

I flipped open the notebook and wrote down everything I knew about what had happened with Maya.

There wasn't much. So I decided to start looking up stuff about JT. Maybe if I could find something, the police would listen to me. I searched and searched, taking occasional sips of my peach smoothie, and took notes whenever something seemed potentially interesting. There was nothing that really stood out, but I was going to be methodical.

"There you are!"

I turned to see Will. "Oh, hi. Is it one?"

"One-oh-one." He was smiling. "What are you doing?"

"Oh, I don't want to bore you with it." I knew he wouldn't want every time we talked to be a borderline therapy session.

He looked at my phone. He leaned forward to look more closely at it. "Is that John Johnson?"

"Who?" I had done an image search on JT and several different images had shown up.

"The basketball player. You know, 'Hoppin' John'?"

"I ... don't care about basketball." Hopefully Will didn't see that as a bad thing. I remembered that TV spot with the team with the kids at the hospital.

"Oh, me neither." He stuck his tongue out and made the gagging sound, which made me laugh. He continued, "But my brother is on the team. Demetrius is pretty good so he gets a lot of court time. Hoppin' John is the star."

"I didn't realize your brother was on the team." That was a really big deal. "I wonder why this image showed up in my search." It was confusing. What did JT have to do with OIT basketball?

"Who's the other guy?" Will asked.

"That's JT. He's ... a guy."

Will laughed. "Illuminating. I'll be back in a minute." He disappeared around the corner of the booth in a second.

I looked back at the image and and read the caption. Apparently, Hoppin' John and JT were cousins. I wrote this in the notebook, but I couldn't imagine how that would be helpful.

John Johnson was lucky he was an athletic superstar, because he had a large birthmark on his neck, a port-wine stain. But he was blond and blue-eyed like JT.

There were some other pictures of JT. He got some academic award in seventh grade and won a science fair in ninth grade. That was the year Lauren first met him. She probably was impressed with his brain. Imagine being white, smart, and charming. It didn't matter that some of us saw through it and knew he was a douche. I'd only met him a handful of times, but it was still patently clear that he was, in fact, a douche.

Will abruptly slid into the booth across from me, sliding a smoothie across the table for me, a coffee in his other hand.

"Oh! Thanks. I didn't mean for you to get me something."

He pointed to my clearly empty smoothie cup from earlier. "I thought it would be awkward if I sat here drinking my coffee while you had nothing."

I smiled, charmed. "It probably would have been, but there's a good chance I wouldn't have noticed."

"But I would have felt the awkwardness. So why did you have a picture of John up?"

I sighed. "I don't want to drag you down this rabbit hole, so I'll only give you a summary. I'm kind of obsessing about Maya. And Friday the cops told me she had been sexually assaulted some time before Halloween, which makes me want to die, but also I'm convinced it was JT."

"Oh, wow. That's horrible. Why do you think it's him?" He took a sip of his coffee.

"Kind of just a feeling. I know that doesn't sound very logical. But two days before, Saturday evening, I saw him leaving their house, and Lauren wasn't at the door giving him a kiss goodbye. It was weird."

I took a sip of my smoothie. He'd even remembered I liked peach.

"Yeah. That's not much to go on, though."

"I know." I sighed. "So, your brother plays basketball, then."

"Yep." He started flipping through something on his phone and then turned it around and showed me a picture of a very obviously Black man posing with John in a very cheesy staged picture, each with a red Solo cup in hand.

"That is your brother?" I said, stunned. Will truly looked white and he did not.

He laughed.

"From the same parents as you?"

He laughed again. "Yep. And I know. There are a lot of pale people on my dad's side of the family and I actually look a lot like them, so nobody thinks my mom cheated or anything. But yeah."

"Genetics is so weird. I look just like my dad."

"Is he around?"

"Oh. Uh, no. He died a few years ago." The hole in my heart reappeared.

"That's rough. I like both my parents. It would be hard if they were gone."

"Yeah. It was really horrible. Fortunately, my mom is

great, and also Lauren's family was really supportive. Her dad was best friends with mine."

"So who's Lauren? You mentioned her with JT."

"I never mentioned her?" That made me feel really bad. "She's Maya's older sister. We all grew up together."

"Are you still friends?"

I exhaled. "She's not responding to my texts." I gave the Cliff's Notes' version of how I'd ghosted her at first, but now she was MIA.

"Now hold on," Will said, a serious expression on his face. "That was kind of shitty of you. Maybe she's just mad at you for ghosting her. She's just a kid herself, right? Why is she fully responsible for her sister? What about the parents?"

"They had to work," I explained, feeling like the worst heel.

"She just made a mistake, right?" He was talking with his hands. "Those happen. She probably feels terrible about it."

I nodded. "Yeah, she does. I know she's devastated. But she won't respond. I've tried to tell her it's not her fault."

Honestly, her family wasn't very nice to her. Dana didn't really like her, and Dana's mom had always been mean to Lauren. Her own mom abandoned her and her dad when Lauren was a toddler. Her dad wasn't a bad guy, but he wasn't very emotionally engaged. They were probably being shitty to her right now.

"I think you need to figure out a way to talk to her."

I frowned. He was right. I should really try to catch her before or after school some day. I was quiet, thinking about when I could do that.

"I'm all set to read Chapter Five tonight," Will said.

The book. "You like it?" This was a better topic than Lauren being mad at me.

"I do. Are you ready for Tuesday?"

The sociology test. "Not quite, but if I can get through the reading tomorrow, I should be."

"Same." He shrugged and took a sip of his coffee. "I have to work tomorrow, so I'll have my book with me."

Then he added, "Hey, do you want to go on that little outing with the group next Saturday?"

"The LGBTQ Student Alliance one?"

Will nodded. "I have the day off."

"Sure." Was that like a date? Was I a terrible person for wanting it to be, and wanting to have a little fun and get to know other people? It was so hard to know what I should feel. I sucked down some smoothie, which made me feel minimally better.

"Cool, cool." He smiled at me, for no apparent reason, so I smiled back.

I really liked this guy. Maybe I could be officially out.

I just needed to really work up the nerve, and also to be officially dating him. Maybe after Saturday.

12

———

Lauren

I stand in a doorway, looking out into the hall. I know where I am. I'm at home. A man wearing a mask showing a face with silver eyes is walking toward me. The mask morphs into a grin and he waves. I don't move. A girl in a pink dress is across the hall from me. She leans her back against the wall, one bare foot pressed against it. Something is odd about her—I can almost see the wall through her.

He stops in front of me and reaches forward to lightly touch the top of my head. He hooks his thumbs in his belt loops and the mask's grin widens.

"Do you want to see a one-eyed snake?" he asks.

I stare up at him. His hair is tucked behind the mask by the rubber band that holds it on. I think it's a trick but I don't know what to say and I can't move.

He unzips his jeans slowly, grasping the waistband with his left hand until a green and brown snake slithers out toward me. It has one yellow eye in the middle of its head and it opens its *jaws wide. I can see the fangs and try to step back, but he reaches up and grips my shoulder so tight I can't move.*

He laughs and says, "Do you like it?"

Lauren

Monday night Tenny, Brandon, and I were at dinner. I was teasing Brandon over his four slices of pizza, but my heart really wasn't in it. I was still thinking about Maya and the dream and all the horrible stuff. I still didn't know why the reporter thought Maya's case was related to the missing girls.

"I still don't think soup and one piece of garlic bread counts as a meal," he said to Tenny, who had admittedly always been a light eater.

"You know I'm never that hungry," she said. "Anyway, question. Lauren's phone is possessed, and we wondered if you had any idea what to do."

The alarm had gone off exactly at five this morning again, waking me from that horrible dream about the pervert. Why was I having these disgusting dreams?

"What's it doing?" Brandon asked.

"The alarm keeps going off even though it's not set. Last night we made sure it wasn't set and even turned the phone completely off, and it still went off at five."

Brandon furrowed his brow. "That's not possible."

"I know, but it's true," Tenny said.

I was working on my salad during this back-and-forth.

"You must have turned it back on in the middle of the night, Lauren," he said. He folded a slice of pizza and took a big bite.

I knew that was the logical answer, but Tenny and I knew something else was happening, but not how or why. And Brandon was totally right that it made no sense.

"I know it sounds like that," Tenny said, a little defensively. "But it was really off."

"A phone can't spontaneously turn itself on," Brandon replied.

I nodded. "It's weird, because every time it happens, it wakes me from a horrible dream."

"What kind of dream?" he asked.

"So gross. I'm dreaming about being molested, even though I never was. The guy is in a mask. I don't know if my brain is trying to tell me something, or what."

"Last night's was about a one-eyed snake," Tenny said.

Brandon looked confused and Tenny waited a moment and said, "It's an analogy."

His eyes got big. "Why would you *dream* that?"

"I don't know! It was so gross."

"Don't think I'm crazy," Tenny said sheepishly, "but I think dreams do mean something sometimes. It's like they're trying to tell you something."

"But what?" I asked.

"That I don't know," she said. "But they keep escalating, so maybe you'll find out."

"I hope it doesn't get worse. I mean, what's next?" I shuddered. I thought about what my brain was trying to tell me. I didn't think I had ever been molested and repressed the memories.

"I think you need to try to take his mask off," she said.

"I don't have any control in the dreams," I said, still a bit confused that my science-y and rational friend wanted to believe dreams were real. I stabbed some lettuce and a tomato and began working on it.

"If you can lucid dream, you would," Tenny said before taking a spoonful of soup.

"What's that?" Brandon asked.

Tenny swallowed the soup. "Basically, where you're aware that you're dreaming so you can control what happens in the dream, especially what you do."

"I've never been able to do that," I said.

"Most people can't," Tenny said. "But you can learn how. Basically, get into the habit of asking yourself all the time if you're dreaming—like, when you're awake—and then you're more likely to think to ask yourself that during a dream, and once you're aware, that's lucid dreaming."

Brandon's brow was furrowed. "That's weird."

I shrugged. "I guess there's no harm in trying. It might be kind of fun to lucid dream. You could fly and do other cool stuff." I ate some more salad, getting a fairly big glob of ranch dressing.

Tenny nodded. We ate in silence for a couple minutes—Brandon finished off piece number four, and I was happy to see that Tenny scooped up all her soup with the garlic bread. I used to genuinely worry she had an eating disorder, and I wondered if I was going to have to be the friend who intervenes. But I really didn't think she did anymore. I assumed she just genuinely wasn't that hungry most of the time. My impression was that people with anorexia usually stayed away from carbs and fat like they transmitted the plague, and Tenny didn't. She liked my fudge and divinity at Christmas as much as any sensible person.

I finished my salad just as Brandon leaned over to kiss Tenny on the side of her head, which made her smile. She wasn't totally comfortable with public displays of affection, but she was getting better. They'd only been together a couple months.

"Ready?" Brandon asked the table.

We headed back to the dorm. Tenny and Brandon were swinging their held hands, and I didn't even miss JT. He was horrible, and I couldn't believe I'd spent so long admiring him. More than two years. And even when I got close to him, I didn't see him for what he was. Because he had to be the one.

I finally saw it. All uncertainty was gone. With the timing, there was no one else.

When we got to the place where I'd spotted the reporter before she came over to talk to me, I wondered what she knew that made her so sure that there was a connection to the missing girls. Was it the sexual assault that made her think that? Was that just an assumption?

I didn't like her. And even if she was right in some way, I didn't see how we'd ever prove anything. The police were only looking at what happened on Halloween night. I assumed they were considering people who might have abused her as suspects for that night, too, but I really didn't know. I wondered who my parents had told them to check into.

I'd have to text Dad about JT. I didn't want to contact the cops. But Dad was too shut down. Would he even read the text? Should I tell Dana?

I wished my parents were ... better parents. I still couldn't believe I had to learn about Maya's assault from a stranger looking for a story.

But I guessed it was what I deserved. Besides, I thought Dana was genuinely doing really badly. I wondered if Gabriel knew. He was still texting me, and I still wasn't reading them.

I followed Tenny and Brandon inside when I suddenly heard my name.

I looked over toward the general lounge and saw Gabriel standing there. I immediately looked at the floor and headed to the stairwell.

"Lauren, wait."

But I was already on the stairs. I couldn't talk to him.

My heart ached remembering Maya grinning in her costume Halloween night. I would never forget that image.

Gabriel

"I'm gonna beat you, Gabriel!" Maya says.

"No way, niña!"

We're on a Crest Ave. filled with trick-or-treaters again.

I follow her around a corner and see her approaching the intersection ahead. She turns right and I manage to follow her, just in time to see a car shoot out from a side street and crash into her car. She flies out of the car and up onto the hood and her face and braids slap the windshield before she slides back down onto the road. The car backs up and drives off.

When I get to her, her eyes are open and she's looking up at me, pleading for help.

But I can't do anything because I'm stuck in the car and can't reach her.

Gabriel

Just like last Tuesday morning, Tolui and Hansen were waiting in the car in front of my house. I locked the door and tried to ignore them and walk to class, but this time they got out, standing in front of me on the sidewalk.

"Why don't you come to the station with us, Gabriel," Hansen said, not asking.

"That's okay," I said. "I'm good." I took a step forward and so did Tolui, blocking me.

"Gabriel Canul, you're under arrest for the murder of Maya Roberts-Baxter," Tolui started.

"What?" It was like a punch to the stomach and head at the same time.

Hansen got behind me and grabbed my arms, slid my backpack off, and dropped it to the ground, then started handcuffing me as Tolui continued. "You have the right to remain silent. Anything you say can and will be used against you in a court of law. You have the right to an attorney." Hansen cinched the handcuffs tight enough that they already hurt, and Tolui kept going. "If you cannot afford an attorney, one will be appointed for you. Do you understand your rights?"

"Yeah." I understood I had no rights at all. White cops were going to treat me like a criminal just for being brown. Being gay didn't help, but I should have known I was doomed as soon as Maya went missing.

They threw me onto the hard plastic back seat and I landed roughly, wrenching my shoulder. Hansen sort of kicked my lower legs to get them in the car and slammed the door shut. There was a little alcove in the back where my cuffed hands were, so I wasn't smashing them, but the cuffs were so tight.

What was the point of working hard and being good my whole life, staying away from lowlifes and hoodlums, if I was going to end up in this seat anyway?

It was all too much, and I started crying, which was

humiliating because I couldn't wipe my eyes so it was going to be obvious to everyone. And I was going to miss the sociology test, and seeing Will.

The jail wasn't very far, just about ten hellish minutes of driving through Burnside.

I saw the front of city hall, but they drove around to the back and parked. Hansen got out and Tolui opened the door, exposing me to the bright sun. A rush of air hit me, really cold on the wet spots on my cheeks.

Hansen came around and reached in and grasped my shoulder and roughly pulled me so I scrambled to get out.

"Were you crying?" Tolui asked with a mean laugh. "Little fag."

I said nothing and fought more tears. They walked me into the back of the building, and we were in a bright area. I was getting increasingly queasy with each step. They made me go down a short hall and pushed me into what looked like an interview room, filled with a cheap-looking dark faux-wood table and three cheap plastic chairs.

"We're just going to talk to you first, so sit down," Tolui said, pointing me to the orange molded plastic chair. He didn't offer to take the handcuffs off. My left hand was completely numb.

But I sat. Hansen had gone somewhere, but Tolui sat in one of the chairs on the other side of the table. He stared at me hard, so I just looked down at the table and tried to ignore the pain in my wrists.

Hansen returned with two coffees, setting one in front of Tolui, closing the door, and then sitting down.

Somewhere within me, I'd gotten mad. Defiant even. "You can ask me anything you want, keep me here as long as you want, but I never hurt Maya and I'm not going to say anything. I want a lawyer. I get a public defender, don't I?"

Tolui laughed, and Hansen said, "We'll get you one, we just want to know what happened first, Gabriel. Your side of the story."

"You're actually going to play good cop/bad cop? Not participating. I'm done."

"How long were you abusing Maya?" Tolui asked.

It took everything within me not to protest, but I knew not responding was better. "I want a lawyer. I have a right to a lawyer."

"She was a cutie, with those black braids," Tolui said.

It made me want to puke. She had been cute, but sexualizing an eight-year-old was sick. "I want a lawyer. Get me a public defender."

Tolui exhaled in annoyance. They looked at each other and got up and left me in there.

I waited and waited. There was no clock in here—obviously missing as part of the psychological warfare these *cabrones* carried out on people.

I waited some more, what must have been hours. They just left me sitting here. My left arm was entirely numb all the way from my hand past my elbow. I leaned forward in the chair to take pressure off my hands.

What did Will think when I didn't show up to class? Dr. Wetherspoon was convinced I was a loser, I was sure. You can't just miss a test. Would Mamá bail me out? How long would I be in here?

Was I going to go to prison? This whole thing was so stupid, and I felt rage building, but it quickly turned to desperation, because innocent people went to prison all the time.

They couldn't have any evidence against me because I hadn't done anything. How did they even get an arrest warrant? I'd never asked to see one. Could this whole thing be fake? What counted as false arrest?

Suddenly, the door burst open, making me jump. Which was obviously the intention. Tolui sneered at me while a white woman in a navy skirt and blazer stepped in.

"I'm Kay Waters. I'll be your state-appointed lawyer." She reached the table and Tolui started to shut the door, but she stopped it with her foot and faced him. "Fix his handcuffs. What is wrong with you?"

Tolui smirked and walked toward me. "Stand up."

I stood and he moved behind me and uncuffed me. I instinctively shook both hands.

"Nope. Sit back down. I'm cuffing you to the table."

There was a metal loop in the center of the table and he handcuffed me to that. Was it really all necessary? I'd never done anything violent. Why did they hate me so much? Still, this was an improvement. My left hand was starting to wake up.

He left, and Ms. Waters shut the door behind him with a glare. She set her leather folio on the table and sat across from me. She had perfect makeup and looked intimidatingly professional.

"Hi, Gabriel. Tell me what happened. Why you're here."

I closed my eyes and leaned forward, head almost on the table. Was this woman going to believe me? Would she help me?

I sat up. "I didn't do anything wrong. I didn't hurt Maya and I certainly never killed her. Losing her has been the worst experience of my life, even worse than when my dad was killed, and getting blamed for it while the guilty person is walking around scot-free is driving me crazy."

She nodded, and it was clear she was really listening to me, which was gratifying. "The evidence they used for the arrest warrant is really weak. Can you tell me what happened Halloween night and why they think you killed her?"

"They told me that she was assaulted some time a little before Halloween, and they seem to think it was me, so I'm guessing that they think that was my 'motive' for killing her. Also, I happened to be the one who found her on the search, and they think that was suspicious. It was just horrible. She had on an ankle bracelet with a flashing light and I saw it flashing inside the trunk because it was ajar."

I had to pause and close my eyes to regain my composure, even though more tears leaked out. I flashed back to the dream I'd had last night, another of the *Mario Kart* ones. "But it doesn't make any sense. I don't even have a car, and I know she was hit by a car that night."

Ms. Waters nodded.

Was the dream right? Did she get hit by a car that drove off? If so, what happened after? I had no idea.

"So, can you go through Halloween night for me?" she asked.

I walked through everything, just as I had with the cops when they first talked to me. Homework, Maya coming by for a picture, handing out candy, seeing cops outside, joining the search for her, finding her, and the dazed walk home. But then I thought she needed the context of our history, so I told her about how I'd grown up with Maya and Lauren, and why it was all so devastating.

After I finished, she nodded thoughtfully, and I asked, "Do you believe me?"

She nodded. "I do, actually. There's a lot of bias in this department."

I was stunned that she'd come out and say that. She

must really believe it. Which was scary because it probably meant it was really bad, which was bad for me.

"Okay, look." Ms. Waters clasped her hands together. "I'm going to do my best to get these charges thrown out, and I'll defend you if I can't do that, but I can't make any promises, Gabriel."

I nodded, more terrified than I'd been yet. She was talking about real things that could really happen.

"Do you have someone who can bail you out?"

"I think my mom can." Except, where was she going to get the money? How much would it be?

"Okay. They're going to book you and you'll get your phone call. Call your mom. Your arraignment will probably be at nine Thursday morning. Give me your and your mom's phone numbers so I can get in touch with you once you're out."

I nodded dumbly.

Ms. Waters stood up and touched my shoulder gently. "I'm going to do my best, Gabriel." She left me in there, and Hansen came back, removed the handcuffs and walked me further down the hall into a white room with various devices. The booking room.

My heart was beating so hard I thought it would burst. They fingerprinted me, took mugshots, and the next thing, I was in a big holding cell, sitting on the cleanest spot on the floor that I could find, where I could also lean against a wall, because the bench was occupied by men much larger than me. This was another moment when I hated being so small.

Getting beat up would be the icing on the cake, wouldn't it? I looked around and spotted a clock. 2:05. The sociology test was long over, and I hadn't been there. I was in a much worse placed, destined for hell.

13

———

Lauren

A man with silver eyes under a mask with painted rosy cheeks is standing in front of a white sheet cake perched on a black card table. The cake has writing on it but I can't read it. It's written in a funny language. He takes a large butcher knife and makes a single cut across the whole cake.

He holds the knife up, eyes flaming red. "You heard me, right? You know what I'll do to her if you tell."

A blonde girl in a pink dress stands behind him and blinks. Each time she does it she fades, like she's turning invisible for a second. It distracts me from the terror in my gut.

He makes a stabbing motion and says, "Right?"

I nod. I'm vibrating with fear. I look down and watch as my pounding heart jumps out of my chest and smashes onto the floor, splashing blood everywhere.

He walks over and steps on it, bloody goo spraying up and covering his foot over his flip-flop.

Lauren

Wednesday, we were playing soccer for PE and I was distracted from thinking about the dream, which I'd been doing all day long. I'd felt queasy all day, reliving the guy slamming his foot down on my heart and the blood going everywhere.

I avoided having to kick the ball as much as possible, and Tenny, Brandon, and I headed back to the dorm when it was over.

"Meet in fifteen?" Brandon asked.

"Sure," Tenny said.

As soon as we got back to our room we fell into our desk chairs, grabbed our phones off our desks, and checked them like any living teenagers. Nothing for me. Who would be texting me? Certainly not my family. I no longer had a boyfriend. I lived with one of my two best friends, and the other one wasn't talking to me. Though he had shown up Monday, probably not just to yell at me. I just couldn't.

"Oh, my God, Lauren!" Tenny said.

I jerked my head up from my phone. "What?"

"Gabriel was arrested yesterday!"

"For what?" I was utterly stunned. He was one of the most law-abiding people I knew.

She scrolled down on the text. "Maya!"

"They think Gabriel killed Maya?" How could they think that? He would never in a million years hurt her.

Or could he? Could he have been the one who assaulted her, too? He could have had access. The queasiness that had plagued me flared up. I grabbed the trash can because I really thought I might throw up.

"It doesn't make any sense," Tenny said.

I closed my eyes. No, she was right. Something else had happened. It couldn't be Gabriel. He was with his mom giving out candy.

"My mom said several people helped his mom bail him out."

The Latino community stuck together here. I doubted his mom would have been able to pay for bail herself. But more to the point, why were the police doing something so stupid?

"He doesn't even own a car." This was true. It really couldn't be him.

"I know." Tenny was still scrolling. "Everyone knows he didn't do it."

"What evidence do they have? They must have had something. They can't arrest somebody with nothing."

"You don't think he did it, do you?" Tenny's eyes were wide with shock.

"No. I don't know. I can't imagine him hurting her. But isn't it always someone in or close to the family?"

Tenny stared at me for a second. "You're talking about the assault. He would never."

I rested my face in my palms. "No, you're right. He couldn't have done anything to her." As I said it, my doubts did clear. There was no way he assaulted her. And murder her? It was impossible.

"I would trust Gabriel with any kid. He's so obviously a good person. I can't believe you even thought for a second."

"I know." I started crying. I was a terrible friend.

"Okay, sorry, I'm being mean. You are right, though. Most abuse is done by someone in the family. They obviously have to have easier access to the kid alone."

"Yeah." Something in what she said triggered mental

feelers in the back of my brain. But they didn't connect to anything. "You are right. I was just freaking out. But seriously, they can't convict him. They can't have any real evidence against him. Everything has to be circumstantial."

She was still looking at her text. She jerked her head back in surprise. "Did you know he was the one who found her?"

"He was?" That was a surprise.

"Apparently so."

"That must have been horrible for him." I realized I had never seen her after she ran off. My last image of her was as a happy pirate. He actually had to see her all beat up. I had been spared that horror, but a wave of desperation washed over me. I was the one who deserved to see how bad it was, not him. It was my fault.

"I'm really scared for him," Tenny said.

"Why? He didn't do it. They can't have anything real on him. His mom can say he was home all night. And all the kids who got candy at the door."

"This is still one of your blind spots, Lauren. They obviously had enough to convince a judge to give them an arrest warrant. Probably white cops, and a white judge. And whatever it is might be enough to convince a mostly white jury."

That stunned me. Tenny and Gabriel were always on my case for not seeing the racism they dealt with all the time. I had gotten better, but I just hadn't seen it here. She was probably right. And now I was terrified for him.

"Seriously, this is really bad, Lauren. They're just going to dismiss whatever his mom says as her lying to cover for him. And how is Gabriel going to find all these people who got candy from him at his door?"

"No, no, I totally believe you. We have to do something.

How can we help him? Should I call the police and tell them he didn't do it?"

I didn't really think it would help. I'd finally called yesterday and told them about JT, but I knew they didn't believe me. It was so frustrating.

Tenny shook her head and put her phone down on her desk. Her eyes glistened and I knew she was crying, too. "They won't care what you say."

My feeling of powerlessness switched to anger. "But they have to! He can't go to prison for something he didn't do. And that would also mean the person who really did it won't go to prison. How can that be right?"

"There's a lot that isn't right in the world. But I'll tell my mom you're willing to help. Maybe they would listen to you in some context, since you know him so well."

"I could definitely be a character witness." I couldn't do nothing. This was horrible. Everything was horrible. I'd lost Maya forever, and maybe Gabriel, too. If he went to prison for something that he didn't do—something that was my fault—I didn't know how I'd live with myself.

Tenny nodded just as her phone dinged. She picked it up. "Brandon's downstairs."

"Okay." I thought about not going to supper, since every-thing was falling apart, but I was hungry and I sometimes got headaches if I didn't eat, especially when I was stressed. Maybe Tenny and I could figure something out to help Gabriel, or maybe Brandon would have an idea. But he was as white as I was, so he'd probably think Gabriel would be fine, just like I had.

∼

Gabriel

"I'm gonna beat you, Gabriel!" Maya says.

"No way, niña!"

Trick-or-treaters run from house to house on Crest Ave. and we fly down it.

I keep up with her around a corner, and then one more corner. I'm just behind her when a car comes flying from the side and hits Maya in the intersection. She is launched out of her kart and slams into the car's windshield, then falls off the hood in front. As I get to her, the car backs up and guns it away from her.

She looks at me for help, but I'm stuck in my fucking kart, despite frantically trying to pull myself out.

Suddenly, someone runs up and scoops her up and takes off to the right. I turn my kart to follow him and see we're almost at the 7-Eleven. He takes her down an alley and I turn just as he's putting her in the trunk of a car. He reaches in—is he strangling her?—and I scream but no sound comes out.

Then he turns, and I can see as clear as day that it's JT.

Gabriel

I gasped when I woke up from the dream. I'd known it was JT! But why? And what had really happened? Was the dream right that someone else had hit her and JT just stumbled across her after it happened, and just decided to kill her instead of helping her? Why?

But how would a dream be right? I knew it was probably just my mind making up a story since I didn't like him.

And then I remembered my arraignment was this morning. I looked at my phone. 6:43. I had to be there at eight thirty. My mom was taking me.

She was trying to put on a brave face, but she was terrified. Which meant I was terrified, because things were terrifying.

On the drive home from the jail Tuesday, she'd cried almost the whole way, and she kept saying, "Why didn't you *tell* me they were bothering you, mijo?"

I hadn't told her because I was trying to pretend it wasn't real.

Lying in bed, I thought about what it would be like for her if I went to prison. First she lost Papá, and then it would be me. They'd wanted to have more kids, but she had complications when I was born and she couldn't have any more after that, so all she had was me. I felt kind of guilty about that. She had her parents and siblings, but they lived in Texas. My parents had moved here when Papá was stationed at Tinker Air Force Base, after they got married.

Then the image of the car hitting Maya's kart shot across my mind and I wanted to throw up. I needed to get up. It was a dream. A terrible one, yes, but I had to shave and dress nice to deal with the terribleness that was my life now.

I'd definitely be wearing one of Papá's shirts. Maybe it would help. I know if it were possible, Papá would help me from heaven. I had some nice blue slacks, so I'd wear those.

I heard Mamá in the bathroom so I gave her some time. She put her makeup on in her bedroom, so she'd be out soon.

But lying here waiting was not relaxing at all, because my brain kept generating all sorts of horrible scenarios of what would happen to me in prison. I was so short, and I'd never had an ounce of machismo. It would be really bad.

I saw the go-kart get hit again, and then I was crying.

Which just pissed me off. I threw the blanket off and went over to the closet. Papá had a white button-up that Mamá managed to keep bright with her laundry ninja tactics, so I decided to wear that. I grabbed the blue slacks and boxers and tossed everything onto the bed, sitting down next to it. I heard the shower turn off in the bathroom.

I was missing my second sociology class this week, after missing the test on Tuesday. Will had blown my phone up on Tuesday and I didn't respond until that night. I thought he would be mad at me, but he was still being supportive.

My phone dinged and I picked it up. Another text from him.

—*Good luck today*—

There wasn't really much luck needed. All we were doing was entering a not guilty plea, which meant it would go to the next stage. But the sentiment was nice.

—*Thanks.*— I texted. —*Do you want to meet later?*—

—*I have to work this afternoon, but what about tomorrow?*—

—

I might not have very many tomorrows. The thought made me tear up again. But I had to just pretend that my college life was still happening.

—*I'm going to see Dr. Wetherspoon to see if anything is salvageable at this point*—

—*Good. I'm sure she will work with you*— he answered.

It was nice that he was so confident. I wasn't sure.

The bathroom door squeaked open, so I headed in and went through all the normal morning prep, even though this wasn't a normal morning at all.

Soon, I was waiting for Mamá on the couch. She came in and tried to put on a brave smile, but I saw right through it. She looked so freaked out, her eyes a little wild.

"Ready, mijo?" she asked.

We headed out and didn't talk the whole way to the courthouse. I think if I had tried to speak, my voice would have been shaking so much that she wouldn't be able to understand me. Eventually she pulled into a parking spot and we looked at each other and both teared up. She took my hand in both of hers and said, "Everyone is praying for you, Gabriel. God won't let you go to prison."

We looked at each other, knowing it was unlikely He'd intervene here, but she always looked to Him when things were bad. I didn't really believe anymore, but if it helped her cope, so be it.

"Okay." I turned away and she let go, and I opened the door.

Ms. Waters met us at the courthouse after we went through the metal detectors. She took us into the courtroom, where we took seats and waited. I looked around the room. There was a section over to the left with several chairs in two rows behind a short wall. Where the jury would sit, I guessed. God, a bunch of white people would look at me and decide how the rest of my life would go. How could I have ended up here? I never did anything wrong. Other kids had teased me for being a goody two-shoes.

I couldn't think about it. I continued looking around the room. The judge's area was up higher, like on a stage. It was like a big, wide desk and ended on the right with what must be the witness stand. Who would be witnesses in my trial? What would they say?

The judge was in black robes like they were supposed to be, and he was white with peppery gray hair, although he didn't look that old. Then there were two long tables facing the judge, which is where the lawyers and defendants went to hear the charges and enter a plea.

Suddenly, they called my name and Mamá squeezed my

hand. Ms. Waters and I went up there, standing behind the table on the left. My heart was pounding so hard that I felt like I couldn't hear properly.

Soon, the judge began reading the charges, and he said it was first degree murder with malice and I wanted to throw up. But I kept my face mostly neutral, even though I was borderline crying, but I held it in.

The judge asked me how I pled, and Ms. Waters had to prompt me to say "Not guilty" out loud.

Eventually, it was over and they set a date for the preliminary hearing—November 28—and we went outside the courtroom into an open area, with doors leading to other rooms and the metal detectors at the front.

Ms. Waters and Mamá talked for a bit and finally we left. I was in a perpetual daze.

14

Lauren

I sit cross-legged in front of my bookshelf. All the books are stacked on the floor. I brought in sheets of colored stickers from the desk and they sit next to the stack. I make two smaller stacks from the first—one for true books and one for made-up books. Then I divide the true book stack into two, one for animals and one for everything else. I start putting red stickers on the spines of the made-up books because red is my favorite color. When I'm done, I put them back on the top shelf one at a time. It's so pretty once it's filled up.

The front door shuts and I can hear talking and laughing. My stomach is twisting and I'm so scared. It's like I'm being pushed into the floor. I get up to close the door. When I sit back down I see that the only thing I have on is a bikini even though I don't own one. My legs are skinny and I'm a little kid again.

I jump up and throw my closet door open, but it's empty except for stacks of books in the back. I walk in and start looking through them and see that every one of them is borrowed from the library. It looks like a sideways bookshelf. More books appear in front of the others, forcing me to step back. A girl in a pink dress sits on top of the first heap of books, her back to the wall, but I can barely see her because she's so faint. She holds out her hand and I reach up to take it, but another stack appears in front of me and I can't reach her. Then there's another, and another, until the whole closet is full of them, and the girl looks small as a Barbie doll perched in the back.

I go back to my bookshelf and sit down. I start putting green stickers on the animal books but they won't stick. They keep sliding off and landing on my leg. They stick to my skin fine, and then my leg is covered with green dots.

I can still hear laughing in the living room. I tremble so much I can't even peel the stickers off the paper. I keep wishing I had a place to hide, but there's no room for me in the closet. I look at the window and see bars covering it.

I stare at the stickers covering my leg. They look like dragon scales.

The talking and laughing has stopped, and when I look around, I see that the whole room is full of thick fog. My stomach is twisting even more. I hear my door open and I'm shaking so much I can hear my teeth rattle, but I can't turn around.

Strong arms pick me up from behind and throw me up in the air. I want to stay up, but then I'm falling and falling through the fog and can't see anything.

I look down and there's the pink comforter on my bed, but it's covered in bath towels. I land softly on it and then I can't breathe because something is pushing me down, holding me in place and tugging on my swimsuit.

∾

Lauren

I jerked awake to the sound of my phone alarm.

"Oh, my God, Lauren. This is insane." Tenny's voice was thick from sleepiness.

We had actually run my phone battery completely down in the afternoon. It was impossible for the alarm to ring.

I couldn't answer because I was so horrified by the dream. I turned the alarm off and the phone was a brick.

"Tenny, this dream. Oh, God." It was real now. They'd said she'd been assaulted and I rationally knew what that meant, but it hadn't fully registered that it was rape. I was queasy from the sense of horror that permeated my entire body.

"What happened?"

How would I say any of this out loud? I took a deep breath, wiped some tears, and told her everything that had happened, and as I was recounting it, it became obvious what else it was telling me.

After I finished, Tenny was silent. I knew she knew, too.

I sort of wished I could see her face, but the light was still off and the only thing I could see was the bottom of her top bunk from the light that leaked in through the blinds.

"That's when it happened, that's when she was assault-ed," I said. "She was hiding in her bedroom and was terri-fied because it had been escalating, and he came in and did that because there was nothing she could do to stop it." Saying it out loud was absolutely horrifying.

"Yeah," Tenny said, sounding so sad even through her tiredness. "But who was it? And when?"

I was quiet for a moment. It was the Saturday right before Halloween. "I never told you this because it was weird. I told you I fell asleep that last time JT was over."

"Yeah." Her voice was shaky.

"I didn't tell you how weird it was to fall asleep while he was there, and that it seemed to be for a really long time. We were watching movies so I wasn't paying attention to the time. But it was afternoon. And then when I woke up, I was in my bed and several hours had passed."

"Were you drinking?"

"Yeah. But only a little, and I didn't think I'd had that much, so it was weird."

We lay there in silence.

"He drugged you." Tenny finally said.

"I know."

"I thought he was a bad person, but not this bad." Tenny sniffed.

I had brought him into Maya's life. I was an even worse sister than I'd thought. I loved Maya. How could I have destroyed her?

"It's all my fault." I groaned and the tears started.

"It's not your fault," she said after a moment, her voice as thick as mine. I wasn't the only one crying.

It was nice of her to say that. Loyal Tenny. But she wasn't right.

There was no way I was sleeping after this. I got up and got my shower stuff and my towel and robe, shaking the whole time I moved around. I almost dropped my shower caddy when I reached for it in the closet.

"Are you getting up for real?" Tenny asked.

"Yeah."

"I can't sleep either." Her bed squeaked as she shifted on her bunk.

"I can't even think." I stood there, cold and shaking despite my flannel pajamas. "All I can do is picture the things in the dreams and try to imagine what it was really like. Probably close, but not exact. I didn't leave her alone with him that many times." My heart twisted. "Obviously still too many. More than zero."

"I know I keep saying this, but it's not your fault. How could you have known? I thought I had a pedophile radar, but I didn't see it either. I just thought he was a douche and didn't care about you, or anyone. But you always take too much responsibility for bad things that happen, even when it shouldn't be yours."

That might be true in some cases, but not this one. "I'm going to take a shower."

"Okay." The bed squeaked when she sat up as I headed out the door.

Nobody was in the bathroom at this hour, so I got the rightmost shower, with the best water pressure, and I turned it all the way up to almost scalding.

I closed my eyes, and the water hitting my face and chest hard and hot felt both good and like punishment. I washed myself absentmindedly, my mind still constantly cycling through the various dreams.

I faintly heard the bathroom door open.

"It's just me." Tenny.

"Okay," I said.

We didn't speak again and I finished, dried off, and donned my robe, then brushed my teeth and headed back, obsessing all the while.

I would never forget this.

I put the shower caddy in the closet and pulled out some jeans and a shirt. I sat on the bed and started working on pulling on the jeans.

And what should I do with this information? I had no actual evidence, and it would be weird if I only just now realized what was happening the whole time. I obviously couldn't tell the police I'd figured it all out from dreams.

But this meant JT was going to get away with it. This type of guy didn't just do it once and never again.

Once I was dressed, I sat at my desk and looked at my books. How was I going to be able to concentrate enough to study ever again?

I couldn't imagine how I was going to live my life at all. It seemed impossible.

Gabriel

Friday, I went to my morning classes and then sat on a bench in Dr. Wetherspoon's building, but in a different hall from her office. I was trying to force myself to not chicken out, but I didn't want her to see me in case I did.

Once her office hours started, I steeled myself and knocked on her door, which was ajar. My heart was beating crazy fast. What if she told me to fuck off?

"Come in."

I opened the door and headed in, queasy with worry.

"Hello," she said, but her eyes widened once she saw it was me. "Gabriel."

"Hi. Can I talk to you?" My voice was shaking from thinking about everything that was wrong in my life.

"Sure. You missed an exam, though."

"Yeah." I was just standing there, uncertain.

"Come sit down."

I sat.

She looked at me while leaning back in her chair, hands tented in front of her. Her eyebrows were slightly raised and she clearly wondered what bullshit I was going to spew.

It occurred to me that I had absolutely nothing to lose here. She couldn't think any less of me than she already did.

"Can I give you the whole story? It's relevant." And what she believed about me was wrong. I wanted to fix that. Nobody else was going to do it for me. Still, as brave as I was trying to be, the chicken in me wanted me to get up and leave.

"Sure. But if someone else shows up, you may have to wrap up." She sounded matter-of-fact and obviously still thought I was a piece of crap.

"Okay." I took a deep breath. I wasn't going to leave. I had to do this. "You know Maya Roberts-Baxter?"

"The little girl you had a picture of." Matter-of-fact again, with a small amount of judgment.

I wanted to cry, seeing that picture in my mind. "Yes. I grew up next door to her. I've known her and her sister, who's a couple of years younger than me, my whole life. Her sister and I basically raised her. I mean, Lauren much more than me, but summers, we all spent together. They were both like my sisters. Lauren's really my best friend. Or was." I missed her so much. How could I get her to talk to me again?

My voice was a little shaky, but it was getting better the more I talked.

Dr. Wetherspoon nodded. "So it was a personal loss."

I nodded, tears still threatening. "I was part of the search that night, and by chance, I was the one who found her." I had to close my eyes to maintain control, but the image of her in that trunk was vivid in my mind. "I was searching with two other guys, and it was just a coincidence that that was our assigned area. I saw the car with the messed-up trunk, with a flashing light coming from inside, and I knew Maya had flashing lights on her ankles, so I just lifted the trunk lid, but I really wasn't expecting anything." At this point, I lost the battle and tears started falling.

She nodded, giving me grace.

"It was the worst moment of my life." I wiped my eyes and looked over her shoulder. My pulse was still pounding because I had no idea how she was taking all this. "From the moment the cops got there, they treated me like I was guilty. They arrested me Tuesday morning. But they have nothing on me because I didn't do any of what they're accusing me of."

She nodded again.

"That's why I missed the test on Tuesday. I was ready for it, but they arrested me when I was on my way to class. And then yesterday morning was my arraignment. I have a public defender and she said the evidence they have against me is all circumstantial. But she also said that a white jury might not care."

I teared up again, thinking about spending the rest of my life in prison. I glanced at her at that point.

Dr. Wetherspoon nodded thoughtfully and tapped her fingers together. I could tell she was trying to determine if she believed me or not.

"Okay," she said, obviously still thinking, because she didn't say anything else for a moment.

I looked down, wiping my eyes again. It seemed I was finally done crying. I wished I could just suppress all emotion like so many guys did. But I wore it on my sleeve.

"Okay," she said again. "I will allow you to retake the exam. Monday. Are you able to take it on Monday after-noon? You can sit in here and take it."

"I have a class one to two, but I can come by after that."

"Two p.m. then. I'll modify it slightly from the one I gave Tuesday."

"Okay." Thank God. The first good thing that had happened in my life since Halloween. I started to stand.

"Hold on. You said you have a public defender. Are you getting a lawyer?" She sounded invested in this, a tiny bit intense.

I nearly blushed and quietly said, "I can't really afford one."

"I have someone who might be able to help. Let me reach out. I know some lawyers who can work pro bono in some cases."

I was shocked. Would she really help me?

She sat forward in her chair and typed the code to unlock her computer. "I can't promise anything, but let me talk to someone. When is your next court date?"

"The twenty-eighth." God, that was close. My stomach was instantly in turmoil.

"Ten days." She made a note on a stickie. "I will let you know Monday what I find out. How are you doing otherwise?"

I wasn't sure what she meant at first. "You mean because of Maya?"

"Yes." Her face was full of sympathy. "You must be grieving."

I shrugged. "Not great."

"How's her sister? Lauren, you said?" She had that caring expression adult women got when they were going into mama bear mode.

"Yeah. She won't talk to me. I was mad at her at first and didn't answer her texts, but then I finally texted her and now she won't respond. I think she's punishing me for ghosting her."

"I see," Dr. Wetherspoon said, sounding a little surprised. "I thought she was your best friend?"

"Yeah."

"She probably feels terrible. You should keep trying to reach her so you can help support each other."

I nodded.

There was a knock on the door.

"Just a moment," she called. She looked back at me. "Are we good?"

"Yeah." I stood.

"I will see you at two on Monday."

I nodded and headed out, passing a young woman I didn't recognize. As soon as I got outside, the air was brisk and a little calming. I pulled out my phone. There were several texts from Will.

—*Did you go to her office hours?*—

—*How did it go?*—

—*I'm assuming you're in there and that's why you're not answering*—

—*Do you want to get a coffee afterward? I'll be in the union at 1:30*—

It was one thirty-five right now. I whipped off a quick text. —*On my way*—

Seeing Will would make me feel better. I would not think about the preliminary hearing a week and a half away.

Lauren

"You guys, I know something is up," Brandon started. "Maybe talking about it would be better. The silence is killing me."

Tenny and I looked at each other. We were having lunch on Saturday, and I knew they'd gone out the night before, so she must have told him something, but I didn't know what.

"It's up to you," Tenny said to me.

Brandon looked at me curiously but I ignored him.

Should I tell someone who didn't even know Maya about the horrible things that had happened to her because of someone I brought into her life? Would I be betraying her trust?

Brandon took a bite of his pizza, clearly trying to not pressure me. He was a nice guy.

I thought Maya would want me to tell. This was something that had happened to her, not something she did. I figured I could share. Maybe it would help somehow.

"I guess there's no harm in telling," I said to Tenny, glancing at Brandon. "Except he'll think we're crazy."

"It's got to be more than the phone thing," he said.

"That's the thing," I said. "If you can't believe us on that, you won't believe this, either."

"Okay. I promise I'll keep an open mind."

I looked at Tenny and she said, "This is definitely your story to tell."

I set my fork down, giving up on the chicken for now. "So, the phone has continued to go off at five a.m. periodically. Thursday night we completely ran the battery down on my phone. It was a brick before we went to bed. And it still went off at five. This time it woke me from a dream that made all the other dreams make sense. I told you about them."

"You told me about one of them," he said. He didn't say anything else about the phone.

"Okay. So, all the dreams were about sexual abuse, where I was on the receiving end, and it got worse with each dream. And the dream I had Thursday night made it clear that I was dreaming from Maya's perspective. And it was clear when it was, and that made it clear who it was." I paused, closed my eyes, and rested my forehead on my fingers. Brandon stayed blessedly quiet.

"It also made it clear exactly how bad it was. And that it's all my fault."

"How can it be your fault?" Brandon asked.

Tenny reached across the table and touched my hand. "It's not, and I keep telling her, but she can't hear it."

I stared at the table.

"So who do you think it was?" Brandon asked.

I looked at Tenny. I couldn't say it. I gave her a nod, and she knew what I meant.

"It was JT," she said. "The Saturday before Halloween. He drugged Lauren."

The color drained from Brandon's face, which surprised me. Tenny looked confused.

"What?" she asked.

"Uh, he has a ... reputation."

"For being a pedophile?" Tenny asked skeptically.

"Actually, yes. He's got a ton of porn on his computer, and there are rumors that some of it is a bit ... sketchy. Maybe with kids."

My heart nearly stopped. Tenny and I looked at each other, our mouths hanging open.

"Why didn't you *say* something?" she asked.

Brandon put his hands up. "I don't know. I wasn't sure it was true, and guys don't rat each other out for most things. It's how you get beat up."

Tenny looked at me again and said, "That's something they can prove, that he can get into trouble for."

"Yeah. It is." I was thinking. "But we don't have any proof."

"Maybe I could get some," Brandon said.

"How?" Tenny's eyes were narrowed. "You're no hacker."

"If I could get him to show it to me, I could report it."

"You would do that?" Tenny asked.

Brandon wasn't a particularly bold guy, so I was skeptical, too.

"Sure." He shrugged, even though it didn't seem like a small thing to me.

"So does that mean you believe us about the phone and the dreams?" I asked.

"Dude, I don't know. It sounds so crazy." His hands were up to emphasize this. "But neither of you is all woo-woo, and you're smart, so if you both believe it, and the puzzle pieces fit, it's hard not to consider it possible. And maybe you're not psychic—maybe Maya's spirit is somehow communicating with you."

"Her spirit?" Tenny said, mouth hanging open. I was equally surprised.

He shrugged. "Makes more sense than Lauren being psychic, you know?"

"That actually does make some sense," I said. "Even though it makes no sense."

Tenny and Brandon both cocked their heads to the side in unison, looking thoughtful.

I crossed my arms and watched Brandon. Maybe he was the ticket to JT getting punished for something, even if not for the right thing.

15

———

Gabriel

Saturday, just two days after the arraignment, I was in Oklahoma City with Will and several other LGBTQ Student Alliance members, including Orion and Simone from the meeting a couple of weeks back. Back before I'd been arrested. My stomach twisted at the memory of that and the arraignment.

We were checking in at a place called Factory Obscura that supposedly had a multimedia immersive art display, whatever that meant. I was obviously just here for Will. And for the distraction from thoughts of the hearing.

The outside of the building was bright and painted with all sorts of colorful designs, including a welcoming rainbow. Orion got us all checked in and handed out these glasses we were supposed to wear, then we all came in together through this weird hallway with the walls covered with red bubble-like poofs, lit only with black lights.

"Ooh," Will said, eyebrows raised.

"I agree," I said, which made us both laugh.

We emerged in another dark room with lights only coming from the displays, kind of like being in a psychedelic cave, with separate mini-cave areas you could crawl into and some rock like structures with many colors and dim lights everywhere in every color, everything lit with a black light. There was soft instrumental music with some kind of subtle beat.

"Put the glasses on," Will said to me. He already had his glasses on and an amused expression on his face. I wished for more light so I could see his face better, but I already knew that he hadn't shaved this morning, and that was pretty hot.

I put them on and immediately laughed. They turned all the lighted areas into heart shapes, like looking through a kaleidoscope, hearts pouring out of every light source.

Will pointed to one of the little caves to the side and said, "I'm going in."

He got on his knees and crawled into it, and I followed him inside, trying not to be distracted by his butt in his Levi's. He sat cross-legged and I sat across from him, our knees touching in one spot, to observe the weirdness of the space we were in. The light changed, with louder EDM music I didn't recognize, and I studied his face in the silly glasses, still seeing hearts everywhere, which really captured how I was feeling at the moment.

He was also watching me, and I got nervous because I was having too many feelings, so I glanced around. The space was lined with a furry, bunched-up fabric everywhere but the floor, with a single light that was changing color: purple, silver, red.

I glanced back at him and he was smiling at me. It felt like we were the only people in the world, because even though I knew there were people outside this little cave, I couldn't hear anything but the music playing and couldn't see anything but Will grinning at me. My heart was going way faster than the beat of the music, and I was glad for the music masking it.

We continued looking at each other and I wondered if he would kiss me. I'd only kissed one person, a girl at a dance back in eighth grade, and neither of us enjoyed it. This would have to be better, but I was nervous, because what if I messed it up?

"Are you leaving?" a voice said from the entrance to our little cave. Will and I both turned and someone's head was nearly upside down as they leaned over to see inside.

"Sure," Will said after glancing back at me. "Let's go."

I followed him out and had to adjust for a moment to being amongst other people again. Some of the other alliance members were still in the room. One guy waved at us and then went into a cave.

We moved into the next room, which had these white bubble-like structures on the wall, like clouds, and pastel rainbow lighting over the door. We played with a vertical liquid display that let us press these giant buttons to make bubbles that floated up from the bottom.

"This is all kind of weird," I said unnecessarily.

Will laughed as we wandered into another colorful room. "I think this is where we're supposed to not think too much about it and instead live in the moment."

"You sound like a wise old man."

"Or a rich white lady who's just opened her own yoga studio after leaving her husband because he cheated on her with the nanny."

I laughed. "That was oddly specific." We were in a room with a purple and yellow wall that was like a giant Lite-Brite. Will was trying to put these yellow rods into holes on the board, but they didn't fit, even though they looked like they should.

"Eh, you know. I'm a man of great specificity." Then he gave me a goofy smile.

There were lots of colorful, random things in different rooms, some that you could interact with—like a weird old-timey Space Invaders-type video game—and we just made our way from room to room, climbing stairs, going down slides. We continued our banter, but the whole time, I was obsessing about the almost kiss.

Was it my fault? Had I hesitated too much?

The next room was really dark, with just a few lights, and we had another moment of staring at each other. I couldn't see his eyes because of the glasses, which were still throwing off dozens of hearts.

We passed through a hallway that was lined with plushies of various types, which eventually turned into lined fabric, the black light still giving off that weird ambience. Then the walls turned into books stacked up floor to ceiling.

The next room had a bunch of slides, which required crawling into a tunnel before sliding down. Will got into one covered slide and I followed him, but it wasn't that slippery and we had to scoot ourselves down.

Once we finally got out, Will said, "I think that one needed some lube."

I snorted, a little shocked, but I still managed to say, "It definitely wasn't as pleasurable as it was supposed to be."

He laughed, and we went on into this strange creepy-bedroom-like room. No one else was in there. We scoped the place out—the flashing lighted flamingos hanging on the vanity were interesting—and I turned to follow him out and crashed right into him. He'd stopped.

He turned around and studied me. Suddenly, I felt very alone with him and watched for a millisecond while he leaned toward me, bending down a bit. My brain finally turned on and I met him in a light kiss—not bad, but not amazing. But then he gripped my shoulders and gave me a proper kiss, tongue and all. I surprised myself by not hesitating, and we kissed for a while. And I wasn't even worrying about someone else coming in.

He pulled back. "Good, I'm glad we finally did that."

My face was hot but I wasn't embarrassed. "Me too."

He took my hand and led me out of there, and we soon emerged in a gift shop, which was jarring because it was all normal light, sun shining in through the windows, psychedelia all behind us.

He held my hand while we wandered around the shop until the last alliance member went outside, and we followed them. We piled into the two vans we'd rented and headed over to the 39th Street District, which was OKC's gay part of town. I'd never been here before, even though it wasn't far from Burnside. Although there were gay kids at both of my high schools, I wasn't really friends with any of them. I was in a whole new world.

Which made the fact that I might go to prison now, of all times in my life, such bullshit.

My phone rang on the drive, but I didn't recognize the number, so I didn't answer. I waited while they left a message and read the transcription after. I nearly had a heart attack. It was the lawyer Dr. Wetherspoon said she'd get in touch with. They wanted to know if I could meet on Monday.

"Is everything okay?" Will asked, obviously sensing my tension.

"It's the lawyer," I whispered, my pulse racing a mile a minute. "They want to meet."

"Are you going to?"

"Definitely. I need to call them back." Maybe this would make a difference. It *had* to. I'd never needed something good to happen more than now.

He scanned the van. "Not here."

"No." I was antsy the whole rest of the drive, my heart pounding. Will tried to distract me.

Eventually, we parked and everyone got out. I looked around. Across the street was a '70s-style mural around the bubbly words "Summer of 66" in yellow. And 39th Street was actually a stretch of the famous Route 66.

But I had a phone call to make. I stepped away while Orion talked about the mural.

The guy answered, "Thompson."

"Hi, this is Gabriel Canul. You called me ..." I sounded so wimpy. I hated being as scared as I was.

"Hi, Gabriel. Muriel told me about your situation. I can't make promises yet, but I'm happy to talk to you to see if we can take your case. Are you available on Monday?"

"Uh, yes. But I was hoping my mom could be there, and she works during the day."

We talked through possibilities and eventually he agreed to meet us at his office at six. Mamá wasn't always home by then, but I could go on my own if I had to.

We hung up and I scrambled to catch up with the group.

"Is it all good?" Will asked when I rejoined them. He grabbed my hand as Orion talked about this other mural, a wide one with a couple of colorful faces and lots of circles, all in rainbow colors.

"We're meeting Monday," I said.

He squeezed my hand. "Great."

My heart was finally slowing down, but now I was queasy. What if I was getting my hopes up for nothing? But to be fair, Ms. Waters didn't seem bad at all. I just knew public defenders were always overworked.

My phone vibrated and I checked it, hoping it would be Lauren. Just Mamá telling me she would be running late tonight. I needed to try to catch Lauren in person again Monday.

We followed Orion around as he showed us more murals, Will holding my hand the whole time. It felt so good. I'd had no idea. It was like a warmth spread from my hand through my entire body.

Orion also pointed out the various bars, all friendly to gay people, and several with drag shows, though some were 21+ only.

"In two and a half years, we'll hit all those places up," Will joked.

"It's a date."

He laughed and kissed the side of my head, which made my face heat up. I was not used to this.

Orion then took us to the only restaurant, Rainbow Bistro. There was a pride flag hanging off a generic brown building, and it was colorful inside, too. With twelve of us, it took a while to order and we were crammed into these two booths, but I loved being squished up against Will. Will and I talked, but we also talked to everyone else, and it was such a range of people. There was one lesbian couple who were both really femme in our booth, and they were really friendly. One of them snorted whenever she laughed, so everyone was dying laughing.

Afterward, we filed out onto the street, and Orion said we had an hour to explore before we needed to meet back at the vans.

Will and I decided to go to the edge of the district and walk the whole thing. It was not very big, and it was odd because it wasn't all entertainment and restaurants. There was a car shop, a therapy center, a realtor, a bunch of pot shops, and an office building.

He kissed me again in front of the car shop, and I was more happy than embarrassed. I could get used to this. For the next ten days, anyway. I hated the cops.

Lauren

I'm sitting at a folding table in our house, Maya in the chair next to me, and we're working on a puzzle. But there's no box on the table, so I don't know what we're putting together.

It's tough because the top of the puzzle is really dark, almost black, but she has put the border together intensely and quietly with preternatural speed. I keep looking for pieces but I'm hardly finding them. But not her.

She methodically tries pieces and puts one in when it fits, so I start doing the same thing, looking closely at the shape of the pieces. She's unusually quiet and calm and I don't know what to make of that.

I keep working on it, but I'm mostly watching the picture emerge. Maya's working top down, and it appears to be a room with concrete walls, not the kind of place anyone would want to be in. So when I pick up a piece that is clearly part of a face, I shudder. What is this?

Maya keeps going, focused but not really engaged, and suddenly I see where the face piece goes.

It's two young girls, one on either side of the room. I can't tell what they're doing because all we have is their heads and shoulders. She keeps going, and I start to see where the pieces go, and soon we have the horrific picture complete. Two girls sitting on dirty beds in a concrete room. They look despondent. There's nothing else in the room with them.

Then I realize—wait!

❦

Lauren

Is this a dream?

Dammit! I was in the dream but now I was awake. I was filled with a sense of horror from the image in the dream, poking through the grogginess from just waking up.

But I also noticed that the alarm didn't go off. Was that because I woke myself up by trying to talk to Maya?

And why did I dream *that*?

I lay still, thinking about the previous dream and how this was so different, but also horrible. Those girls were obviously being held prisoner. But who were they? Was it real? How could it be real? But why would I be dreaming that? It's not what happened to Maya, and she wasn't either of the girls.

I tried to go back to sleep, but I couldn't get the horror out of my head, and instead I just lay there, sort of resting, obsessing about the girls in the dream.

Then it hit me. Were these the missing girls? But how would Maya know any of this?

I picked up my phone and opened up the browser. I started searching Burnside and OKC missing girls, and soon I had several pictures of them up. The problem was I didn't remember the girls in the dream very well. I kept looking through the pictures.

OMG! This one really looked familiar! My heart started pounding like crazy. A little blond girl with blue eyes, smiling in her school picture. Maddy Banks, nine years old. She'd gone missing eight months ago, in March. I was almost positive she was the girl on the right in the dream. I closed my eyes and tried to picture the dream puzzle. But I'd clearly tainted the memory by looking at the pictures. Still, I was still pretty sure.

Why was *I* dreaming this? Why was Maya in the dream? Did it have something to do with Maya, like that reporter thought? I still couldn't see how. I kept looking through the pictures, committing the images of these poor little girls to memory. As much as I dreaded it, I might dream about it again.

I went down the rabbit hole reading about these girls. It was all so sad. Most of them seemed to come from poorer families, but that was a lot of people in Burnside, everybody but the professors. There were ten in total, starting about two years ago, almost one every couple of months.

Eventually, I knew everything there was to know. All but two of them were from Burnside, with a couple from northwest OKC. Half of them were white, two were Black, and three were Latina. The youngest was eight and the oldest was the one from the summer, twelve. The last one had disappeared in August and it was almost Thanksgiving, which probably meant there would be another one soon.

What a horrible thought.

I put my phone down and turned toward the wall, trying to fall asleep on my side, but I couldn't. Some little girl somewhere in Burnside was sleeping happily on a Sunday morning, and eventually she'd be taken and no one would know what happened to her.

If I did have another dream about it, maybe I could talk

to Maya in it. Maybe she'd give me useful information I could share with the cops.

Anonymously.

As soon as Tenny was up, I'd tell her about the dream, and maybe she'd have some thoughts about what it meant and if there was anything I should do.

Gabriel

I left Dr. Wetherspoon's office after taking the makeup test Monday afternoon, heading over to the dorm to try to catch Lauren after class.

I managed to get there just as the first kids started filing out of the classroom building. Eventually, Tenny came out, but no Lauren. Tenny looked tired.

"Hey," Tenny said as she approached me. "How are you?"

I shrugged. "You know, not great. But I'm meeting with a lawyer tonight who might take my case for free. How are you?"

"I'm okay. But that would be good. I hope they take your case. Are you looking for Lauren?" She brushed her long black hair behind her ear.

"Yeah. She's still not answering my texts. Is she mad at me for ghosting her at first? Or does she think I'm the one who hurt Maya?"

People were filing past us, but no Lauren.

Tenny looked toward the classroom building. "No. I don't think she's mad at you, and she knows you're not the one. I think she just blames herself and can't face you."

I grimaced. She must feel really bad. But it wasn't right.

"Can you please tell her it's not her fault and I really want to talk to her?"

She sighed. "I keep telling her it's not her fault, but she doesn't believe me. You know Dana totally blamed her that night, right? I assume she still does."

"That's horrible. Dana should have been the one taking Maya trick-or-treating in the first place, not Lauren on a school night." Dana had always been kind of shitty to Lauren, and I never knew why. When you'd ask Lauren, she'd defend her. I never thought Dana deserved it.

"I know. I went over there that night and Dana yelled at her to leave. We came back to the dorm."

"Oh, wow. What about Nick?" I already knew the answer, though.

"You know how he is. He's disappeared."

"Yeah." I looked toward the classroom building. "Is she hiding from me?"

"I don't know. Let me talk to her. I'll try to get her to respond." She adjusted the backpack hanging off her left shoulder. "Maybe you could talk to her over Thanksgiving."

"Okay. That's a good idea. Let me know if there's any news."

"Will do." She turned to head inside. "See you."

"Later."

I looked at the classroom building again for a minute, but nothing. So I headed to the union to meet Will. I beat him, there so I snagged a table in Booth Forest after getting my smoothie and some burritos from Taco Bueno.

He found me and slid into the booth, coffee in hand. "How'd it go?"

At first I didn't know what he was talking about. "Oh, the exam. Good. But now I'm stressing about the meeting tonight."

"It's going to go great. I have a good feeling about it." He grinned at me, and it was infectious. How did he have such an overall positive effect on me? He was so hot, but somehow nice, and extra nice to me.

Turning my frown upside down did actually make me feel slightly better, so we just smiled at each other for a moment.

Eventually, my brain started working again. "So, tonight's Chapter Twelve, right?"

"Yes, I'm excited to finish it."

"So are you into comics now? Do you need to borrow all my books?"

"May ... be."

Before I could answer, my stomach growled, and even with all the background noise, we could both hear it.

"You obviously need to eat your food," he said solemnly.

I nodded. "Yes."

"I'm going to get something too. He left his backpack and went back to the food court.

We studied a little, but I was hugely distracted by his very sexy presence and my increasing anxiety about the meeting, so it wasn't exactly productive.

I got a text from Mamá at four saying she'd be home at five thirty so we could go to the meeting together, and that was a relief. I was so glad she'd be there.

"I'm going to have to leave at four twenty," Will said while I was texting her back.

I snorted. "Four twenty."

He laughed. "It's just a coincidence. No drugs involved, just my boring library job."

I told him Mamá would be at the meeting and he was relieved for me, then we chatted about some of his coworkers, who I was getting to know through his stories. Always drama. And I was going to bring him a Batman graphic novel the next day.

At four fifteen, he got up and slid onto the seat next to me. My pulse picked up at having him so close. He looked around, then turned back and kissed me.

It was nice and deep, and when we came up for air, I noticed the girl in the booth across from us looking away. She looked embarrassed, not like she cared.

Will got up and grabbed his backpack. "See you tomorrow in class."

I nodded, still a bit dazed from the kiss. "See you."

Then I sat there, my head swimming, for a few more minutes before heading to the house. It was a fifteen-minute walk, and I couldn't believe it, but halfway home it started raining. I jogged the rest of the way because I was afraid my books would get soaked.

After I got home, I changed into dry clothes and waited on the couch for Mamá.

Then it was time. We didn't talk in the car until she randomly announced that she loved me.

"That will always be true," she continued. "I know you didn't hurt Maya, and I'm sorry this is the world we live in."

I didn't say anything.

"Have you talked to Lauren, mijo?"

"She still won't answer. I went by the dorm today and talked to Tenny, but Lauren was hiding. Tenny's going to try to convince her to talk to me. And I'm going to try over the break." I looked out the window.

"You need to. You know how much I love her parents, but Dana is still blaming her, and you know Nick shuts down when he's upset. And she's all by herself at that school."

"She has Tenny." I knew it was weak.

"But she doesn't have you."

I watched the dreary roadside pass us by, an Arby's, car shop, and beauty salon in one shopping center, then a tax shop and sandwich shop in the next.

"Promise me you will get through to her, mijo. What happened is not her fault. People lose track of their kids all the time, and usually nothing bad happens, even though it's always terrifying."

I knew it wasn't Lauren's fault. It was JT. It was his fault because he was the one who actually killed Maya, not Lauren.

"I have gone by the dorm and she won't talk to me," I finally said. "But I'll talk to her when she's home this week."

"Thank you, mijo."

She was right, of course.

Soon, I spotted the building we were going to, and she pulled into a parking spot. We took a creaky elevator up to the fourth floor and found the door. It was locked but a man opened it after we knocked.

"Raj Thompson," he announced, sticking his hand out toward Mamá. She shook it, then it was my turn. I felt so small next to this tall guy who had fairly pale skin despite the Indian first name. My whole family was so short.

"Come on in. Normally the door is open and the receptionist would greet you, but it's after hours." He stood to the side and we walked in.

"Thank you very much for being able to meet us late in the day," Mamá said.

"Happy to oblige," he said. "I understand what it means to work for a living."

There were a couple love seats in a small area with a receptionist's desk in the back. We followed him down a short hall into an office and he motioned for us to sit down.

Once he'd also sat down, he started, "Muriel told me a little about your situation. I understand you have a public defender."

"Yes, Ms. Waters," I said.

"She's very well-respected. But let's see if I can help out. Can you tell me what they've accused you of and what happened? Don't leave anything out." He was leaning back in his chair, resting his forearms on the arms of the chair.

I went through everything just like I had with Ms. Waters. Mr. Thompson nodded at appropriate intervals and asked a few questions, but I couldn't tell what he was thinking. So there was this deepening pit inside my stomach as I talked. Mamá interjected a few times with info I'd missed, and eventually I got through everything.

"Okay, thank you. I think Ms. Waters is right and they do not have a strong case against you, but I need to see the documents. I'm going to reach out to her. I do believe I will be able to help you."

The pit fell away with relief. Mamá reached over and squeezed my hand.

"Thank you, Mr. Thompson," she said, since I'd lost the ability to speak.

I managed a nod, but I was on the verge of tears. Maybe it would be okay.

But I did not want to get my hopes up. I'd have to text Will on the way home, even though he wouldn't get it until he got off work tonight at eight. Then we could finally talk.

16

____

Lauren

Maya and I are doing another puzzle. This time she's expertly building from the bottom left corner. A red roller suitcase in a dark room emerges.

I feel useless because I can't see where any of the pieces go, so I start organizing them by color and content, and Maya keeps picking the right pieces, so it does feel like I'm helping. But there's this constant sense of dread making a pit in my stomach at what is going to emerge.

The suitcase is standing upright in front of a metal bed. Eventually, I can see a girl in dirty pink pajamas sitting on the bed, staring at the suitcase with haunted eyes.

Maya keeps building the puzzle, and once she gets to the bed on the right side, I can see that it's empty. It's metal just like the other one and there's a thin blanket half hanging from it.

I am sick to my stomach because I know what's in that suitcase. But I still don't really know what's going on and why I'm dreaming this—

Shit! Maya!

Lauren

I jolted awake from the dream, heart pounding and sweat on my forehead. I'd figured out I was dreaming, but it woke me up instead of letting me talk to Maya, just like the last one. Even though the idea of talking to her was new, it seemed hugely important because it could explain what was going on with these puzzle dreams. They had to be important.

I couldn't believe I was thinking dreams were *important*. I closed my eyes and stretched, trying to slow my heart. I was in my bed at home Wednesday morning before Thanksgiving. We obviously weren't doing anything for the holiday. Last year had been a normal Thanksgiving with Maya still here, turkey, mashed potatoes, green bean casserole, pumpkin pie. Not this year. I was only here because the dorms were closed. Dana was still mostly in bed, and I was going to stay in my bedroom except to go to the bathroom and get something every once in a while from the kitchen. It would be a long five days of granola bars and peanut butter sandwiches. Hopefully the bread wasn't moldy.

I couldn't believe I wouldn't see Gabriel tomorrow either. Usually our parents would get together in the evening to drink tequila and watch movies while Gabriel, Maya, and I entertained ourselves with other things. Puzzles, reading, our own movies.

I closed my eyes again. I had no reason to get up. Why was I having these dreams? And how could I even be considering the fact that they could really mean something? I was supposed to be this logical, rational person, so I wasn't supposed to believe in dreams. At least not that they represented reality.

Was it possible that JT really wasn't the one who assaulted Maya? Had my brain just made all that up so I could have some kind of closure? JT was pretty obviously a horrible guy, given the way he dumped me, so it would make sense that he'd be the one I'd subconsciously blame. But actually doing that stuff to Maya was next level.

And I just felt like it was true. It all made so much sense. Very few men had regular access to Maya. And if it was someone who simply assaulted her out of the blue, Maya probably would have told us. But I knew that when kids are abused repeatedly, it usually escalates, and each incident is a little worse than the last. But the kid is already manipulated and gaslit enough to not say anything, so even when it gets all the way to that kind of assault, they don't really understand how severe it all is. Tenny taught me that. She was molested by her uncle repeatedly when she was little, and the only one in her family who believed her was her grandma, who died a while ago. A few years later, in her freshman year of high school, Tenny became a little obsessed and read all these psychology books about child abuse. It was shocking to me how much abusers messed with their victims' heads, and how it did lifelong damage. Tenny promised me she would go to therapy when she had control over her own medical choices.

My stomach rumbled and I thought I really should go get some food. Hopefully, I wouldn't run into Dana. I threw the covers off and swung my legs off the side of the bed.

I grabbed a sweatshirt and threw it over my pajamas and headed into the hall. I looked left toward my parents' bedroom, and there was no movement, so I should be in the clear.

Tenny thought the dreams were real, too. And even Brandon thought it was feasible. Maybe I subconsciously knew the whole time, and that's where it was coming from.

That just wasn't what it *felt* like. It felt true.

By the time I got to the kitchen, my bare feet had collected a bunch of crap. I looked at the bottom of my foot. Hair and dirt that hadn't been vacuumed in a month.

I checked the bread and of course there was mold on the three slices that were left.

Suddenly I was crying.

Why did there have to be another pirate Halloween night? If there hadn't been, I would have noticed she was missing right away. Why did JT have to show up? Why did I think he was such a great guy? Why had I even brought him into Maya's life?

I crossed my arms and stared at the counter, trying to stop crying. Maybe there was something else to eat. I looked in the fridge. There was some old yogurt, moldy cheese, and grape jelly. A couple six packs of Milwaukee's Best in the bottom. I checked the jelly and it was still in okay shape. We had peanut butter in the pantry and some canned vegetables. I'd have some vegetables later. I opened the peanut butter and ate a spoonful, holding it away from me so I wouldn't get tears in it.

After three bites, I put it back and turned the sink water on hot. Once it was warm enough, I rinsed the spoon and left it there.

This break was going to be torture, thinking about Maya and the dreams. But how could I not? I might even have more dreams. I did have some homework, but not enough to fill every day. I should go to the library and get a couple of books and try to just exist without thinking of all the horrible things in the world.

Gabriel

"Mamá, I'm going to go next door now, okay?" I called from the kitchen Thanksgiving day. She was sitting in her room working at her sewing machine.

"Okay, mijo. Please don't leave until you talk to Lauren."

"I know. That's why I'm going." I held covered dishes of *pepián de pavo* and chiles rellenos, two of our traditional Thanksgiving dishes. *Pepián de pollo* was a national Guatemalan meal, a creamy chicken stew, but when I was little, I wanted to have turkey on Thanksgiving like everyone else, so Mamá started making the dish with turkey. Just on Thanksgiving. Lauren loved both of these. I didn't know if Dana and Nick would want any, but I'd promised Mamá that I'd offer. Mamá had already been over there to spend some time with Dana this morning, leaving me in charge of the oven for a bit.

I got out the front door without dropping anything and locked the door. I looked over at Lauren's house, a bland tan color that was chipping off of the siding in some spots. Nick's car wasn't in the driveway. Seeing the house—a place I'd spent so many hours with Lauren and Maya—made my heart hurt. Was Lauren going to talk to me? Or was she still mad at me for ghosting her?

I stepped off the porch and started next door through the short grass, my heartbeat increasing with every step. The back of my neck grew damp from nervous sweat.

It was so wrong that I was nervous about seeing Lauren. This was entirely my fault.

I walked past the big window of the front room, the light off, with no signs of life. I reached the porch and went up the step. My hands were full so I hit the doorbell with my elbow.

And I waited. It seemed like for a long time, and I wondered if I should just leave, but instead I rang the doorbell again. I wasn't going to let myself chicken out.

Finally, the door started opening, and my heart was in my throat again, but then Lauren was looking at me with wide eyes. She had on pajama bottoms and an OIT sweatshirt. She started to shut the door but I stopped it with the dishes I was holding.

"Hi," I said. "Please don't shut the door on me, Lauren. I need to apologize to you."

She looked so tired, and she had no makeup on even though she usually wore some if she thought she might see people.

"I brought some dinner," I said, holding up the dishes.

"Pepián and rellenos?" She smiled a little.

"Yep. You hungry?"

"Starving. We have nothing but peanut butter, and the bread is moldy." She stepped to the side to let me in. "Do we need to heat it up?"

I stepped inside, relieved that this seemed to be going okay. "No, it's ready to serve. Should we ask Dana if she wants some?"

Her face fell and she looked away, then turned toward the kitchen. "You can ask her. I don't want to risk it. She still hates me. It's my fault." She sounded so beat down when she said that last bit.

"Tenny told me she blames you. Is that true?" I looked around the front room. Empty beer cans on the table next to the chair Nick always sat at, two on the floor. The carpet looked grungy, and there was a plate with a half-eaten sandwich on the coffee table, growing mold and with flies circling.

Lauren hadn't responded to my question, which was answer enough. I followed her and my stomach twisted in guilt. Lauren's family wasn't the most supportive. They always sort of used her without appreciating her. So of course they blamed her. Just like I had. She had nobody but Tenny and JT, and I was guessing JT wasn't very helpful, either. I was an asshole. I should never have abandoned her, even for that short time.

We got to the kitchen and she pulled out two plates and two bowls. Without saying anything, she turned and walked back toward the bedrooms. The kitchen looked abandoned, nothing but crumbs on the counter. There were a few spoons in the sink.

From the back of the house, I heard Lauren say, "Dana, Gabriel brought food. Do you want a plate?"

Of course, she'd bit the bullet and asked Dana herself. She was such an adult and kind-hearted, and always had been.

Lauren stared at the floor as she walked back. She grabbed a third plate and bowl and put them on the counter.

"Is she really still staying in the bedroom all the time?" I opened the containers, and Lauren nodded and handed me a spoon, which I used to dish the soup into the bowls and put the chiles next to the bowls on the plates.

She nodded. "That's what Dad said. I haven't seen her out."

How was Lauren the most adult person here? Her dad just disappeared when bad things happened, and Dana obviously wasn't going to step up for Lauren. Even though Lauren was obviously incredibly down, it still felt right to be here with her. I should never have ghosted her.

"Where's your dad?" I asked.

"Who knows. Probably driving."

I nodded. Nick drove for Uber and Lyft. I hated both him and Dana for not being supportive of Lauren.

"Let's eat in my bedroom. Can you take the plates in there?" She closed her eyes for a moment and picked up the third plate, obviously preparing to take it to Dana.

"No, let me." I set the other plates down and took the third one, fork and knife laid across it.

Lauren nodded and took the other plates. When I got to Dana's room, I called her name. She eventually answered.

"It's Gabriel. I've got a plate for you." When I went in, she was so pale and thin, dark circles under her eyes. She was a mess. I'd never seen her like this.

"Thanks," she said, barely getting it out. She put the plate on the nightstand and I stood there for a second, but then it was obvious I should leave.

I went into Lauren's room. The hot pink of the walls seemed so wrong right now. Lauren had let Maya pick the color because she'd begged, and now Lauren was stuck with it. The small desk was behind the door, and she just had one dresser and a small closet. Her suitcase was open on the floor. She was probably living out of that.

I pulled the black folding chair from behind her dresser and sat at the side of the desk.

She was sitting in her chair, and pulled up to the desk. She glanced at me. She took a spoonful of stew.

I felt like such an asshole.

"Lauren," I started, nervous again.

She turned toward me. Her eyes were so sad, but I could tell she wanted me to say something nice.

"I'm sorry I ghosted you. I was so upset I wasn't thinking right, and I blamed you. But I know it's not your fault. But why wouldn't you return my texts? You obviously had every right to be mad at me, but I really needed to know if you were okay, and I needed you to know that I was sorry."

Tears welled in her eyes and she wiped them away.

"I miss Maya so much, but I've missed you just as much," I said.

She was still crying but she looked at me. "Me too."

I felt such a surge of emotion—guilt mixed with affection. "Can I hug you?"

We both got up and did this awkward hug, but then we looked at each other and did it right the second time.

She sniffed, which made me tear up. But we sat back down. I wiped my eyes. I didn't want to cry right now.

"Tenny told me they arrested you," she said. "Why? They don't usually do that for no reason."

That made my heart nearly stop. "They absolutely do. The preliminary hearing is Monday. I will have a better idea of why after that." I took a bite of the rellenos.

"What does that mean?" she asked.

I had to finish chewing. "That's where they decide if there's enough evidence to go to trial."

"What do they even have on you? Weren't you home with your mom the whole time?"

"*Nothing.*" I couldn't keep the anger out of my voice. "I didn't do anything wrong. They think Mamá is lying to cover for me."

"Tenny told me they arrested you because you're Latino, and I believe it."

I nodded, and the image of JT putting Maya's body into the trunk and strangling her played in my mind. "Can I tell you something crazy?"

"Okay." She looked wary and spooned more soup.

But then it occurred to me that she was dating JT. How could I tell her that her boyfriend was a murderer?

Still, it was obvious that I had to tell her, because she should not be dating a murderer. How had I not thought of this before?

"Are you still ... with JT?" I asked.

She shook her head as a dark look passed over her face and she stirred the soup absentmindedly. "He broke up with me my first day back in class."

"What?" Who would do that?

"I know, but that's not really the important thing." She looked at the ceiling.

"What do you mean?" I ate a spoonful of soup.

"Do you promise to not think I've lost my mind?" she asked, voice shaking a bit.

"I already know you're not crazy."

She nodded, avoiding eye contact. "Promise you won't change your mind?"

"Okay, yes, I promise. You have to promise the same thing because of what I'm going to tell you here in a minute."

"What was it you were going to tell me?" she asked, suddenly remembering.

"You first." This conversation should be funny, but neither of us was laughing. What on earth was she going to tell me? My stomach was roiling with nerves from being about to share this wacko idea and wondering what she might be about to say.

"So there's a little more to it, but I started having these dreams after ... Maya."

My eyes widened. "You had dreams about her, too?"

She jerked back in surprise. "You did too?"

Lauren

"Yes, I dreamed about her," he answered. "And they weren't normal dreams. What were yours?"

We had been friends for nearly all of our lives, and neither of us had ever had a dream we took seriously. We were nerds, not dream people. This really was crazy.

Still, thinking about the dreams made me feel bad again, queasy and cold. Would I ever escape these? "They were horrible, and it took me and Tenny a while to figure out what they meant. But, um, the message in the end was very specific and horrible. They told me who assaulted her."

"They did?! Who was it?"

"JT." I couldn't look at him. He would hate me again.

"Oh, my God, Lauren! He was the one who killed her— that's what my dreams showed!"

My mouth hung open. But then my eyes welled up with tears again. How could everything be this horrible? "It *is* all my fault."

"No, no, it's not. It's *JT*'s fault. We always do this—let men off the hook and blame the victims and any women in the vicinity. He's the one that killed her and the one that assaulted her. None of us knew."

"I guess." I didn't believe it. "What happened in your dreams?"

He shuddered. "They were horrible, like a horror version of *Mario Kart*. I was stuck in my kart and couldn't do anything." He explained how he kept chasing Maya in his dreams, culminating in the last one, where JT made his appearance. Then I told him about my dreams.

His face was red. "How could all that happen right here? How did we not notice?"

"I know, I feel the same. But Tenny said those people are really good at manipulating kids." I still should have noticed.

"I don't understand why he was even there Halloween night, and why he did it," he said.

"I think I know." I grimaced as a wave of desperate regret passed over me. "It all finally makes sense. And it is still all my fault. I *hate* myself."

"Lauren, stop. JT's the one who did it, not you."

No one was going to convince me that was the complete story. Also, he probably didn't know that JT was there with me at all. "Maybe you don't know how the whole thing started that night."

"When he was coming over to hang out with you?"

"No, on Halloween night," I clarified. "We were going from house to house, and Maya had connected with this other group of kids. I was watching her, but I didn't realize there was a boy dressed as a pirate, too. Then, out of the blue, JT called my name. He was out jogging." I had to rest my forehead in my palm, queasy all over again. "We talked for a minute, then he took off again. And I watched Maya as we went on to different houses, but then I realized it wasn't her—it was the other pirate. Fuck." I relived that moment and my stomach turned over. I took a breath. "And Maya was nowhere. She must have taken off running after seeing JT. That has to be what happened."

Gabriel finished the story. "And then she ran into a street and a random car hit her and drove off. Then, because JT had been chasing her, he came across her injured, and probably was afraid she'd tell on him, and he killed her."

I nodded, freely crying. Then Gabriel started.

"We have to tell the cops something," I said. It had to matter who'd actually done it.

He shook his head. "I already told them to look into JT, before they arrested me. They said they'd talked to him and he'd had nothing to do with it."

"But he had *everything* to do with it!"

"But he's a pretty white boy and I'm not," Gabriel said with a surge of anger.

"Oh, my God." I was still crying. "What can we do? You cannot go to prison for this! JT cannot get away with all of it!"

"I know, but we have no evidence. Dreams won't count. Even if they tell a story that explains everything."

"God. What can we do?"

He shook his head. "I have no idea. I'm supposed to meet with my new lawyer tomorrow afternoon. I can tell him this, but he'll think I'm crazy. People will just assume our brains made this up based on we want to believe."

"We have to figure something out." I tapped my lip. Then something he'd said finally registered. "Wait. Why did you tell the cops to look at JT?"

He nodded. "You know I didn't like him, but it was because right before Halloween I saw him leaving your house, and his face was just so smug. I hated him in that moment."

I felt my eyes go wide. "What day was that?"

"The Saturday before."

My heart was racing. "Do you know what time that was?"

His eyes narrowed. "Don't you know what time he left?"

"Just tell me!" This could be it. I leaned forward in the chair.

"Maybe seven? I was getting the mail. Why? What happened?"

My heart nearly stopped. "He drugged me. That was how he did it. But you are a witness—this could prove that he did it! At least make them look at him again!"

"Lauren," he said, far too calmly. "They won't. They won't believe me as a witness. They will think you're just making it up to distract them from me. And there would be no other evidence to tie him to her. Us just saying we saw things isn't enough."

I deflated. He was right. But shouldn't we at least try?

His face was grim, but he didn't say anything.

It seemed like there was nothing we could do. What was the point of even talking about it?

There was that one possible thing. "Tenny's boyfriend told us that JT might be into child porn."

Gabriel grimaced. "That's horrible. But not shocking, considering."

I nodded. "He's going to see if he can find out for sure so he can report it."

Gabriel's eyes went wide. "Oh, my God, Lauren—do you think JT filmed Maya?"

The blood drained out of my face and I was instantly queasy. How had I not thought of that?

He looked as freaked out as I felt.

"Can we do anything?" I asked weakly.

"I don't think so." He stared at the desk, a faraway look in his eyes. "I don't understand how life can be so awful."

"I don't know." What had any of us done to deserve this?

We were quiet for a moment, until he asked, "Do you think Tenny's boyfriend will report it?"

"He doesn't want to unless he's sure. He's still afraid it will come back on him."

"He should just fucking report it."

I nodded. "I agree."

Then we sat there again, looking at each other. I'm sure I looked as shell-shocked as he did.

He broke the eye contact. "Let me take this stuff back to the kitchen to reheat it. We should at least try to enjoy one good thing."

As he left, I suddenly felt something that was long overdue—anger. This was wrong. None of this should have ever happened. And even though I'd brought JT into my and Maya's world, I didn't know he was bad. Everybody else thought he was great, too. Gabriel was right—JT was the bad guy. And whoever hit Maya with their car and drove off. And the cops for letting JT off the hook, and for pinning it on Gabriel even though there was no way. If Brandon wouldn't report it, I was going to talk to Ms. Patton myself. I was going to figure this out.

Lauren

Maya and I are sitting at the folding table working a puzzle again. This time, the picture is outside, in what looks like an alley. There's a grungy brick wall across the top of the puzzle and a dumpster in the middle of it. The sides of the dumpster aren't filled in yet.

She's working away, adding pieces in a fast cadence on the right side. I try to help, seeing some shoes that seem to go on the left side. Eventually, a girl emerges on the right. She looks young and has silver sneakers, shorts, and a pink backpack over a white t-shirt. She's smiling and facing the other side of the puzzle, which is still empty.

That side complete, Maya starts filling the other side in. She does the area around the shoes first. These look familiar, but I can't place them.

Then she works from the top, and before I know it, she's filled the face in and my heart stops when I see that it's JT.

It's a dream!

"Maya!"

"Lauren," she says, turning toward me in the dream, nearly expressionless.

"What is going on? Is this real? Are you telling me something that's really happening?"

She nods, still with a flat expression. "He's the one who finds the girls for them."

I don't know what she means. But then it registers. "The missing girls?"

"Yeah, all of them."

I look at the picture. JT is facing this girl, his most charming face looking open and welcoming.

I'm so queasy. Maya reaches over and rubs my back, in such a weirdly adult move that it devastates me. She's here in my dream, but she's really gone. Even in my dream she isn't herself anymore.

"What can I do, Maya?" I ask desperately.

"Find them."

"But how?" She looks at me and says nothing.

～

Gabriel

"So what do we do?" Lauren asked Tenny and me. We were all in my bedroom going over what we knew from the dreams. Lauren leaned against the foot of the bed with my laptop in her lap, while Tenny had the beanbag, and I sat in my desk chair. There'd been a shift in Lauren. She didn't seem all beat down, but instead had energy to spare. She wanted to fix everything herself, but we'd convinced her it wasn't that simple.

She'd gone over the three dreams she'd had about the girls being kept prisoner, including last night's, where she finally talked to Maya, who was only minimally helpful. None of us understood how this ghost dream thing worked —how would she know who the girls were and how they were being kept prisoner, but not be able to just tell us where or by who?

"Did you tell him about the reporter?" Tenny asked.

Lauren shook her head. She was scanning through articles, trying to find pictures of the missing girls to see if she recognized any of them. "A reporter came up to me one time when we were going back to the dorm. She said she thinks Maya's case is related to the missing girls. And now we know she's right. She's the one we should go to. The police are worthless."

"My naive self a few months ago would have said we have to go to the police," I said. My phone dinged but I ignored it. "But you're totally right. In addition to pinning it on me, they completely dismissed JT being involved."

"Oh, my God!" Lauren exclaimed. She pointed at the screen. "This girl. She was in the first two dreams!"

"Oh, my God," I said as both Tenny and I went over to look. I read the name. "Lola. Where are they being held?"

"I have no idea! It's just a room. It could be anywhere. It's like a concrete room."

I realized Tenny was crying, probably from just thinking about this poor girl who'd been missing for over two years. We all knew what that meant.

"We have to do something," Lauren said. "They're not killing them right away. Some of them might still be alive."

"I agree." My phone dinged again.

"Call the reporter," Tenny said, sniffing. "Maybe she can investigate it."

"Yes." I nodded emphatically.

Lauren opened a new search window. "Her card is in my

desk at the dorm. I don't remember her name. Do you, Tenny?"

Tenny looked at the ceiling, thinking. "No, I can't remember. Maybe it started with a C?"

"You know what she looks like, though," I said. "Is she local?"

"I think so." Lauren tapped her lip. "I can see if I can find any of her stories with a picture."

"Yeah, do that. Maybe she even reported on some of the missing girls. Maybe one of these in the results?" My phone dinged yet again. Although I felt this little emotional boost because it had to be Will, that was nothing compared to what Lauren and I were looking into.

"Is that your mom?" Lauren asked, clicking on the first story.

"No, it's ... a guy." I was embarrassed for sounding embarrassed.

Lauren and Tenny both spun to face me. "Are you seeing somebody?" Lauren asked, sounding surprised but subdued.

"Sort of, yeah. Yes. But this is not the right time to talk about it. I'll tell you later. His name is Will. You'll like him."

"Well, at least answer him." There was no author picture on the story she was looking at, and Tenny jumped up and went to my desk.

I responded to Will. His texts were just ones detailing his family's second Thanksgiving—it was complicated because they had to visit two sets of grandparents—so I just told him that I was finally talking to Lauren and that I'd text him later. But then I added a few heart emojis.

Tenny handed Lauren some stickies and a pen.

"Okay, I replied," I announced. "I'm good for now."

Lauren looked over and smiled at me. Why had I stayed

away from her at the beginning? I was horrible. I needed to make it up to her somehow.

We kept looking through the different stories and ruled them out if they had a picture that didn't match, or were written by a man, and wrote down all the other names. Then we started looking them up and eventually found her. Candace O'Brien.

"I'll email her right now," Lauren said. "If she doesn't respond before I get back to the dorm, I'll call her."

She wrote an email without saying what the information was, just that she had something important to share. She sent it and we all sat there, like we were waiting for a response.

"It is a holiday break," I said.

"Yeah," Lauren said.

We all looked at each other, and Lauren and Tenny looked as freaked out as I felt. None of us said anything as we stared at her email inbox. I didn't know what some reporter could possibly do, but she was our only hope from the responsible adult world. But if she couldn't help, we'd really have to take matters into our own hands. Lauren was right.

~

Lauren

We didn't have to wait long for the reporter's response. Tenny and I were still in Gabriel's room with him when the email came in.

We all heard the inbox ding, so Gabriel handed the computer to me and they got on either side, still at the foot of his bed.

I opened the email. She just asked if I could call her and gave her number.

I dialed it on my phone, nerves firing all over my body.

"Candace," she answered. Very abrupt, but this wasn't about becoming best friends.

"Hi," I started. "I've got you on speaker with my friends Tenny and Gabriel because they know about this and have helped me piece things together."

"Okay, that's great. Is that Gabriel Canul, the one the police have charged?"

That made Gabriel look away, so I answered. "Yes. And he had nothing to do with it."

"That has been my belief, too," Candace said.

Gabriel looked back toward me, but his face was unreadable.

"So why don't you tell me what you know and what you believe," Candace said.

I wondered if I really should tell her all of this. But it really was obvious that the police wouldn't listen, and she already thought there was a connection between Maya and the other girls, so maybe she would believe us and be able to do something.

"Okay," I said, a little unclear where to start.

"Start with how we aren't tarot card people, in the first place," Gabriel said quietly to me.

Tenny and I nodded, so I said, "First, I have to warn you. This is all really weird. Gabriel, Maya, and I all grew up together. He lives next door, so we've always been close. But we also are not woo-woo people. We don't sit around and talk about our dreams or read tarot cards or whatever."

My nerves were still firing all over the place.

Candace said, "Understood," like she might be losing interest.

"You already know how everything that happened Halloween night was just so confusing. Gabriel and I have both been having dreams that explain what happened." I almost lost my nerve at this point because I was so terrified she wouldn't listen and we'd get nowhere, with no backup plan. Gabriel squeezed my hand. "Neither of us thought much of them at first. But they were so specific, and when combined, they make everything make sense. I never really believed in ghosts, but I think Maya came to us in our dreams like a ghost."

It felt stupid saying it all out loud, but Candace just said, "Perhaps you dreamed things based on things you subconsciously know."

"Yeah, maybe." It wasn't true, but at least she hadn't hung up on us yet. "So, let me tell you about mine. I basically dreamed about being on the receiving end of escalating sexual abuse, leading up to the final ... incident, which happened the Saturday before Halloween. The dreams weren't literal, but I was able to map them to things that happened in real life. So, they told me how the final assault happened, and who did it."

I paused, stomach roiling again at the memories.

"And?" Candace said.

"It was JT," I said. I couldn't say anything more.

"JT Comstock?" she asked.

"Yes. I was dating him, and he used to come over sometimes when I was babysitting over the summer and on the weekends. They got along so well that sometimes when Gabriel and I needed to do something, we left Maya with him. Not a lot, but enough."

"Okay, I'm following along. What else?"

"Something weird happened that Saturday that I didn't understand, but now I do. JT was over, and we were drinking some beer he'd brought, and I fell asleep. And it was just really weird. I thought I'd accidentally gotten way drunker than I'd intended. But I'd only had one beer. Now I know he drugged me. And then he went back to Maya's room. She had been working on organizing her bookshelf around that time, and the dream showed her working on that when JT came in. And then it showed the beginning of ... what he did."

"Okay," she said. "Was that it?"

"For the moment, yes. There is more, but that is all I have about what happened to Maya. I'm going to have Gabriel tell you about his dreams."

"Yeah, so mine weren't as involved as Lauren's," he said. "I had basically the same dream over and over, but it just went a bit further each time. It showed how Maya ran away that night, but she was in a kart like in Mario Kart, because she and I used to play that game all the time. I was trying to follow her, but I was also in a kart. She was speeding ahead of me and not looking where she was going, and she drove into an intersection right when a car came through. The car hit her, then backed up and drove off. Right after that, JT came running up, picked her up, looked around and spotted the car with the bad trunk latch. He dropped her in, and strangled her. I saw all of it in the dream, stuck in my kart."

I wanted to sum up the point. "So we think that because he assaulted her, she was terrified of him, and when he showed up Halloween night, she ran away in fear, got hit by a random car, unrelated, but that car didn't stick around. Then, JT had been chasing her, so he reached her, and saw that nobody was around, and he was afraid she would tell on him, so he killed her. We don't think it was planned at all."

I thought about how I'd called him after she was missing, and he'd wished me luck, even though he must have already killed her by the time I called.

"This is largely what the police already know, minus the who," Candace said. "But obviously you can't tell the police about these dreams. They'll just assume you know stuff because you were involved, and are lying about it."

We all looked at each other. I hadn't even thought about that aspect of it, just that they wouldn't believe us because they were dreams.

"Can you do anything with all this?" I asked.

"I can look into things. The problem is that they've already ruled JT out, and unless he tells them, there's no way to connect him. And the car that hit her is a total unknown. The security footage around there didn't capture anything useful."

I nodded, disappointed, but she was right. "There's more."

"Tell me."

"So, first, there are rumors that JT has child porn on his computer, and Tenny's boyfriend is trying to see if he can get some proof so he can report it."

"Mm-hmm," Candace said. Did she already know about that?

"The other thing, and this is way crazier than anything else so far, is that I have been having dreams about the missing girls."

"Okay." She perked up with that.

I explained the frame of the dreams as something important being revealed in a puzzle image, and that, based on the last dream, JT was involved. I told her about finally talking to Maya in the dream, and how she gave me some info, but not a lot.

Candace said nothing at first, and I wondered if she

thought I was off my rocker. But then she said, "Do you have any visual cues from the dreams at all?"

I shook my head. "The room in the first two dreams was like a concrete cell with no windows. There was a single naked lightbulb hanging from the ceiling, and those two metal beds, and that was it. The alleyway and dumpster would be more recognizable, but I wouldn't have any idea where to look. There were no street or shop signs."

"Okay, this is helpful," Candace said. "Let me know if you have any additional information."

"Why did you think Maya was connected to the missing girls?" I asked.

"I can't give you details, but JT has been on my radar for a while. I knew you two were dating."

"Really?" I said, stunned. Tenny's and Gabriel's faces looked just like what mine must have looked like, wide-eyed.

"Yes. So, nothing tangible so far, but this gives me a bit more to work with. Thank you. Please let me know if you get more information, even if it comes from a dream. The human mind can surprise us."

"Okay, I will. Bye." She said goodbye, and I hung up.

Tenny, Gabriel, and I all looked at each other. I was tense but a little hopeful.

"Do you think she can do anything?" Tenny asked.

"I have no idea," I said. "Hopefully?"

"I wish she could do something to convince the police it wasn't me," Gabriel said.

He was so down. I couldn't blame him at all. I couldn't believe he might actually go to prison for something he didn't do.

"Gabriel, I think it's going to work out," Tenny said. "I have a feeling."

"We're science kids," he said. "We're not supposed to have 'feelings,' or believe in ghosts or psychic dreams."

I frowned. "I know. I keep thinking I'm losing my mind, but then I think what the dreams are showing me just seems to be true. Maybe there's a scientific explanation somehow."

Tenny nodded. "I read this book once that said that people's souls continue to exist to some degree as energy after they die, and that that might explain ghosts. Maybe it's true."

"Maybe," Gabriel said.

"It also said that some people believe life in the afterlife is different enough that ghosts or whatever aren't all there mentally, which is probably why she didn't explain it to you, Lauren."

"Huh," I said. But then I realized something. "Candace already suspected JT and knew he was dating me, and she never warned me."

"That sucks so much," Gabriel said.

"But would you have believed her?" Tenny asked.

We were quiet for a moment. I didn't want to think about it anymore.

"You probably want to text your boyfriend, don't you?" I teased Gabriel, trying to end the somber mood.

"Actually, yes. Get outta here."

Tenny and I laughed, although it was weak. She said she needed to get home, and although I didn't want to go back to my house, he needed his space.

"I'm just kidding, Lauren," Gabriel said. "You can stay if you need to."

"No, it's fine. I'm going to read."

We all got up and Tenny and I headed out. I started toward the house of depression, every step making me feel worse. In that house, everything was my fault. But then I remembered. This wasn't my fault, and somebody needed to fix things as much as possible. And right now, my friends and I—and a reporter—were the only ones working on it.

It was mostly dark when I went in, and no one was around, so I didn't have to see Dana. I looked at the living room, and through the dim light I could see how trashed it was. Beer cans all over from Dad sitting out here and not cleaning up after himself. I rage-cleaned and tried to think of other things I could do. This wasn't easy, but I knew there had to be something.

18

Lauren

The puzzle scene comes alive and Maya is nowhere. I'm lying in the dark on a mattress that smells like pee. It's so thin I can feel the cold metal frame under me. The chain is around my ankle, like always. I'm so tired and sore everywhere, but especially in the middle. My face is wet with tears, as it usually is.

I can hear the crying of the other girl on the other mattress I know is in the room. I'm not going to be generous today.

"Stop it," I say.

The crying stops and there's a sniffle. "Is someone there?"

"Yeah, I'm here, but it won't do you any good. The only way you're getting out of here is dead in a suitcase. Just accept it."

The crying starts again. "Where are we?"

"In hell."

"I'm scared of the dark."

"You'll love the dark soon. When the lights are on, it's the worst hell. When it's not one of them, it's the other. They take *turns taking pictures and being in the pictures. The old one's the worst. The younger one is usually nicer."*

That was all I had to say. She didn't answer except for her sniffles.

~

Lauren

I'm shoved into the blue car by the older boy who's been so nice to me. I catch my arm on the roof of the car and my other hand on the door, but he peels them off and pushes me inside, slamming the door behind me. I never thought he'd be so rough. Now I was really scared. A white-haired man is in the back and he looks at me the way men look at my older sister. I look toward the front. A blond man whose head touches the top of the car is looking at me the same way. I can see his face clearly from the headlights of a passing car. He has a moon-shaped scar just to the side of his right eye and a large birthmark on his neck.

~

Gabriel

Last night Will and I decided he'd come over Saturday and we'd study for the upcoming sociology test together. He'd said he could really use a break from his family. So he was coming over at ten, and it was nine forty and I was freaking out, standing in the living room for no reason. I'd changed my shirt four times. And my socks twice. I thought socks might be dorky in my own house, but we kept the heat low, so I was cold without them. I decided to be practical and put on some blue ones.

Now I was thinking about how stupid it was to care about this stuff when Maya was dead and I might go to prison.

But this was *Will. In my house.*

Or it would be soon.

I went into the kitchen and looked in the fridge again. We had nothing interesting. We had some Cokes and a fruit salad Mamá had made for Thanksgiving. I'd have to warn Will about the papaya if we ate that—a lot of people didn't like it.

I ended up basically pacing from the kitchen to the living room, but then I stayed in the kitchen in case he saw me through the window, walking around like I had nothing better to do.

Then my heart nearly stopped when there was a knock on the door. A very confident, manly knock, I couldn't help noticing.

I raced to the door and threw it open, and there was Will, a big smile highlighting that powerful jaw of his. He had on a red North Face jacket and jeans that hugged all the right places.

"Hey," I said, a grin stretching across my face, too. I was hoping he would kiss me again.

"Hi." He stepped inside as I moved to the side.

He stopped in front of me and got deliciously in my personal space, and then he kissed me. No tongue, but lots of soft lips.

"You taste like chocolate," I stupidly said.

He laughed and walked inside. "I did you a favor by eating a chocolate bar on the way over here."

I shut the door and stood there for a second. "We can sit on the couch. And I'm sure eating it was a great burden. Thanks for taking that on for me."

He laughed again and fell onto the couch, dropping his backpack on the floor next to his leg.

"So, before we start working—graphic novels," I said, sitting on the chair. "Are you ready for some new ones?"

"Sure."

"Wait here." I went into my bedroom and pulled the two most important Batman ones off the shelf, *Year One* and *The Killing Joke*. I didn't actually own that many graphic novels, because I usually got them from the library, but I had the most important.

I headed back into the living room. "Here. Read this one first." I pointed to *Year One*.

"Gotcha." He took them from me and set them next to his backpack.

I realized that I should introduce him to Mamá. "Do you mind meeting my mom?"

He smiled. "Nope."

"Okay." I went back to her room, the whirring of the sewing machine loud as I reached her door. "Mamá, Will's here. Come meet him."

She looked over and smiled at me, trying to look supportive but not totally landing it. "Okay, mijo. This is your special friend?"

I laughed, feeling a little proud. "Yes, my special friend."

We reached the living room and Will jumped up to shake hands with her.

"Will, meet my mom, Adelita, and Mamá, this is Will from my sociology class."

That hedge made Will smile.

They exchanged nice-to-meet-yous, and Mamá asked him some boring questions about college, then offered some fruit salad, before finally saying, "Okay, I'm going to get back to my sewing. Learn a lot so you can do well on your test."

"Thanks, Mamá."

Will sat back down and I sat on the other end of the couch. I was pretty sure we were at least going to try to study.

He threw his arm across the back of the sofa, which would have been very cool if I'd been sitting next to him. "Your mom seems nice."

"Yeah, she is. She's, like, a genuinely good person. Which I think is rare." I turned sideways and sat cross-legged so I was facing him. He cocked an eyebrow and did the same.

The cocked eyebrow was so sexy. I had tried to do it when I first read that in a book, but I couldn't do just one, only both together, which made me look confused or curious, not sexy. I left my eyebrows alone.

"So, what do you want to study first?" he asked.

"I guess we could start with the gender chapter." The test was covering gender, the sociology of the self, and deviance and criminology.

"Sounds good." He nodded and pulled his book and notebook out of his backpack.

I did the same. Will was really studious and always went over his notes and book after class to take secondary notes that were organized and logical. Mine were messy in comparison, so we usually worked off his notes.

"So, gender roles," he said.

"I'm fairly familiar with those," I joked.

"Same." He laughed. "Why don't you see if you can name the ones we talked about in class."

There was a knock on the door. It sounded like Lauren's and my special knock, a triple-knock with a delay, a hangover from childhood.

I looked at the door and back at Will. "I guess I need to get that."

"No prob."

I opened the door and found Lauren standing there rubbing her forehead. "Oh, my God, Gabriel."

I was instantly worried about her. "What happened?"

"I had ..." She looked past me. "Do you have someone over?"

"Yeah." I opened the door. "Lauren, this is Will. Will, Lauren."

Will smiled and waved, and Lauren returned it. "Sorry, I'll go. Could you call me later?"

"No, you look upset," I said. Her hair was mussed and she didn't have any makeup on. "Are you okay?"

She grimaced. "I had two more dreams last night—I just woke up from the second one. They were horrible."

"Did you want to talk about them? Will sort of knows what's going on. Are you going to contact Candace?" I looked at Will and mouthed, "Sorry."

"I think so. One of them had someone that looked familiar, and I'm wondering if you could help me identify him."

"Come in. We can talk about them. Will and I can take a break. We've been hard at work studying for ... five minutes." Will and I laughed.

Lauren came in and sat in the recliner no one ever used. "Okay, I'm sorry, I won't stay long."

"You're fine," I said. Now that she was sitting, I could see that she was shaking a little. As upsetting as my own dreams were, I couldn't really imagine what it was like for her to be dreaming these awful scenes.

"So—" she started, but I cut her off.

"Hold on." I looked at Will, who looked confused, but not like he was about to pack up his backpack, so I figured it was safe to proceed. "Will knows about Maya, and the police, but not the dreams."

"Okay," Lauren said.

I sat back on the couch and looked at Will. "So, uh, this is kind of weird. First, I have to preface this by saying that Lauren and I are not woo-woo people. We didn't spend our early teens analyzing each other's dreams. But since Maya died, we've both had weirdly specific dreams that give us information that we could not possibly know. And it seems to come from Maya herself." I grimaced. "We sort of think Maya came to us in the dreams, kind of like a ghost." I grimaced again and held it as I watched Will's reaction.

He frowned a little but nodded. "O ... kay. I guess there are weirder things people believe."

I laughed awkwardly and glanced at Lauren, who was staring at her hands in her lap. "I know. We kept trying to figure alternative explanations, and we just can't. Mine were basically me chasing Maya in a Mario Kart-style scene following the path we think she ran that night. There was a little more each time, and the final one showed her getting hit by a car that drove off, and then being picked up by JT, put in the car trunk, and strangled."

Will's eyes widened. "That's so horrible."

"But Lauren's told another part of the story." I looked at her. "Do you want me to tell him?"

She nodded, still staring at her hands. "Yeah, just give a summary. I don't want to relive everything."

I went through the main points of hers that related to what happened to Maya.

"That's also horrible," Will said.

I looked back at Lauren and she was wiping tears from her eyes. Then I told Will about the more recent dreams, and how we'd talked to the reporter. "We were surprised because she seemed to believe us. She already thought that

Maya's case was connected to the missing girls, because she suspected JT somehow."

"This is all so crazy," Will said. "How would anyone figure out what really happened if a ghost wasn't telling you?"

"I know," I said.

"Makes it all even more bullshit that they've pinned it on you."

I nodded. "So, do you want to tell us, Lauren?"

"Yeah. So there were two." She told us about the first one, with the girl being mean to the newest one, and basically saying what was happening. We were all silent after she finished, and I had to hold my queasy stomach. Will looked totally rattled and vaguely ill, as well.

I exhaled a breath I'd been holding. "Lauren, I'm so sorry you have to go through all this. But I really believe that it will help us get justice for Maya and the other girls."

"It *has* to," she said, full of power. "The second dream wasn't so horrible, but it finally showed the other men involved." She told us about getting shoved into the car and seeing the two men. "I've never seen the old guy, but the younger guy looked familiar. I'm wondering if he goes to OIT. He's definitely college-aged. White. He has to be really tall because he filled the front seat, but not fat. Short blond hair, not curly. Kind of a square face, from what I could see from the side. Birthmark on his neck."

I glanced at Will, who was on his phone, and I wondered if he was texting someone to call him with an emergency so he could get out of here.

Lauren continued, "And he had this scar just below his right eye."

Will's eyes widened when she said that last bit. He

jumped up and squeezed between my legs and the coffee table to show Lauren something on his phone. "Is it him?"

"Oh, my God, that's him!" Lauren said, looking at me in shock.

"Who is it?" I jumped up to see and Will turned the phone toward me. "It's that basketball player!"

"Hoppin' John. John Johnson," Will said, excited. "OIT's star baller. I told you about him before. He got that scar in a DUI last year."

"JT's cousin," I added as I remembered.

"They're cousins?" Lauren asked.

"Apparently," I said.

"That's why I thought of him. And the birthmark. And then you mentioned the scar. Oh, my God." Will sat back down. He looked totally shaken, all the blood drained from his face.

"You all right?" I asked.

"Dude. You know, you could have made all this up—not consciously, but like, you made up these stories based on people you saw in real life, and it just happens to make a coherent story, unlike most dreams. But I think it actually makes more sense that you are both haunted."

My lip curled. "I know."

"What do we do, Gabriel?"

I cocked my head to the side. "You obviously have to contact Candace."

"Yes," Lauren said.

"You know," Will said thoughtfully, "Demetrius told me Johnson was gross and people said he was into child porn."

"What is with everyone just being cool with this?!" Lauren exclaimed with a huge burst of energy.

Will jerked back in surprise.

"Sorry," she said, hands up in apology. "My friend said

the same thing about JT. He's actually trying to see if he can see it so he can report it. We're hoping he can manage to because that would at least be one thing he'd get in legal trouble for. Even though it's nothing compared to rape and murder. And potentially putting an innocent person in prison." She looked at me and frowned.

Will nodded. "He absolutely should do that. They take that stuff seriously." He paused. "As they should."

"Okay, I'm going to go back and contact Candace," Lauren said, standing. "I didn't even bring my phone over. I just had to tell you about the dreams."

As I was getting up I noticed her feet. "You didn't even put shoes on." She just had these cheap slides she wore around the house.

She looked down at herself, almost surprised. "Also, I'm still in my pajamas, I just put a sweatshirt on."

Will chuckled a little. "Own it."

Lauren looked at him, face a little red. "Nice to meet you, Will. I'm sorry I made us talk about something so awful."

I hugged Lauren. "I'm glad you did, because I wouldn't have figured out who that guy was."

She hugged me back tightly, obviously needing it.

We let go, and she headed to the door. She waved awkwardly and was out the door. I shut it and turned around. "I'm sorry our study session got so messed up."

"It's really okay. This stuff is no joke. You're at risk of going to prison for something you didn't do, and somebody is kidnapping and murdering little girls. Fixing that is way more important than some sociology test."

I nodded and rubbed the back of my neck.

"But I do think I need to go." He started packing up.

I was so disappointed, but how could I blame him.

I stood by the door watching him. He finally stood up and came over.

"Don't worry, I'm not mad at you or anything, I just feel gross. And kissing you feels wrong given all the talk of child porn. So, I'm just going to go now, but let's study at the union on Monday, okay?"

"I have the hearing, but if you could meet in the late afternoon or evening, then yeah." I hoped he was being honest. I thought he was.

"Oh, yeah. I hope they figure out they have nothing on you. It's such fucking bullshit."

I nodded and then he hugged me. Although it wasn't as nice as a kiss, it was still good. Then he was out the door with a casual bye and a wave. I watched him get in his car, a maroon Honda of some sort.

And I sat back on the couch, knowing that I wouldn't get any more studying done for a while. I was going to deal with it like any reasonable eighteen-year-old—I was going to take a nap. Maybe I would wake up in a better world.

Or at least one where I wasn't on trial for a murder I didn't commit.

19

____

Lauren

I'm being driven through downtown. The white-haired man is next to me, talking, but I can't listen. Buildings I recognize are flying past.

The car stops. The driver gets out and unlocks a padlock holding a rust-colored gate shut, the right door hanging at an angle. He pulls the car in and gets out to relock the gate.

The white-haired man looks at me again and smiles and I know I'm in trouble.

∾

Lauren

Monday morning I woke from the dream, the picture of the place they took the girl etched in my mind. My first thought was to tell Gabriel, but then I remembered his preliminary hearing today,.. They had to realize they didn't have enough evidence against him, because it didn't exist.

I was desperate for Tenny to wake up so I could tell her. Finally, her alarm went off.

"You up?" I asked. "I had another dream."

"Yes," she said with a thick voice.

I told her about the dream and she got out of bed.

"Would you recognize it in real life?" she asked. She looked at her phone.

"I think so. But it's hard to know where to look. I'm sure it's OKC, but I don't know it well enough to know where the buildings are, even though they were familiar."

She looked at me with wide eyes. "Brandon said he has news. He sent a text late last night, but I didn't hear it come in. He's going to wait for us downstairs at eight twenty."

My stomach roiled. Had he seen something? Could this be the thing that starts real consequences off for JT? "Does he say what the news is?"

"No." She opened her closet and pulled out her shower caddy. "But for your dream, maybe we could look at Google Street View?"

"That's a good idea. I think I might recognize the area from the satellite view, then I could do the street view."

She pulled some clothes out and grabbed her towel. "Yeah. If you can describe it to me, I can look too, just for a second pair of eyes."

I yawned, hating that I could feel tired when there were girls out there being abused and maybe on the verge of being murdered. I should be energized with anger. "That's a good idea." I shifted and sat up, feet on the ground.

"Be back," she said and left for the shower. I needed to do the same thing, but there was a little time, so I opened up my computer and started searching downtown OKC. After several minutes, I had nothing. I gritted my teeth in frustration. I definitely needed to tell Candace about it, so I texted her and said I could talk right now or after school. We had talked Saturday after I found out about JT's cousin, and it sounded like that had been new information to her. She was looking into it.

I decided to draw what I had seen in the dream, as much as I could remember, so I did that. Nothing from Candace. I grabbed my own caddy, almost throwing half of the stuff out of it because I picked it up so fast. I passed Tenny in the hall and we nodded to each other and got on with getting ready.

Brandon was waiting for us when we got downstairs. He gave Tenny a quick kiss. But he was antsy and I knew he had something real. My whole body was tense. What did he have?

Once we got outside we walked out onto the lawn away from the buildings, and he looked left and right and behind us, and then he leaned in and quietly said, "I saw it."

Tenny and I both gasped.

"Not on JT's computer," he continued, "but Lewis's, and he hinted that he got it from JT. And, at least one of the girls was one of the missing girls I remember seeing."

We were still staring at him in shock. I shook my head to clear it. "Did you report it?"

He had this awkward grimace on his face. "No, I wanted to talk to you first. How do you think I should report it? To the police? Or to Ms. Patton?"

I was buzzing with energy now. Ms. Patton would have to care. "Maybe her? I think they'll take this very seriously. I don't think even JT will get a pass. And if he does, you can contact the police."

"I agree," Tenny said. "Although you could probably report it anonymously to the police."

His eyes widened. "You don't think anyone would find out I told, do you?"

"Brandon, this is bigger than some kids being mad at you," I snapped. "Little girls are being assaulted and murdered. If you don't tell Ms. Patton by lunchtime, I'll do it myself."

He frowned but nodded. "You're right. If I come over at lunch nobody will see me." He rubbed the back of his neck. He wasn't even wearing a jacket despite how cold it was.

"Text us as soon as you report it," Tenny said.

He nodded. "Let's go to class." Tenny and I followed him into the classroom building and headed to our classes. I was going to be completely on edge waiting to hear what would happen. I'd probably have to wait until after school. And I'd also talk to Candace then and hear from Gabriel about his hearing. This was a big day.

~

Gabriel

The drive to the preliminary hearing Monday was pretty much the same as the drive to the arraignment, both Mamá and me scared and nervous. She again said God would take care of me, and I again felt skeptical.

We met Mr. Thompson when we got there. We were about twenty minutes early so we stood awkwardly in the hall. Mr. Thompson told me what to expect while we waited, but it was hard to pay attention. The upshot was that the prosecution would bring in witnesses and present whatever evidence they had against me. The judge would decide if it was enough to go ahead, then a trial date would be set. Finally, it was time to go in. He and I stood behind the table until we were told to be seated. Mamá was right behind me, being her supportive self.

The district attorney went over his evidence, and then they brought up their first witness, that guy who'd joined the search right before I found Maya. He said it was obvious that I knew where her body was. Mr. Thompson questioned him, but he was really insistent. Then they brought up the two cops I first saw after finding her, one at a time, and they both testified that I behaved like someone with something to hide. Mr. Thompson also questioned both of them, but they were the same. Then they brought up the two detectives. I was so overwhelmed that I stupidly started crying again because I couldn't believe all these people really believed I could have killed Maya.

I was struggling to really listen throughout because I felt disoriented, but I got enough. I knew that they were going to send me to trial. Mr. Thompson said it was very rare for charges to be discharged at this point, and it was no reflection on how good the evidence was for me being the murderer, as the burden of proof was low at this point. The judge set a date for the trial. January 16. This was really not ending.

Once we could leave, we did, and ended up standing in the hall outside the courtroom again. I was so queasy from the stress, which apparently was obvious.

"Gabriel, don't worry about today," Mr. Thompson said. "We knew there was almost no chance of a discharge, but I still think their evidence is incredibly weak. I can't predict what a jury will do, but this is not a slam dunk for the prosecutor. We are going to mount a solid defense."

"Okay," I said. While he was talking, Mamá had hooked her arm around my elbow, which calmed me a little.

"Thank you, Mr. Thompson," she said.

We all walked out of the courthouse together, then went

in different directions to get to our cars. Once we were in, Mamá said, "We're going to get through this."

"I hope so."

"You will not be forsaken. You have always been a good boy."

I looked out the window at all the other cars in the lot, probably some belonging to real criminals. She started the car.

I pulled out my phone and turned it back on, then texted Will.

—I'm free for now. Heading over—

He responded right away. *—I'm already at the union and have a choice booth claimed. Waiting impatiently—*

That made me smile. "Can you drop me on campus? I'm going to go meet Will. We're going to try again to study for the test tomorrow."

"Okay, mijo." She pulled out of the parking lot onto the street and we started heading toward campus.

She was quiet for a moment. "You really like this boy?"

"I do."

"Okay." She sounded uncertain.

"Does that make you uncomfortable?" I asked, wishing she was just a bit less religious.

"I want you to be happy." She turned right. "That's what I care most about."

I nodded. I really couldn't complain. So many people, especially in Oklahoma, had parents who treated them like shit when they came out. A mom who was a bit uncomfortable was not the worst.

We drove the rest of the way in silence. Eventually she pulled into the bus lane on the north side of campus. I got my backpack out of the trunk and said goodbye, anxious to get to Will.

At least for a few hours, I could pretend like I was a normal college student whose biggest problem was an upcoming test.

~

Lauren

After school Monday, I was lying on my unmade bed, taking a moment to chill out, even though my mind was going a mile a minute. Tenny was with Brandon, but she'd texted that he had told Ms. Patton today at lunch, and she'd been shocked, and he was sure they would do something about it. Now I just had to wait, not able to do anything while horrible stuff was happening in that warehouse in the city.

I texted Gabriel. —*You have a minute? There's news*—

I set the phone on my stomach and closed my eyes, trying to calm my mind, which hadn't let up since this morning. When would something happen?

The phone vibrated and I checked. Gabriel said he was walking across campus but could chat.

I FaceTimed him and he answered. "Hey. You have news?"

"Yes! Brandon told us this morning that he saw some of the porn!"

Gabriel's eyes widened. "On JT's computer?"

"No, on another guy's, but he basically said he got it from JT, and Brandon reported it today at lunch. Nothing's happened yet, but he said Ms. Patton was really freaked out and he's sure they're going to do something."

"They better." He was looking up instead of at the phone, but I could tell he had on his serious face.

"How was the hearing?" I asked, instantly feeling like an

idiot. What was he going to say—oh it was great, we knocked back a couple of Cokes and passed around some chips.

"Shitty." He looked off to the side.

Obviously. My perpetual sense of queasiness flared for him. I slid my feet under the blanket at the foot of the bed.

He explained what had happened, and how horrible it was to have people saying all this utter bullshit about you, and other people believing it. "The trial starts January sixteenth."

"We have to get this all figured out before then!" I sounded a little frantic.

"I know. I don't know how." A loud group walked by him, cutting off what he was saying next.

"What did you say?"

"It just feels so hopeless, Lauren." He looked at the phone for a second before looking up again.

"I know. I wish I could fix this for you."

"You're always fixing everything." He smiled at the phone.

"Not this." If only. It was driving me crazy to be so hamstrung, having knowledge but with no one listening. "Maybe Candace can come through. I am so out of ideas. Even if JT gets in trouble, it probably won't bring down the whole ring. But I can't stop thinking about those girls."

"I know. We have to figure it out." He turned a corner and I knew he was heading to the student union.

"I both dread another dream and am desperate for one. I keep thinking maybe there will be something that the police would believe." My stomach twisted from all of those possibilities.

"Yeah." He paused. "How's school going? Are you keeping up even with all this shit going on?"

"I'm okay. I wasn't too ambitious when I registered for this semester, so my course load isn't terrible, compared to some kids'." This was a slight exaggeration, as I wasn't doing great in my classes, although I had kept up with most of the homework.

"That's good. It was such a shock going from Burnside to OAMS."

"Yeah, at least I had a heads-up from you. How are your classes? How's Will?"

His mouth stretched into a smile and he looked at the phone again. "Will's great. Well, I assume. I'm going to meet him now. We're going to study for our sociology test tomorrow. But overall, classes are fine. Calculus is a pain."

"That's good." I looked at the bottom of the top bunk. "It's still so weird that we have to keep doing everything—after Maya, and with your trial and everything. Just pretend like things are normal."

"I know." He stopped outside the union and leaned against a wall. "Dana's not, though. Your dad isn't. I don't know what's wrong with your parents."

I felt a little defensive. "Dad just doesn't cope well with really bad things. And Dana ... I guess, you know, she really loves Maya."

"I know. But you know, you've always been the most adult person in that house whenever things aren't great. They're fair-weather parents. I'm glad you're at OAMS so you don't have to deal with them not being around."

He was right, but I didn't like to think about it. "Yeah. It could be—"

Gabriel looked up grinned, and said, "Hey! Sorry, I'm talking to Lauren."

Will appeared behind Gabriel's shoulder, smiling and waving.

"Hi." I managed a small smile. "You guys go study and be smart. I'll talk to you later. Bye, Gabriel."

"Bye, Lauren. We'll figure this out somehow."

I hoped he was right, but I couldn't think of a single other thing we could do that might help.

20

———

Gabriel

Will and I were in Booth Forest at the union, where we'd been for a couple hours since the test, which we both felt good about.

We'd been studying, actually getting work done, even though all I really wanted to do was kiss him. But we'd made ourselves sit on opposite sides of the table to be good.

I looked over at him, reading his chemistry book. His black hair was cut in a fade and it really made his facial features look strong. He was so hot when he was focused like that. He wasn't as much of a nerd as Lauren and I were, but he cared about doing well, and I liked that about him.

"What?" Will said, not looking up, but with a smile.

"I was just staring at you for no reason."

"I think there probably is a reason," he said, looking up.

I rolled my eyes, unable to stop the huge grin from spreading. "Probably, but this is not something discussed in polite society."

He laughed. "What made you think I was a member of polite society?"

"Oh, I just assumed, with us being members of the aristocracy."

"Yes, I forgot about that detail." He tangled his feet in mine and we just stared at each other for a bit.

This was definitely a hot look and it suddenly felt wrong with everything going on, and I looked back down. Food trash littered the table and I decided to collect it all. "I need to take a piss, so I'm going to clean all this crap up and do that. Back in five."

"Okay." He leaned back against the booth and yawned. "I wish we didn't need sleep. I was up too late playing Fortnite and thinking about those girls."

"Yeah. I couldn't sleep because of the news from Lauren." I collected the trash and stuffed all the wrappers into the Taco Bell bags.

"I felt bad playing a video game, but we are stuck, right? There really isn't anything we can report." He frowned.

"You've already helped us so much by identifying the basketball player. It's okay to relax and enjoy yourself." I stood up and grabbed the two empty drink cups.

"I guess." He sounded deflated and I felt bad for ruining the good mood.

"I'll be back." I gave him a nice smile to try to fix the mood shift, and headed toward the trash bin. I made the obligatory pit stop and headed back.

Will was back in his chemistry book, but he looked up when I got back. He looked happy enough and said, "My turn."

I slid into the booth just as my phone dinged. "I'll be here, waiting."

He got out and headed off and I checked my phone. A

text from Lauren. She must have snuck into the bathroom to send the text. —*OMG, Gabriel, they raided the boys' side of the dorm. A bunch of guys were pulled out of class. I think they arrested them!*—

—*Did they take JT?*— I asked, heart pounding.

—*We aren't sure exactly who it was, but someone said he was one of them*—

I checked the time. 2:15. —*You're still in class, right?*—

—*Yeah, about to start the second to last. We should know more when we get back to the dorm. I will let you know when I find anything out*—

—*This is great, L*— It really was. It might help break up the ring if JT revealed where he was getting it.

But it still didn't help me any.

—*I know. But we still have to figure out how to make them see what else JT did*—

Lauren knew what was up. My stomach twisted with guilt for ghosting her for so long.

—*Gotta go*— she texted.

—*Okay, let me know what's up*— I set the phone down and opened up my calculus textbook. I needed to try to get that homework done, even though my heart was racing and it was going to be hard to care about differential equations when I was picturing JT in that same room I'd been in at the police station.

Abruptly, Will returned, two cups in hand. He put the smoothie down in front of me and I couldn't help but grin. This guy was something else.

"You look kind of spooked," he said as he sat down and took a sip of his coffee.

"It happened." I told him that they had raided the school and it sounded like some boys had been arrested, but I wouldn't know until Lauren had more info.

"I have to work at four," he said, frowning again. "What time do they finish?"

"Four-twenty."

"Seriously?" He laughed.

I cocked my head to the side. "I know, adults are so clueless. But it will still take a while to find out, probably. I will text you."

"I don't finish until nine, so I'll text you after that." He pulled another textbook out of his backpack. "I wish I didn't have to work tonight. Or at least I wish we were allowed to use our phones."

"Yeah, me too." We smiled at each other.

I was so desperate for this to be my life, just this time with Will without all the other shit going on. If I didn't go to prison, maybe it would be.

~

Lauren

"Stand still, girl."

I'm freezing, standing naked and barefoot on a cement floor. My toes are ice cubes.

There's a flash.

"Uncross your arms, mamacita."

I know it's best to just do what they say, so I uncross my arms and any warmth that was in my chest evaporates.

There's another flash and then the man not working the camera walks up to me. He's the old one, with the white hair and kind face, but he is anything but kind.

"Turn around and lean over on the table, mamacita."

Maya appeared in front of me, shaking my shoulders. "Lauren, you have to do something."

Lauren

Thursday morning I woke from that horrific dream—I *was* doing something, or at least I was trying. If Maya could give me more info, maybe I could do more.

I spent the rest of the day sick and panicked at our lack of power. JT had been arrested Tuesday along with four other boys, and the whole school was reeling. But that didn't mean anything would happen with the imprisoned girls, even though we knew that at least one girl in the images was one of the missing ones. I was hoping JT would reveal where he was getting the porn and they might find out that way, but I didn't expect it.

Classes took forever, but then I got back to the dorm and couldn't do anything there, either. We went to dinner. Brandon was happy that no one seemed to know who had reported it.

Tenny and I tried to work during study time that night, but it was hard. Right before study time ended, I got an email from Candace with some images of properties that Hoppin' John's dad—who also named John, apparently— owned. This was it! The images were small on my phone, so I opened it up on my computer to see better. Tenny looked over my shoulder as I pulled them up. The first one was a house, obviously not the warehouse from the dream. The next one was an empty storefront on an urban street.

"These don't look anything like what you described," Tenny said.

"No." I flipped to the third one. This one was a warehouse with a rusted door, but it had corrugated walls. Then I looked at the fourth one—this was it! I gasped.

"Is that it?" she asked.

"Yes!"

"Where is it?" Her voice was high.

I looked through the email but there were no addresses. Heart racing, I opened up the texting app and sent Candace a quick a snapshot of the right one. —*This is it! There are girls there now! Where is it?*—

"How do we get in there?" Tenny asked.

I turned around. "I don't know. We need the police to do it to make sure evidence isn't messed up and stuff. But how? They don't believe anything I say!"

My phone buzzed with a new text.

—*Thanks, I'm going to do what I can*—

She wasn't going to give us the address. It was so frustrating.

"We're just sitting here, doing nothing while those girls are suffering!" Tenny cried. She put her palm to her forehead. "How is this happening?"

"I know, this is all insane." I was so queasy and sweat was beading on my forehead. "Let's call Gabriel. What time is it?"

"Ten forty-seven," Tenny answered.

We only had thirteen minutes before it was lights and noise out, so we had to be fast.

I FaceTimed him and thank God he answered.

"What's up? Is everything okay?" Gabriel was adjusting the phone, obviously sitting at the desk in his room.

"Candace just sent me some pictures of properties that Hoppin' John's dad owns and I recognized one from the dream!" It came out fast and my heart was beating like crazy.

"Where is it?"

"She wouldn't tell us," I said. "What should we do?"

"Can we find it on Google Maps?" he asked. "Did you try a reverse search yet?"

"No! I'll try that. Maybe I can send it to you and you can start looking, too. I know it's downtown OKC, but not really where."

"I can look, too," Tenny said.

I got the image sent off to them and we signed off. What we would do once we found the warehouse was still up in the air. But we had to do something.

Gabriel

Saturday morning Will pulled up in my driveway and I scrambled into the car so we could go get Lauren and Tenny. We had a plan.

"I know this is serious and important, but can I have a quick kiss?" he asked, melting my heart.

"Uh, obviously." I leaned toward him and we shared a nice, relatively chaste kiss that melted me even more. I pulled back, feeling a tiny bit dizzy from happiness, which fizzled right out when I remembered what we were doing. "Alright, to the dorm."

"I actually don't know where it is," Will said, smiling.

"How do you not know everything?" I teased. "You seem like you know everything."

"If only."

Now we had to be serious. "So, head back to campus, the southeast corner."

"Gotcha." He backed the car out and we started over there.

Lauren and Tenny were waiting at the end of the dorm

by an open parking spot. They got into the back as soon as Will pulled into the spot. I introduced Tenny and Will, and then we got down to business.

"Thanks for driving us, Will," Lauren said. "Do you want the address? Or I can do it on my phone." She'd actually been able to find the location after spending some time on Google Maps.

"Give it to me," he said, pulling his phone out of his pocket.

She recited it, and Will entered it into his GPS. He headed out of campus and drove toward the short highway that led into northwest OKC.

"What is the plan once we get there?" Will asked. "Are you going to knock on the door or something?"

"I'm not sure," Lauren said. "There's a gate, anyway, so we probably can't get to the door. I just feel like I need to see it. What if we hear something suspicious? We could report it."

I didn't think that was very likely, and no one else said anything while Will merged onto the highway. They'd probably agree with me if I said it out loud. But I also felt the same as Lauren. Seeing the place seemed really important.

We traveled in silence, and soon we were heading into downtown, in the forest of tall buildings. It looked mostly deserted because it was the weekend. Will followed the GPS, and we ended up in the left turn lane to turn onto the actual street where the building was.

The green arrow lit up and we turned. Will drove slowly down the street. There were a couple of office buildings on the left side of the street. I glanced back at Lauren and her face was white. She must feel sick with those dreams going through her mind.

We were getting close to the end of the street when we

saw a car pulled into a driveway in front of a gate on the left. The car was a gray Honda Accord. A man was fiddling with the top of the gate. As we got closer, Lauren said, "That's it! And that's him! Hoppin' John."

"Don't slow down," I told Will, pulse already racing.

Still, we all looked at the gate and building when we passed, knowing the horrors that were going on inside, despite how mundane—and run-down—it looked. There was a janky faded red gate with two doors that sagged where they met in the middle, a chain with a padlock hanging at the top.

"That was definitely Hoppin' John," Will said. "But that wasn't his car."

"Yeah," Lauren said, gripping my shoulder. "We need to go inside and rescue them! We have to do something!"

My heart was trying to beat its way out of my chest. "How? What should we do?"

Will got to the end of the block, signaled, and turned right.

"I don't think we can do anything, as much as I also want to," Tenny said as Will turned right onto the next street.

"Yeah, if we go in, won't it be illegal? And wouldn't we mess up the investigation?" I turned around to face Lauren. "I think that's the core problem. Well, other than the fact that we can't tell the police you saw it in a dream, and they wouldn't believe us anyway. But there has to be something."

We were approaching the next corner, but this street had some traffic.

"Okay, guys," Will said. "What about this? You know my brother knows Hoppin' John."

I looked at him.

Will continued as he turned right. "Maybe I can claim to know something through the grapevine. I'd have to make it like I found out myself, rather than 2 hearing it and telling me, because I'm not going to get him in trouble. Unlike me, he actually looks Black. And we know how well being Latino worked out with Burnside PD."

How did I find this perfect guy? I'd only liked him at first because of how he looked, with no idea how perfect he was. Did all relationships start so superficially?

"Are you Black?" Lauren asked, obviously surprised.

"Yeah, I just take after my white mom. My brother takes after my dad." He pulled up behind a car at the next intersection. One more right turn would take us past the warehouse again.

"Huh," Lauren said, trying to process it.

"Now you and Tenny are going to be staring at me, trying to figure out if there are any signs," he said ruefully.

Tenny laughed lightly, but then she asked seriously, "What could you claim to know about Hoppin' John?"

Will turned right again, brow slightly furrowed. The gate came into view but he drove at a normal speed, not slow.

We all looked over, and to my horror, John was loading a suitcase into his trunk, back toward the street.

"Oh, my God!" Lauren cried as Tenny gasped. "We didn't save her!"

I felt sick.

"Could she still be alive?" Will asked.

"No, they're already dead by the time they go in the suitcase," Lauren said between sobs.

We got to the intersection and I looked over at Will again. He was white as a sheet. Tenny was trying to comfort Lauren but her voice was thick.

"God," Will said. "We can't let it get any worse. I'm going to pull over. We need a plan."

"If he's leaving, should we sneak in?" Lauren asked, high-pitched and frantic.

"No," Tenny and I said together.

Will turned right, then pulled into a parking spot along the curb, hands at ten and two. "Okay, so I report something." He was staring ahead, tapping his thumbs on the steering wheel.

I looked back at Lauren and Tenny, both crying and pale with shock.

"It has to be Will," Lauren said. "They won't hear anyone else."

"Yeah," he said. "It has to be enough to make them investigate, but not so much that they're suspicious of me or my brother."

"Right," Tenny said. "But let's think what they don't know, and what the most convincing information is that would make them act."

"I think that's him!" Will said. "He's just turned toward us." He put his car in gear, and after John and a couple other cars passed, pulled back onto the street. The light turned red and John pulled to a stop, with us three cars behind him.

"Are we going to follow him?" I asked.

"I think so," Will said. "Don't we have to? I feel like we're in a movie and the plot says follow. Movies always end well for the good guys, so let's do it."

"Yes," Lauren said with force.

Will hit the gas as the cars ahead started moving. He changed lanes to get closer to John. Was this really going to work?

21

Lauren

Somehow we managed to stay behind John through downtown, despite the many traffic lights. We trailed him onto the highway that went into Burnside.

My mind was spinning so much that there was a ringing in my ears.

"Do you think he's just going home?" Gabriel asked. "With a body in the trunk? That's crazy."

"This whole thing is insane," I said. "Who could do this to actual little girls? And then throw them away like trash. All while being this famous college basketball star. No one would believe this."

"What if we rear-end him?" Tenny asked.

I looked at her. She was such a genius sometimes.

"That ... might work," Gabriel said.

"I'm not entirely opposed to it, but I don't think it would actually work," Will said. "Even if we got a cop there, they'd have no reason to look in the suitcase. We'd have the same problem of telling them what we know."

"Dammit," I growled. There had to be something we could do.

We were quiet for a bit, watching John's car. He wasn't driving like you'd think a macho-type college guy would, but he was probably trying to make sure he didn't get stopped.

"I just realized why he's driving a different car," Will said. "He wrecked his car last weekend. Another DUI. I bet it's in the shop."

We got to the first traffic light officially in Burnside and followed John into the left turn lane, two cars back. The light turned green just as a fire truck pulled out, with sirens on, just beyond the intersection. John was already halfway through his turn, so he made it through, while the car in front of us had to stop for the fire truck and the light turned red.

My heart fell. "No!" I said, just as Gabriel said, "Shit! We'd been so lucky!"

"He's probably going home, right?" Will said. "I know where he lives. We'll drive by and see."

"AirTag," Tenny said, just as the fire truck blew through the intersection.

I looked at her. "You're so smart."

Tenny shrugged. "Does anyone have one?"

"I'm sure we can get one at Walmart," Gabriel said. "But how do you know where Hoppin' John lives, Will?" He sounded curious.

"He has parties. My brother has been, but a lot of people know." He paused. "And no, my brother's not going to end up being involved."

You had to wonder.

"Your brother is definitely turning out to be very useful to us," Gabriel said, reaching over to lightly punch Will's arm, which made Will turn and smile at him. They really were cute together.

But I couldn't get distracted by that. We finally made it through the intersection, and Will started driving through town, heading to the edge of downtown.

"This is his street." He turned right onto a street lined with cars on both sides. "His is the last house on the right."

We all watched as we got closer.

"I see his car!" Gabriel said.

"Okay, now we have to figure out how to get an AirTag on it," I said.

"I'm driving to Walmart right now," Will said. He turned right just past John's house.

"What about a magnet of some sort?" Tenny asked. "Isn't the inside bumper of cars metal?"

"They're usually aluminum," Will said as he pulled to a stop in the left turn lane. "Magnets don't stick. But the exhaust tubing should be steel and would work."

"Would it stay on as he's driving around?" I asked.

"Neodymium magnets are really strong," Gabriel said.

Will turned onto the main street.

"I think I know what we can do," Gabriel said.

He detailed the plan on the way to Walmart. Once there, we split up. Tenny and I went toward the grocery side, and Will and Gabriel headed to electronics. We met back at the car, where Tenny and I had plastic cling wrap and duct tape, and Will and Gabriel had two AirTags and a plastic bag filled with damp paper towels.

We got in and got to work prepping the two AirTags. We figured that having two gave us a better chance that one wouldn't fall off, and also, if he found one, he wouldn't necessarily find the other.

We set the tags up on Tenny's account because my iPhone was ancient. Then, for the first one, we used the cling wrap to attach the tag to a bunch of small magnets. For the second one, we made a little pouch for the tag and duct-taped it shut. We didn't totally cover it because we thought the tape might interfere with the tracking.

"Okay, are we ready?" Gabriel asked, turning around to look at us.

In response, Will started the car, and Tenny and I nodded. My heart was already racing.

He drove us back to John's neighborhood and parked down the street. He was going to stay in the car because he might be recognized. So the rest of us got our supplies in two different Walmart bags and headed toward John's car, parked on the grass in front of his house.

My pulse was pounding in my ears as we walked down the sidewalk, and I felt like I couldn't see anything except John's car, like it was at the end of a tunnel.

We had worked out a detailed plan, but I couldn't believe we were actually going to do this. Gabriel and Tenny must be as freaked out as me. We were definitely not the kind of people to do something like this. Eventually, we got to John's car. We all looked toward the house and around, and saw nobody, so we crouched down behind the trunk, where we couldn't be spotted from inside the house. But we still had to act fast in case someone else looked out their window.

Tenny leaned toward the trunk and said, "Hey, is there anyone in there?"

Nothing.

Gabriel rolled on his back and pushed himself back,

under the bumper. "I'm glad this is a rental. Otherwise he'd probably have an alarm."

My heart lurched. What if this one did? But there was no alternative plan, no going back. I handed him the magnetic tag.

We heard a clink. "On the exhaust pipe," he said. Tenny handed him the other tag. He searched around a bit, and I was queasy with nerves, my ears ringing from stress.

"Okay, give me one of the wet towels."

I handed him one, hand visibly shaking. He wiped some area under the car. "Dry one, please. And a piece of duct tape about 6 inches long."

While he wiped the spot off, I tore off a piece of duct tape. He fiddled with it a bit, then slid out. We all looked at each other for a second, then Tenny and I helped him up and headed back toward Will's car.

"Oh, my God," Tenny said, out of breath. We were walking quickly, but not *that* fast, so it had to be from nerves.

"I know," Gabriel and I said at the same time. We sounded as freaked out as she did.

We made it back to the car and scrambled inside.

Will asked, "Success?"

"We need to test it," Gabriel said.

Tenny pulled up Find My on her phone, and we saw the two tags on the account, showing just down the road from us. My heart twisted. This might work. "Yes, success," I said, finally answering Will.

Gabriel nodded and Will pulled out onto the street, and that was that. Now we just had to wait and see where the AirTags went.

❧

Gabriel

Will and I were at my house later Saturday evening, long after sunset, sitting hip-to-hip on the couch, and trying and failing to watch Superbad. He was holding my hand while I kept my phone in my other hand, fielding Lauren's texts. Tenny had her phone open and was watching the AirTags, but they hadn't moved.

—*It's moving!*— Lauren finally texted.

"It's moving!" I shouted, which made Will flinch, but then his eyes got wide.

"Oh, my God," he said, looking at my phone.

But there was nothing to see except my texts. Three dots appeared at the bottom, but I was impatient. I FaceTime dialed Lauren.

"It's moving!" she said when she answered, her own face full of shock.

"Show it!" I said.

"Everything okay, mijo?" Mom said from behind the couch. It nearly gave me a heart attack and made Will jerk. I turned the phone over.

"Yeah, sorry, we're fine." There was no way I could tell her what was going on.

"Hi, Will," she said.

"He just—" Lauren started, and I quickly turned the phone and took it off speaker.

Mamá looked at it, but then Will said, "Hi, Mrs. Canul. How are you?" He sounded so strained. We were desperate to get back to the phone.

"Good." She looked from him to me, back at him and then back at me. "What is going on?"

"Nothing," I said. "Just chatting with Lauren."

"Okay, I'm glad you are talking again. I'll leave you to

your Saturday night." She squeezed my shoulder and headed back to her room, even though she knew something was up.

"Are you going to tell her?" Will asked as I flipped the phone back over and turned the speaker on.

Lauren was talking, voice excited. "—stopped. I think he's at a stoplight."

"Sorry, Lauren, Mamá came in so we missed what you were just saying."

She looked at the screen. "Nothing really happened. He's just driving. We keep writing down the intersections and taking screenshots."

She paused.

"He's moving again! Let me show you."

The camera swung around until she was showing Tenny's phone in her hand. The frowny emoji Tenny had picked moved along a street. We all watched it in silence. I couldn't get the idea out of my head that he was going to go bury a little girl's body.

"This is so weird," Will said quietly. "This whole thing. How we got involved, and how I know people that are this horrible and I never knew."

"I know." Our shoulders were touching and it was just comforting, not sexy.

Lauren's phone was shaking but we could still see the frowny face moving slowly on the screen. We watched as he pulled off the road, long before he was out of town.

"Where's he stopping?" Lauren asked.

I found the spot on Google Maps and my heart sank. "Arby's."

"Oh, no, he's not going now," Tenny said.

"Maybe he'll go afterward." Lauren obviously didn't even believe that herself.

"He's probably not going to go until way in the middle of the night," Will said.

I nodded. "You're probably right. You are going to have to stay up all night to watch this."

Lauren and Tenny said, "Yeah," at the same time.

We continued to watch the frowny face as it barely moved on the screen. Eventually, he pulled back onto the street, going back the way he'd come.

"Damn," Lauren said, which matched my own feelings. "We can hang up. We'll just call you if something changes, Gabriel."

"Yeah, okay. I'll have my ringer up as loud as possible to make sure I wake up."

We hung up, which left Will and me looking at each other, feeling frustrated.

"Arby's," he said.

"I know."

He took my hand again and we just sat there for what felt like a long time, leaning against each other.

He eventually squeezed my hand.

"I think I might get going," he said. "But what really happens next? What if he goes out into the boonies tonight?"

I looked at him. His brow was furrowed. He was in this now, whether we'd meant for him to be or not.

"If he does, could you drive us there tomorrow?" I asked, both excited and nervous. This was progress. Something might happen now.

He nodded. "I'm supposed to work in the afternoon, but I'll see if I can switch with someone."

He was so great. I had an almost overwhelming surge of affection for him and nearly teared up. I wanted to kiss him, which made me feel bad.

"Send me a text when you know something," he said.

"Yeah." I sat up, already missing the contact.

Will got up and checked for his wallet and phone in his pockets and smiled at me. "See you tomorrow, probably."

I stood up and hugged him. "I mean, I'm not looking forward to it, but probably."

He gave me a peck on the lips, as unsexy as a kiss could be. Anything else would have been wrong. We waved at each other as he got into his car. I watched him leave, still so hyped up from everything that my head was spinning.

I finished the movie, then started another, some cheesy Lifetime movie about a couple opening a cookie shop. When that ended, I started another one, and finally my phone rang. I answered FaceTime instantly.

"Okay, for real this time," Lauren said. She showed me Tenny's phone, and John was already out of town, heading further into the boonies. "He went to another house for a while earlier. But now we think he's doing it."

"It is Saturday night." I yawned and checked my phone. "Or technically very early Sunday morning. He obviously has a social life. But imagine just driving around with a body in the trunk."

"I know," Lauren said.

I pulled up Google Maps on my own phone to see where he was going, and he was heading northwest, away from Burnside, deeper into the boonies. If he kept on the general route, he'd be heading out into proper country, with long country roads with no side streets, just plains and some remaining parts of the forest.

"Is he going to dump her in the woods?" Tenny asked.

I nodded, and Lauren said, "I think so. This is horrible."

Eventually he did go way out into the boonies, and then stopped. We zoomed in and got some screen shots.

"Hey, zoom out," I said. "We can measure his location along the road from the two intersections to calculate the right spot." My head was spinning at what was happening. I was dizzy.

"Good idea," Tenny said. She zoomed out and grabbed some more screenshots at different zoom levels.

Lauren turned the phone back around. "We're still watching. He's not moving."

We were quiet for a bit.

"Still not moving," Lauren said.

I yawned again and we were quiet again for a while, the car still not moving. Nobody was sure what to do or say.

Finally, Tenny said, "He's probably burying her right now."

I grimaced and Lauren closed her eyes. When she opened her eyes, they glistened with tears.

What was there to say?

"He still hasn't moved," Tenny said.

"Yeah, he's obviously parked," I said.

Lauren wiped her eyes. "We'll keep watching, but what are we going to do? How are we going to get over there?"

"About that," I said. "I asked Will to drive us. He said he would."

"Oh, wow," Lauren said. "We should go early, if we can."

"I'll text him and let you know when he responds." I hung up and texted him, but he didn't respond right away.

I trusted this guy so much. I knew he'd come through tomorrow. But I didn't know what else was going to happen, or what we'd find, if anything.

I knew it was really stupid for me to go looking for this, but I couldn't let just Will go, and obviously it couldn't be just Lauren and Tenny. Besides, even if I wasn't there, the police would still find a way to blame me. I was in this.

22

Lauren

Tenny and I were waiting downstairs Sunday morning. Gabriel and Will were on their way, and Gabriel was coming in to check us out so we could all "go to church." Will would be staying in the car.

He came in and the RA working the front desk said hi to him.

"What are you doing here?" she asked, overly friendly. She was so friendly to all the boys. She was on one of the other floors and was always doing weird leg stretches in random places.

"Hey, I'm just here to check Lauren and Tenny out." He looked tense, but was trying to seem chill.

She noticed us standing next to him and smiled at us. "Where are you going?"

"Church," I answered, not feeling guilty about the lie at all.

She made a note in the computer and waved us off. We

all calmly walked out, but as soon as we were out of view of the front, we ran to the car and scrambled in.

Tenny got her phone out and gave the intersection to Will, who put it in his phone map, and then we were off. My heart was pounding in anticipation.

We were quiet for a bit, but then Gabriel asked, "Do we have a plan?"

"Tenny and I talked about this," I said. "I think we just park the car as close to where he stopped as possible, and then look for an opening into the woods where he might have gone. Then we go in and look for anything off. He was just there last night, so maybe there will be signs of someone walking through even if there isn't a path."

Tenny piped up. "Yeah, and we looked at the area right about where he parked, which was 0.46 miles from the intersection. I got this app on my phone that tracks GPS really precisely, so we can actually measure 0.46 of a mile."

"Very cool, Tenny," Gabriel said.

"We also looked at Street View, but we couldn't see anything obvious in the trees there," I said.

We drove in silence for a while until we got closer.

"It's the next intersection, guys," Will said. "I'm turning right, right?"

"Yes, but stop in the turn so we can measure the distance," Tenny said.

We were getting close enough that Will started braking, and my heart sped up.

He came to a complete stop right at the start of the new street.

"Okay, I'm ready," Tenny said. "Drive slow."

I watched her phone ticking through the distance. 0.18, 0.19, 0.20.

"0.25," Tenny said.

Will nodded.

"These woods look impenetrable," Gabriel said.

0.31, 0.32, 0.33.

After we passed 0.40, Tenny started calling each number out. As soon as she said, "0.46," Will stopped abruptly and we all jerked forward a bit.

"Sorry," he said.

I already had my door open. We all got out and stood on the side of the road, knee-high grass swaying slightly in the cold breeze. There was a ditch between the road and the trees, but I couldn't see anything indicating someone had come through with a suitcase.

"Maybe he didn't go that far in," Gabriel said.

"Let's walk up and down a little," I said. "Maybe we can spot something out of the ordinary."

"Good idea." Gabriel started one direction down the road, staring intently at the woods, and I went the opposite direction. Tenny followed me, and Will went after Gabriel.

"Here, guys," Will called after a moment.

We all ran back to where he was pointing. There were some broken blades of grass that did look a little out of place. My pulse quickened even more.

"Let's go in," I said. I jumped down to the side of the ditch and then jumped across, the dead grass rustling. I didn't wait for the others, but I could hear them following as I passed the first tree. My pounding heart was loud in my ears. I looked at the ground and there was some more broken foliage and old leaves, but I didn't really know what to look for so I wasn't sure. I kept going, following the possible trail, the others behind me.

But then I passed one tree, and there was some flattened foliage and drag marks in the exposed dirt. I gasped and stopped.

Tenny ran into me and everyone else stopped. I stepped aside and pointed at the marks.

"Oh, my God, this is it," Gabriel said, shock sharpening his voice.

As we pushed our way through, following the trail, I looked around some more. It was pretty dark, even though when I looked up I could see sunlight through the branches. It smelled like dry grass and earth, just like winter.

"Look, it seems to end here," Gabriel said.

We all stopped. There were fewer trees right here, like a mini clearing. I squinted to get a clearer look at the ground. There were still some leaves around, but the dirt was mostly visible here. And it looked different, not as packed.

I walked a few feet to a patch of dirt that looked especially loose. There were clear footprints over the dirt. My stomach dropped.

I looked back and everyone else was studying different spots on the ground. Will had a branch he was testing the ground with. After a moment, he said, "Huh."

"What?" I looked at his face, which had a quizzical expression.

"It's caught on something."

I walked over and brushed aside some more of the dirt around the stick with my foot.

There, in the ground, was a small hand. The arm was still underground. The branch was hooked on a torn plastic bag over the hand.

"Jesus," Will said, jerking back and falling.

The rest of us stared in shock at the hand while Will tried to get up, but I turned and saw he was on his knees, head down. I was about to throw up, myself. I couldn't look back. The images from the dreams were flying across my mind and I could have sworn I heard voices coming up from the ground.

Tenny was wiping tears from her eyes, and Gabriel was folded over. "What do we do?" he asked.

I was vibrating from tension and pulled my phone out to dial Candace, some weird auto-pilot taking over.

"Hi, Lauren," she said.

"We found the bodies," I said, not recognizing my strange, foreign-sounding voice, a background symphony of ghostly voices behind it.

"What—where?" she asked.

I looked at Tenny, all business. "Send me the screenshots of where we are and where the car went."

Tenny pulled her phone out and unlocked it.

"We trailed their car and found where they bury all the bodies," I explained.

The images came through and I started to send them.

"Lauren! Get out of there!" Candace said, clearly alarmed.

This jerked me back to reality, but I was just done doing what adults told me when I knew better. I finished sending the pictures.

"Lauren, you need to get out of there," Candace said again. "They're going to suspect you're involved! Is Gabriel with you?"

"Yes, I know, but we couldn't do nothing!" I said, all my emotions unlocking at once—anger, desperation, panic. I looked at everyone else, and they were just standing there, looking shell-shocked. Will and Gabriel were looking at where we'd come from, and Tenny was staring at me.

My heart was beating like crazy because I knew she was right, but none of us was moving.

"We should leave," Gabriel said quietly. "We shouldn't disturb the site."

A rustling sound came from the trees, and JT appeared at the end of the path into the small clearing. His mouth fell open. Before I could react, Hoppin' John appeared right behind him. He blinked while my brain cycled through all the dreams he'd been in. I couldn't believe we were all here at the same place at once.

"What's happening, Lauren?" Candace asked.

"They're here," I stupidly said into the phone. My brain was fuzzy. Why were they here?

"Right now?" Candace asked, sounding confused.

The clouds in my mind suddenly cleared. This was insane—these horrible monsters who kidnapped, tortured, and raped little girls before murdering them. And they were just standing here like we were hikers who'd run into each other in the woods. John had tortured, raped, and killed countless girls, and JT had done the same to my little sister. The air coming through my nose was hot and acrid, and I could feel rage building, but I still didn't know what to do with it. The ghostly voices had gone high-pitched, almost like a siren.

"Sanders?" John said, looking at Will, while JT looked terrified.

"Johnson," Will said.

"It's not what you think," JT said, looking at me.

Something primal snapped in me. "Yes, it is, it's exactly what I think!" I yelled and charged at JT, smashing into him before he could react, and we fell to the ground. I started pummeling his face.

"How could you?" I yelled as he tried to cover his face and push me off. "How could you do that to her? You raped my little sister and then you murdered her!"

JT's eyes flashed.

Someone grabbed my shoulders roughly but then someone else pushed him off.

"She wanted it, you bitch," JT said through gritted teeth. My rage spiked and I screamed, "Liar—" but then his hands went around my neck. I tried to peel them off but he was so strong. Then Gabriel started helping and JT's fingers came loose so I jerked back, and Gabriel landed elbows first on JT's face. Someone was behind us, but then there was a crash, and I realized Will must be fighting John. I pulled back and somehow landed a fist on JT's nose and it gave a little, making him shriek. I was still half on top of him and he reached for my neck again, but Gabriel hit the side of his head and grabbed his hands. Will and John were rolling around, and I wondered if he could handle the athlete. JT was growling as blood poured from his nose, and he rolled to the side away from both of us, making me lose my balance and land on the ground. Gabriel grabbed him from behind, but he pushed him off and went further into the brush, and somehow managed to get up before me. He took off and I tried to follow him, losing track of Gabriel. But JT was too fast and I tripped on some branches.

Somebody grabbed me from behind, arms around my waist, as I got up.

"Don't," Tenny said. I turned around, confused, adrenaline pounding in my ears.

"I have to. He's getting away!" I tried to jerk out of her grasp, but she was holding tight.

"If you catch him, he'll kill you." She squeezed me as I tried to pull away, a weird hug holding me in place. "Listen."

Will and Gabriel were fighting John, and there was yelling and grunting, but the voices were quiet now. Then I heard something in the distance: police sirens.

"Oh." I looked at Tenny, whose face was red from the tears dampening her cheeks.

"The police are coming!" I yelled, which made John jerk to a stop just as Will landed a punch to his jaw.

John pushed back and scrambled away and Will grabbed his collar, but Tenny said, "Stop!"

John ran off down the path and they turned around. Both of them were bleeding, Will from cuts on his cheek and chin, and Gabriel over his eye. They were both panting from exertion and covered in dirt and sweat even though it was cold. I felt like I had to throw up, and turned to the side to retch, but nothing came out.

"I recorded it," Tenny said. "I even got what JT said about Maya."

I stared at her in shock. How could he have said that? How could anyone be so evil? But why was I surprised, given that we were standing in the middle of a burial ground of murdered little girls?

There was muffled yelling and we all looked at the phone in Tenny's left hand—mine.

"Lauren!" It was Candace. Tenny handed the phone to me. I must have dropped it when I charged JT.

"We fought them," I said. "They got away. But we hear police sirens."

"They're almost there. Don't leave the site. It's too late for you all to get out of there. You're just going to have to tell them the truth and hope that they believe you, and that there's enough physical evidence against the others."

"Okay."

We stood there, quiet except for the heavy breaths. The sirens were much closer. My heart was still beating like crazy and I still felt sick, but now I was terrified about what the police would think.

"What made you think to record it?" Will asked Tenny.

"Candace told me to." She wiped tears from her eyes. "I was so scared. I thought they were going to kill us."

"Me, too," Gabriel said. "I've been through some terrifying things lately, but that tops them all. You all know I've never punched anybody in my life."

"Me neither," I said, feeling true shock come on. I looked at Gabriel. He had leaves in his hair, was bleeding from a big gash over his forehead, and had dirt all over his blue bomber jacket and jeans. He'd saved my life. Nothing would ever tear us apart again.

"Do you think they're there yet?" Tenny asked.

We all shook our heads. Will looked back toward the road. "I wonder if they caught them."

I leaned over, holding my roiling stomach.

We'd probably know soon.

Gabriel

I reached out and took Will's hand. He squeezed mine. I couldn't believe what was happening. The police were going to pin this on me. I wanted to cry again—we'd found Maya's murderer and we'd found the men behind the disappearances and uncovered what they were really doing, which was worse than anything anyone imagined. But the police were going to say I was part of it. What had I ever done to deserve this? I held on tight because this might be the last chance I'd have to hold his hand.

Lauren and Tenny were standing about five feet in front of us, looking like they'd just been in a fight, even Tenny. They looked terrified. Lauren's hair was all over the place and there was a leaf in it and dirt around her neck and all over her jeans and shirt. I looked at Will. He was thinking the same thing about how this was going to look. He was also terrified.

There was rustling down the path, so Will and I dropped hands and went to stand next to Lauren. It had to be the police coming. There were loads of sirens now, even though we were far from the road and it was muffled. Had they gotten John and JT? Would they let them go? It would be obvious they'd been in a fight, but they could say they were fighting each other. The police would be desperate to believe them since they were white.

Two cops appeared, one behind the other, down the path.

"What's going on?" the first one asked, a tall, blond guy.

Nobody said anything at first, but then Lauren said, "We found a body."

We stepped to the side and she pointed toward the hand in the dirt.

"You stay here," the second cop, a small white woman, said. She pointed at all of us.

"We're not going anywhere," I said. I was so sick of their shit, even though I knew this was going to go badly for me.

The first cop spoke into his radio. "There's at least one body here." After he finished, he asked, "Whose wallet is that?"

We all looked where he was pointing, at a black wallet a little beyond the body we'd found.

That must have been why John and JT turned up here this morning. "None of ours," I said.

We stood to the side, still breathing heavily from the fight and from fear. I couldn't help but look at that poor, solo hand sticking out.

The woman watched us, glaring. I wanted to get mouthy with her, but I didn't have the energy.

Several cops appeared from the path, and they handcuffed me and then walked all of us back to the street, a line of exhausted teens heading to jail. Or at least to the police station.

"Just tell the honest truth," Lauren said about halfway to the road.

"No, instead, ask if you are free to go," I added. "If not, seriously don't say a single thing without a lawyer."

The cop pushing me said, "Shut it."

"None of us should say anything until I've talked to my lawyer," I finished.

When we reached the street, there were more than ten police cars, John and JT nowhere in sight. Had they really gotten away?

One of the cops grabbed me by the shoulder and led me toward a car. "Did you get them?" I asked.

"Who?" he said, obviously uninterested.

"John Johnson and JT Comstock. The two guys who were running away from here."

"I don't know anything about it." He pushed me into the back of a car, and I couldn't see anything else that was going on. I couldn't move around much. All the other cars were behind me.

After a while, my elbows were sore from the position I was in, but a cop finally got in and drove me to the police station. My face was throbbing and I knew there were cuts and blood, something I'd never experienced before. It stung like hell. Twenty minutes, and I was back in a familiar interview room.

They handcuffed me to the table, and the same two detectives who'd had an ongoing hard-on for me came in after about half an hour. Hansen leaned back and tented his fingers.

"I'm not talking to you without my lawyer," I announced as soon as they sat down.

"That's not smart," Tolui said. "You should know that Lauren is giving you up as we speak."

"Don't try that prisoner's dilemma crap on me. Am I free to go?"

"No," Hansen said.

"Then get my lawyer. I'm not talking to you all."

23

Lauren

They drove Tenny and me to the police station in one car. I saw them put Gabriel in handcuffs into another, and Will in a separate car, no handcuffs. I hated them.

They dropped Tenny and me off in different rooms, and left me alone for a bit. It was obvious I shouldn't leave, but I still had no idea if we were in legal trouble. I also didn't know if they'd caught John or JT, because they wouldn't tell us anything. It was a small room, about half the size of my bedroom, with a large window that I couldn't see through. I assumed someone was watching me from the other side. The table had a metal loop in the middle, obviously for handcuffs, and the plastic chair was really uncomfortable.

My lip was really hurting, and when I touched it, my fingers had spots of blood, and there was blood under my nails, which I hadn't been keeping painted lately.

After at least an hour, a small woman in plain clothes came in, and at first I relaxed a bit because she wasn't a big, intimidating man. But then I realized they were already starting the manipulation attempt. She said hi and sat down across from me, but I said nothing.

"I'm Detective Morrell. We just want to find out from you what happened," she said with a sympathetic smile.

"Am I free to go?" I felt sick to my stomach asking this, defying authority, even though it was my legal right. I always did what everyone wanted me to do.

"You are, but that's not very productive. We need to understand what happened, because from here it's very suspicious. How did you know the bodies were there?"

"I'm going to leave." Even though it was terrifying, I stood up. I was shaking. I never defied authority. I steeled myself. I was in the right here. "Do you have JT and John?"

"I can't tell you anything about the investigation. But you can leave if that's what you really want," she added with a sigh, clearly still trying to manipulate me into staying. But she walked to the door, opened it, and motioned for me to leave.

I stepped through the doorway and saw a big room with desks. "Where are Tenny and Gabriel?" I probably should have asked after Will, but right now I was limited in who I could care about.

"Your friends?" Detective Morrell asked.

"Yes." I stood just outside the door, watching people at the desks and a couple others walking around.

"I don't know where they are," she said matter-of-factly.

Of course she wouldn't tell me. "Where's the exit? And is there a bathroom?"

"That way." She pointed me toward them and I headed into the bathroom. There was a sink area with orange laminate counters chipped in several places along the edge. I wondered what had gone on here for that to happen. I looked in the mirror and saw a cut lip, bruises forming under my eyes, and even some small bruising around my neck. I took some pictures on my phone. Of course the asshole police hadn't given a shit. I pulled off some paper towels and tried to clean my lip and the blood spots on my chin, but it was dried and difficult. I had actual first aid supplies at the dorm. I'd just deal with it there. I went into a stall to do my business, and ended up sitting there and crying for a while. What were they going to do to me? Was I going to go to jail, too? I had a really bad feeling about Gabriel. They'd already used made-up stories against him. Would JT and the Johns get away with it? I couldn't imagine it, but this whole thing had made me understand that the world was not fair, or even logical, much of the time.

Once I had myself mostly sorted, I texted my dad, who said he was on his way. I washed my hands and made another attempt to clean my face, getting some of the dirt off.

Gabriel

They left, and I fumed. I hated them so much, but now I was angry that they were also messing with my friends. Were they going to assume Lauren was somehow guilty, too? I thought Tenny and Will might be okay because they weren't directly involved, or at least they hadn't been. Would they assume Will was white and treat him better? I really hoped so, because I would never forgive myself if he got in even the tiniest bit of trouble because of me. All he'd ever done was support me and try to help. But what if they figured out his dad was Black? Would it change anything?

I wasn't as worried about Tenny, because even though she was Latina, she was a girl and young and pretty timid, so she wouldn't make the mistake of mouthing off.

But what was Lauren going through? They could be accusing her of all of it. I knew they were lying about her pinning it all on me. I was the one who'd been disloyal—not her. Never her.

Mr. Thompson eventually arrived. He had on what looked like golf pants and a light jacket. "Gabriel," he said as he entered the room. He sat down. "What's happened?"

I told him everything, including all the dream stuff, even though I knew it sounded crazy. But it's what happened, and that was his question.

"Do you really fully trust Lauren?" he asked, his eyes narrowed slightly. "You don't think she had knowledge of this through JT?"

"No!" I almost yelled. "Sorry, but no. I know her. She's the best person I know, and she's as weirded out by all this stuff as the rest of us. We aren't woo-woo people. And those dreams tormented her. They were horrific."

He leaned back, nodding thoughtfully. "Okay. I'll be honest, I don't immediately know what to do with information that came from dreams. Normally, this wouldn't be believed, but if there's no tangible evidence tying you to the actual crimes, we may be okay. I'm going to have to do some research. Let me go find out what their plans are." He left me in there, and I had to wait and wait.

Eventually, he came back with Hansen, who unlocked the cuffs and said, "Don't go anywhere, Gabriel."

They gave me my phone back, and Mr. Thompson and I walked out to the front of the station. It was cold, but he waited with me until Mamá got there to pick me up. We were supposed to meet with him Monday afternoon to talk about what to do about everyone. I didn't know if they would need their own lawyers or not, but I hoped not.

"We'll figure this out, Gabriel," he said.

"Thanks." I wondered what he really thought, but I just got into the car.

Mamá had been crying. "Mijo, your face!"

"I know. We fought the bad guys." Pride surged through me. I'd been in a righteous fight—I hadn't backed down. We'd all stood up for what was right even though we could have died. At least somebody in the world cared about all the dead girls. Also, I'd kept JT from killing Lauren the same way he'd killed Maya.

Mamá sniffed and pulled away from the curb, and I had to explain everything to her. She listened, crying more as I told her about what Lauren saw in her dreams.

"I love you, mijo," she finally said.

"I love you, too, Mamá." There wasn't much else to say when we had no idea what the future held.

Lauren

After I left the bathroom at the police station, I went outside, back into the cold December day. I wanted to wait for Tenny and Gabriel, but it really was cold, my face hurt, and I had no idea when they'd be done. I looked back at the glass entrance. I did not want to go back in there.

Dad pulled up about ten minutes later. I got in.

"What's happening?" he asked, still sounding beat down, like he had since Halloween. "What happened to your face?"

"Can you just take me back to the dorm?"

He put the car in gear. "Yes, but you have to tell me what's going on before you go inside."

So I told him everything on the drive back and finished while we sat in the parking lot.

His face was white, and he cried when I told him what had happened to Maya. I didn't tell him what JT had said about her in the woods.

I was about to get out when he grabbed my upper arm. "Wait."

He squeezed and then let go. "Lauren, I know I have been a terrible father. I've left you mostly to your own devices, which was easy to do since you were at the dorm, so I knew your basic necessities were being taken care of. I'm sorry. I just ... you know how bad I am in crises. I shut down. But I'm sorry. I wasn't there when you needed me."

I was stunned. "I've been okay." This wasn't remotely true, but what else could I say?

"You always say that. You always handle things. I think of you as an adult, and that's not fair. We relied on you too much. I know you feel terrible about Halloween night, but I want you to know I do not blame you at all. We've all lost track of a little kid now and again, and most of the time everything's fine."

"Thanks." I didn't really know what to say. I did believe him. But Dana? She still thought it was my fault.

"And I know you think Dana blames you, but she doesn't. I've talked to her. But she is seriously depressed and not getting better and I am really worried. She lost her insurance because she lost her job. And she really never leaves the bedroom except to go to the bathroom. She's lost so much weight. I've had her at the hospital, but they keep sending her home because she pretends to do better so she can leave, and then she just goes back to the bedroom."

He said all this staring straight ahead. He didn't mention it, but that must have been costing a fortune without insurance.

"I'm not asking you for advice, honey," he said, looking at me earnestly. "This is not a problem you can solve for me."

I nodded. He was right—I had no idea what to do. And I didn't entirely believe him about her not blaming me, but he obviously felt bad about it, so there was no point in arguing.

"But really, how are you doing?" he asked. "How is school?"

"I'm okay. I'm not making straight As, but it's okay. The dreams have been pretty horrible, and they made sleeping difficult, but maybe they'll stop now."

"Okay." He was staring at the steering wheel again. "We should talk every week. I can't let this go on. How are your Sunday mornings?"

"Well, not too early, but that would be okay."

"Ten?"

"Eleven. We sometimes don't go to breakfast until ten."

"Sounds like a plan. Now we just have to figure out what's happening with the police." That was obviously stressing him out, because we couldn't afford a lawyer.

Would I even be finishing high school? There was no way to know.

"I'm going to go inside," I said. "I'm going to try to talk to Gabriel to see what his lawyer said. They probably can help us figure out what to do."

He reached over to hug me and gave me a kiss on the side of my head. I got out of the car and went back inside the dorm, checked in, and headed up to my room. No Tenny.

I lay down on the bed and texted both Tenny and Gabriel. I didn't know Will's number.

They didn't respond, and I texted Dad to see if he could find out what was going on with Tenny. Right after I sent it, I heard back from Gabriel. —*Are you okay? Can I call you in a few minutes?*—

—*Yes. I'm ok*— My brain flitted through everything that had happened in the woods.

My phone dinged with a text. I looked at it and was disappointed to see it was only Candace, but she wanted me to call, so I did.

She was able to give me an update. They had all three of the monsters in custody—JT, Hoppin' John, and his dad. I filled her in on exactly what had happened, even though she was so pissed at us for getting involved.

I didn't care. We weren't going to just stand by and do nothing when something that horrible was going on.

"Oh!" she suddenly said.

"What?" I asked, excited by the tone of her voice.

"They entered the warehouse. Two girls were there, alive!"

"Really?" I instantly started crying again, but it was from the biggest relief I'd ever felt.

"Yes!"

I was speechless. I just sobbed and sobbed, but through it, I texted both Tenny and Gabriel.

"Are you okay, Lauren?" Candace asked.

"Yes," I croaked. And I was. Who knew what else would happen, but we had saved two little girls, even if Maya wasn't one of them.

~

Gabriel

When I got home Sunday, Mamá cleaned up my face. I could have done it myself, but honestly, it was nice having my mom take care of me. And I know it made her feel better, too. It was something in our lives that she still had some say over.

Lauren texted me with the news about all the arrests and then we talked. It was such a relief, but she and I were a mess on the phone. And we still didn't think JT would ever be punished for what he did to Maya.

"Tenny has the video of him admitting it, doesn't she?" I asked.

"She's not here, and she's not answering my texts."

"Is she okay?" I asked. I was scared again.

"I have no idea." She was obviously still crying. "I tried her mom but she didn't answer, either, and I asked my dad to find out but he didn't hear back from her."

We talked about the plan for Monday's meeting with Mr. Thompson, but then Tenny suddenly showed up in their room. I could hear them talking and knew they were hugging. Then I could hear them crying.

"I've got Gabriel on the phone," Lauren finally said.

"Hi, Gabriel," Tenny said.

"Is everything okay with you?" I asked. "Have you been at the station this whole time?"

She sniffed. "No, they let me go, but then my mom took me to the church. I had to talk to the priest. It was stupid."

Then Lauren and I told her what had happened with us and about the meeting with the lawyer the next day. She texted her mom about the meeting.

We all seemed to run out of energy at the same time, and finally hung up.

Will still wasn't responding to my texts, so I updated him on the arrests and went to bed. What if he never wanted to talk to me again? All my drama might just be too much for him.

But I woke to a text. From a number I didn't recognize. It was a bit after midnight.

—*It's Will. Are you okay? I lost my phone in the woods and just got one from my brother*—

—*Yes, they let me go for now. I don't know what's going to happen. What happened with you?*— Please let him be okay. I would never forgive myself if he got in trouble because of me.

—*I think kind of the same. They didn't charge me with anything, but it sounded like not the final decision. So I don't know. But I did what you said and they kept trying to convince me to rat you out, even though there was nothing to tell them. They said you were blaming everything on me*—

—*They did that same shit with me, telling me Lauren was blaming me. I called them on it*— Suddenly, I was crying again. Everything was such a mess.

—*Can I call you?*— he asked.

—*Yes*— The idea of talking to him—that he still wanted to talk to me—was such a relief. The phone buzzed a few seconds later.

"Oh, my God, Gabriel. When I saw you walk into sociology that first day and though, hmm, I never guessed where we'd end up." He laughed a bit, an edge of hysteria in it.

I panicked for a second. Was he going to break up with me? But he wasn't going anywhere. "I know. Maya was still here. And everything was normal."

"Except for what those guys were doing to all those kidnapped girls."

"Yeah." And we just went about our lives like everything was okay while those girls were being tortured and filmed in a dingy warehouse in Oklahoma City. How did stuff like this happen?

"As scared as I am, I'll never regret what we did. It was the right thing, when nobody else was doing anything." There was genuine pride in his voice and it made me love him even more. If that's what it was. I had no point of reference, but it felt amazing. He was one of the most incredible people I'd ever met.

"Yeah," I said, trying to keep my feelings out of my voice. It wasn't the time to deal with that stuff. "Lauren said Candace had told them about JT before, and they dismissed her."

"Really?"

"Yeah. He came up in her research because he had a connection to two of the missing girls. The first and third ones."

"Oh, my God." He sounded so pissed. "Why did they ignore her?"

"I guess his other uncle is a cop."

"Of course. And all those guys were just perfect white dudes. I'm so sick of this world sometimes."

I yawned, such a bad moment for it.

"You just yawned, didn't you?" Will said. It sounded like he was smiling.

"I'm so wiped."

"Me, too. Let's hang up and try to sleep. I will see you at the meeting tomorrow."

"Yeah, that sounds like a good idea." I paused and neither of us said anything for a moment. "Will?"

"Yeah?"

"I'm so glad I met you." I sounded raw. "We wouldn't have been able to do this without you. We saved two lives."

"I'm glad I met you, too. I'm glad I could help."

I teared up again. Even though Maya might never get real justice, she helped us bring down the other bad guys, and I know she wanted that. Even from the grave.

"Goodnight, Gabriel."

"Goodnight, Will." My voice was thick, but I didn't care if he heard it. I knew he wouldn't judge me.

We hung up and I tried to sleep, but I was just feeling way too many feelings. Going to class tomorrow like my life was normal was going to be so hard.

24

———————

Lauren

We were all in the lawyer's office, in a conference room that wasn't really big enough for nine people. He started talking and before he'd finished a sentence, his phone rang. He left the room and when he came back in he told us the best news, even though it was so completely messed up.

This whole time, they'd been ignoring a key piece of evidence. They had collected a bloody fingerprint from inside the trunk where they found Maya. It didn't match Gabriel, but they'd charged him anyway and kept this secret. But they'd tested it today against JT, and it matched. So they finally accepted that he was Maya's killer.

"They are dropping the original charges against you, Gabriel," Mr. Thompson said after telling us.

We all broke down. I've never cried more confusing tears. How can you be happy and devastated with sadness all at the same time? Dad was crying, Tenny and her mom were, Gabriel and his mom. Will looked relieved, probably for Gabriel, because now it was over. Will's dad mostly looked confused because he'd just been brought into this mess yesterday.

"So what does this mean for the rest of them?" Will's dad asked.

Mr. Thompson nodded. "Although I can't guarantee anything, I think that with the information that is coming out, you all should be okay. I'd still recommend each of you finding a lawyer, just in case. I can recommend some if you need them."

I looked at Dad. We couldn't afford a lawyer. Tenny's family could, and I thought Will's would, too, but I was screwed if we ended up really needing one.

That was really all there was left for the meeting. We were still in limbo, but Maya's killer was caught, some kidnapped girls were rescued, a horrible child porn ring was ended, and the killers of the other girls were going to go down.

Dad hung back as everyone left until it was just us and Mr. Thompson.

Head hanging low, he said, "Mr. Thompson, we really cannot afford a lawyer. Do you know anyone who might be able to ... help?"

The lawyer nodded and said, "I have someone in mind. Let me contact her and get back to you." He took Dad's number and we left.

Everyone else had been waiting for us when we got outside, and we all hugged. There wasn't much to say. We all knew that we had done a good thing, and maybe we'd also be getting in trouble, but hopefully not. It was still worth it. This was bigger than all of us, and because we had risked everything, we saved two little girls.

EPILOGUE

Lauren

We all got on with our lives. At first we heard a lot of news about the girls, Maya, and the fact that two perfect young blond men with their whole lives ahead of them turned out to be evil. The OIT basketball team wasn't going to do well in March Madness, and there were actually imbecilic fans who claimed Hoppin' John couldn't have really been involved, because why would someone so good at basketball be a bad guy? It was idiocy.

They were right, the team was rubbish in March, but they did better the next year. By that time, JT and his uncle and cousin were all in prison, all convicted. The juries had seen them for what they were. Although there were the basketball fans who refused to believe, most everyone else in the state hated them for being monsters.

But in November, just over a year after Maya, something horrible happened, and I just didn't know if this would ever be truly over. Dana killed herself. Dad had thought she was doing better because she seemed to have more energy and had started getting out of bed, even making food for herself. He'd talked to Adelita about her, and they agreed she was finally coming out of her deep depression. Adelita was spending more time over there. Dad sounded so happy when he told me. But then he came home one night to find that she had taken some pills and was already gone by the time he got there. Dad was destroyed. He couldn't even tell me, and Adelita came to the dorm to talk to me and tell me. I just felt like, how much worse could things get? It happened right before Thanksgiving, and I ended up staying with Adelita and Gabriel over the break because Dad was just gone. Adelita was also a wreck. What had our families done to deserve so much tragedy? I didn't understand.

It left me with a perpetual sense of dread at what could happen next. But eventually Dad came back, and I was at home with him at Christmas. Adelita made both of us come over for Christmas dinner, and I could tell he was trying. In January he decided to train to be part of a volunteer search and rescue team. It was rather random, but I encouraged him because I knew he was trying to find purpose in life. Everyone was gone, and no one would ever really be back. I was already mostly living at the school, and then I'd be going off to college. And I figured maybe it wasn't entirely random, because he'd done some rock climbing when he was younger. Before I was born.

This was just the new world my family existed in.

Although it took several months to know for sure, we were never charged with anything after they arrested the men. Candace's exposé about what happened to Maya and the other girls came out, and told how the police had looked the other way. I guess they hadn't technically looked the other way, except with JT in regards to Maya, because

Candace was the only one who thought JT was connected to the missing girls. However, she also wrote about how she figured that out, and it was something the detectives should have found. But then she revealed that JT's other uncle was a cop in another small Oklahoma city, and so they never took any mention of JT or the other men seriously—not when Candace reported it, not when Gabriel did, and not when I did.

This led to an investigation into the racism and discrimination in the Burnside police department. Gabriel and Tenny were very skeptical at first, but it became a huge story nationwide because of what the investigation exposed. There was clear and well-documented racism and discrimination internally, too. It wasn't a coincidence that there were only three woman in the department, because they ran the others off so fast. It was just a cesspit.

The real thing that pushed the investigation forward was the evidence they'd withheld—JT's bloody fingerprint. It was patently obvious that Gabriel wasn't guilty, but they hid that from his lawyer. Apparently, it was a junior officer who actually exposed it after they arrested JT. Otherwise, he might have gotten away with the murder. Although, he was involved with his uncle and cousin, so he would have gone to prison, anyway. Just maybe not for as long.

We all learned the term "blue wall of silence," which meant it wasn't just Tolui and Hansen who got in trouble. The good news was that in January and February of my senior year, three cops—including Tolui and Hansen—were convicted of a variety of charges related to corruption, favoritism and looking the other way, withholding evidence, witness tampering on other cases, and even more, but I couldn't keep track. They were going to go to prison. One trial was still going, and it had blown up nationally, emboldening whistleblowers at several other police departments across the country. No one else had been convicted of anything yet, but it really seemed like they might be. Gabriel told me one night that he felt like maybe everything he went through was worth it if it really changed things in America. There were just so many bad stories. We hoped it would get better.

It was now March of senior year, and some more crazy stuff was happening at the school that semester—there were some trans and gay kids who'd gotten in trouble for posting some truths about OAMS on TikTok. That was a whole other story, but there was a walkout for them on a Friday, to show support for them and try to convince the school board to not expel them. A lot of kids from the school came out for it, and Gabriel and Will showed up with the college's LGBTQ+ Alliance. They were still together, and even though I was a little jealous of them, I was still happy at how happy they were. They'd finally been able to have a normal college relationship and go around and have fun, instead of worrying about going to prison and chasing murderers.

Tenny and I didn't have signs at the walkout, but we were there, and even though it had nothing to do with Maya, it still felt good to be part of people standing up for the right thing again. So many people were cowards, but we weren't. We chanted and marched to the city hall with the whole group. We also found out that we weren't the only ones doing the walkout—somehow the protest had gotten legs, and kids all over the country did their own walkouts.

Even more importantly, it was the same day that the final cop from Burnside was convicted. People were shocked that all four of them went down.

That night, I was tired from everything that happened with the walkout, but it still took me forever to fall asleep.

Then I woke up in the middle of the night to see a ball of light floating in front of me, and at first I freaked out.

Maya. My heart twisted into a million knots, and when the light pulsed, I burst into tears. But then a sense of peace overcame me. It pulsed again. She was saying goodbye. We'd done the best we could for her. I had overcome my tendency to just do what everyone expected, and had done what I knew was the right thing instead. The light pulsed again and went out, and I knew Maya was finally free to go wherever she was supposed to go.

I'd helped take three monsters and four corrupt cops out of circulation, and now girls were just a tiny bit safer.

THE END

If you enjoyed *Echoes of Maya*, please consider leaving a review on Amazon or another site—reviews are invaluable to indie authors.

For more info about Kelly and their books, sign up for their newsletter here https://qr.fm/wDzYmE or scan the below QR code:

BOOKS BY KELLY VINCENT

Finding Frances

Echoes of Maya

New Girl

Binding Off

Always the New Girl

The Art of Being Ugly

Ugly

Uglier

Ugliest

Fea (*Ugly* in Spanish)

Brutta (*Ugly* in Italian)

ABOUT THE AUTHOR

Kelly Vincent wrangles data weekdays and spends the rest of their time with words. They grew up in Oklahoma but have moved around a bit, with Glasgow, Scotland being their favorite stop. They now live near Seattle with several cats who help them write their stories by strategically walking across the keyboard. Their first novel, *Finding Frances*, is a fine example of this technique, also winning several indie awards. Their most recent release, *Ugly*, was selected as the Honor book for SCBWI's Spark Award in the Books for Older Readers category for 2022. Kelly has a Master of Fine Arts in creative writing from Oklahoma City University's Red Earth program.